The Mustard Seed

The Mustard Seed

David Tracey

The Mustard Seed is a work of fiction. Names, characters
and events are invented or used fictitiously.

Pure Wave Media
1469 Wallace Avenue, Los Angeles, CA 90026
purewavemedia.com

ISBN: 978-0-9865055-1-5

Printed and bound in the United States

Understand that the body
Is merely the foam of a wave,
The shadow of a shadow.
Snap the flower arrows of desire
And then, unseen,
Escape the king of death.
And travel on.

The Buddha

To say goodbye is to die a little.

Raymond Chandler

The revolution is inside.

The XIV Dalai Lama

1

This all started with an odd noise that woke me up. I watched the door, still locked, as I tiptoed naked to the window. Orange rows of streetlights curved towards the black sea. A warm breeze brought in the scent of nightflowers.

Then the sound came back. A distant *pak-paka-paka-pak*. I took it for automatic weapons, maybe M-16s. Not that I would know. I was just a sportswriter, and despite the way the world was going, terrorism had yet to make the Olympics as a legitimate event. But there was an arrhythmic pulse to the firing that struck me as live, and because of that, thrilling.

My excitement at a real shoot-out could hardly have been called professional, not on my first night. I'd been sent to cover the Continental Cup. My paper, the *Boston Post*, No. 2 in the city, was trying to reach No. 1 by adding new immigrant subscribers. When I'd suggested making a splash about international soccer, my editor immediately saw the possibilities. Sri Lanka was her idea.

So it must have been curiosity alone that had me lean out the window, eyes squinting, nostrils flared, searching for the source. I considered waking up one of the hotel staff to drive me to the scene. Not to walk right into a crossfire. I was not that brave or stupid. But close enough to get a shot or two from telephoto range. Maybe some soldiers crouching in an alley, or a guerrilla firing from the roof of a barricaded building. It wouldn't take much to add some blow-by-blow for the copy. Just the basics, no need for details. Our readers had more interesting wars to track than some minor league revolt in remote Asia. But with a trouble-in-paradise hook, I might work it up into a Sunday spread for the Globe and You section. And wouldn't that put the rest of the press box hacks in a spin? Me off the sports page at last.

But an hour later nothing had changed. The dreamy city hung unwavering in its tropical odor of flowers tinged with rot. The sound continued in the same staccato pops. At one point I thought I heard a counterattack in a distant drum roll clatter, and wondered if it might all take off, but no one else seemed to notice. There were no shrieks, no sirens. Even as the popping continued, the rest of the city was quiet.

I took its darkened windows as a summons to go sensibly back to bed. My heart was no longer thumping as I lay back on the sheets. It may have been something entirely innocent. Night construction with a wonky jackhammer, or a Third World factory burdened with some Soviet hand-me-down riveting machine. Yet for some reason I hoped not. When I closed my eyes, the metallic crackle was almost comforting, like falling asleep to rain on the roof.

In the morning I was the only customer in the lobby restaurant downstairs. The barefoot waiter rewarded me with the smile of a sweepstakes winner. I lowered my voice so it wouldn't reach the kitchen.

"Hear anything about a shoot-out last night?"

He was puzzled but eager to go along. "You wish for break-fast?" he whispered back in a practiced cadence.

I tried enunciating. "Break-fast, yes," I said, "but first. One question. What do you know about a shooting, guns, blam-blam-blam, last night? Around 3 in the morning?"

"Ah. Last night I was not here," he said at a normal volume. "Now you would like to see a menu? Order drink only?"

I opted for the cheese and onion omelet after he promised it would be "big enough even for you no problem." In the kitchen he said something in Sinhalese to the cook. They both laughed.

He returned, grinning, with a formidable omelet that overhung the edges of the plate. When I asked whether I might be given a shovel, or failing that a fork, to eat it with, he beamed all the more. With the utensils he handed me the *Island Tribune*.

The first edition wouldn't have had time to run anything on a late-night shooting, but the sports section did carry a four-page preview of the tournament. I copied down a few quotes to use if a game got dull and I needed to pad. Soccer may be a worthy fascination for most of the planet's sports fans, but two defensive teams slogging for a tie can grind an afternoon down.

After that blazing start on the day's work, I felt good enough to settle in over breakfast. The omelet was moist inside without sacrificing any fluffiness, an achievement I hadn't expected from the mid-range hotel I'd been booked into. The paper's purchasing clerk had explained with a smirk that the Moonstone Inn was rated as clean and respectable, but I should take it anyway because it was near the road leading to the national stadium where I wouldn't get distracted. I got his message: the flight and accommodations already made it a pricey venture for a dubious sports assignment, so I would need a damn good reason to run up the tab.

If breakfast was a fair measure, I had no cause to complain. The tea was superb. I closed my eyes and swallowed a mouthful that left a faintly astringent trace on my tongue before warming my gullet. I peered into the cup to gauge how many sips remained. Ten? Maybe more if I took them small. But why deny myself the pleasure of a gum-flushing swig? I had tasted Ceylon tea before, at home, but nothing like this. And no wonder. They probably kept the best for themselves. I made a mental note. The locals were clever enough to bear watching. Well, there were ways around that. I made another mental note. Stuff my suitcase with tea on the way home.

I got a fresh pot with an extra order of jam toast, then turned to the paper with an anticipation that went beyond professional concern. Even the most trivial disasters can seem interesting in a new setting, so I slid down to relax and give the Tribune a full read-through.

It had the nagging tone of a government rag, but it wasn't my government. I didn't even mind when typos suddenly appeared like biblical locusts on the Society page. The gem-laden Sri Lankans photographed at some five-star reception were probably muttering to the help over all the mangled captions, but for me the misprints only enhanced the paper's developing-country charm.

The news itself was rich. My own paper could take lessons in how to liven up some of our duller sections. The Real Estate section in the *Island Tribune* was not just an ad-driven boost to the housing industry; it got personal. My favorite item was on two next-door neighbors, best friends since childhood, who got into a beef over their property line after one received a reading from a local astrologist. He wanted the line redrawn, the other didn't, so they stabbed each other, one time each, a belly for a belly, then shared a cab to the hospital where they settled everything by agreeing to consult a new astrologist.

Good as that was, there was more from the cosmic front. The lead editorial proclaimed planetary indications for Sri Lanka in upcoming 1988 pointed to "continued strife, agitations and a more burdensome life for the common man," all of which reminded me of home.

I continued reading, slicking my fingertips with cheap ink as I learned the island's alpha dog was a president and political one-man band who went by the initials RJ. His rounds the day before were worth four different stories, two on the front page. One of the inside articles included a quarter-page pic with a visiting circus troupe from Mongolia. RJ, glowing in an immaculate white shirt and sarong, blew the effect by staring with his mouth open at a rubbery girl who could pat her head with her own feet. I considered cutting it out for the caption potential on the office bulletin board, but let it go. Nobody knew who the president of Sri Lanka was anyway.

His biggest event made the front page above the fold. The banner head was sharp: "RJ: We Will Crush You." The story described his talk at a fund-raiser for the Buddhist Ladies Benevolence Society. It sounded like a rouser, for a president, and a charity. The reporter described "thunder" in RJ's voice as he pounded the lectern and vowed to "annihilate" a group of radicals known as the JVP.

Front page left was a column of one-para shorts: A rural official from RJ's party stabbed to death. . . Four shotguns missing after a raid on a Kandy police station. . . A newspaper vendor who took a bullet in the head but was expected to survive. . . A minor politician in the southeast held for ransom. The *Tribune* blamed them all on "subversives," which even I understood was their bogey-word for the JVP, a dreaded acronym they would not print unless the president happened to say it first.

After breakfast I took a short walk around the hotel pool, coming back to the lobby in a sheen of sweat. The hotel manager, a surprisingly young man with a spectacular overbite, greeted me from behind the front desk.

"How do you do today, sir?" he asked cheerfully, his top teeth looming.

"So far so good," I lied. Five Sri Lankan men spread about the lobby's mismatched furniture. They stopped talking to watch me, perhaps more by default than with any real interest.

"Colombo is hot, no?" the manager said. Professional decorum probably kept him from staring at the sopping patches under my armpits. "A big change from your country in December, I'm sure."

"It's warm enough." I didn't bother trying to describe the snow drifts I'd waded through to reach my taxi to the airport. "Do you have cold drinks? Or do I ask back in the restaurant?"

"Certainly, sir. We have cola, orange, lemonade, ah, cola –"

"Lemonade sounds perfect. But only if it's cold."

"Of course." He wagged his head yes. Gesturing to the lobby's last empty chair, a red-padded mahogany antique, he added, "If you please."

He said nothing more, but the waiter from breakfast appeared. He listened to the manager speak Sinhalese, aimed a genial head wag in my direction and departed with little slapping noises on the tile floor.

"First time coming to Sri Lanka?" asked a man lolling at an angle on a sofa. A roll of flab pouched out between his sarong and the hem of an undersized polo shirt.

"Yes," I answered, apparently ending his interest in the topic. He stared out the window at the parking lot without bothering to acknowledge the reply.

"May I ask the nature of your trip?" asked the manager. "If it's not an intrusion. Are you here on business or pleasure?"

"I'm a reporter. A newspaperman." At home I would have started out with sportswriter to head off the inevitable follow-up questions about what I write. Maybe here they wouldn't care.

"Oh, you must help Manik then," said the manager, nodding towards a preppie type with modern yellow-frame glasses. On Manik's lap was a clipboard. "He is just now studying to become a journalist."

I was about to say something against clipboards when the flabby one sat up in earnest. He brushed a clump of hair back from his forehead.

"You will be needing the taxi," he announced. "You want to go north, I know, and perhaps east as well. The Tamil areas. Where all the journalists go."

"Actually, no."

In the silence that followed I wondered whether any of them were Tamil. A white-haired man half-dozing on a vinyl love seat had skin that was almost black. I added, "Not that it isn't a good story. I read an article about it on the plane here. Just not my territory."

Again, no one spoke. The manager politely filled the gap. "Very good."

"I don't really do politics," I explained.

The room was silent again. The manager craned his neck towards the kitchen. He turned back to me with a wolverine's grin. "Soon come," he promised. No one else spoke.

"How about that Continental Cup?" I offered to the room in general. "Brazil the team to beat or what?"

No one bothered to catch that one and toss it back, so I let it go. The room was quiet. Were they that disappointed I wouldn't write about their current events?

"I did read something in the paper this morning about some subversive group," I tried. "Is it called the JVP?"

Manik nudged his yellow glasses up in what seemed an obvious signal to the manager. When he saw that I'd noticed, he pulled a handkerchief out from his shirt pocket and busied himself with the lenses. His mustache, a wispy patch that reminded me of high school, twitched.

"From what country are you?" asked the white-haired man from the corner, looking somewhere over my shoulder. His rheumy eyes bulged as he tried to focus.

"He is from America," the manager answered in a loud voice.

"Ronald Reagan," contributed the pudgy taxi driver. "The Big Apple. Beat it just beat it. Michael Jackson."

"America is a beautiful country," explained the man with white hair to the room in general.

"You've been there," I noted, impressed.

"No," he answered, then chuckled. "But it is beautiful all the same."

There was a lull. The parking lot shimmered with heat. I said, "So are the JVP playing in the big league here? There was something about them in the newspaper this morning. A few things actually. The president said he was going to take them down in less than two months. Sounded like the start to the playoffs."

The silence gaped for another awkward moment. Manik came

to the rescue.

"The JVP are active in the villages. Mostly in the south," he answered. "You don't hear about them a great deal in Colombo. Not officially because they're now proscribed. So they don't give interviews, I'm sorry to tell you."

I shrugged. "I'm not surprised. If they're also killing shop owners just for selling the wrong newspaper." With an inflection meant to indicate irony, I added, "If you believe what you read in the papers." No one got it.

Manik improved on his already upright posture. "So many lies are being spread about the JVP."

The white-haired man rolled his eyes. Manik looked again to the manager, then down at his clipboard.

"I would imagine there – " I started to say, but was interrupted by the taxi driver.

"I can take you anywhere you want to go. You like a one-day tour, three-day tour, one-week tour, no problem. I go to Kandy, Sigiriya, Polonnaruwa. Hikkaduwa you will like very much. The finest beach and corals in all of Sri Lanka and even the world. Tourists from many countries say this, not me."

The manager interrupted him in turn. "This must be an interesting time for a foreign correspondent in Sri Lanka, no?" He cupped his hand to block off an imaginary headline in the air. "Small Island: Big Problems." He leaned his head back to admire the creation from a distance, then smiled his overbite at it.

"And are you single or married?" asked the white-haired man.

"Married," I answered. "Legally, that is."

He waited for me to explain.

"Long story," I continued. "You wouldn't want to hear it."

"And what is your age?" asked the taxi driver.

"Well. Not so young as I used to be." I tried to say it wearily, to steer them away from personal questions, but I'm a lousy actor.

"Naturally," he answered, and waited.

"Ooh-kay. I'm 37."

"Have you any children?"

"No."

"I myself have six. Four boys, two girls."

"I'm sure they keep you busy."

He said, "Ask my wife."

"You are very big, no?" noted the white-haired man. He held a palm a foot over his own head.

"I guess." I pointed to my gut. "Problem is, bigger here."

The manager said something in Sinhalese that made everyone look at the taxi driver and laugh. He lifted the shirt to expose more of his belly, then smacked it with his palm before tugging the shirt back down. He stood up.

"Very well. We go now. Come," he told me, walking to the door.

"I'll pass. Besides, here's my drink."

The waiter stood beside me bearing a silver tray with a straw and a bottle of Elephant Brand lemon-flavored pop. Their idea of lemonade. I should have guessed. I took a sip. Warm as a bath.

"By the way, did anyone happen to hear a strange noise last night?" I tried.

The room was silent.

"A kind of popping noise? It was late, around 3 in the morning?"

The men were busy contemplating the potted palms.

"It went on and on," I said, and wanted to add, "like the silence around here sometimes."

"The hotel was noisy?" the manager asked with concern.

"No. Off in the city somewhere. To the east. It sounded almost like gunshots."

No one answered, so I gave up. Just as well. Call it a shutout. So much for my political feature. The first soccer practices of the day would be starting soon anyway.

Up in the room I took my second shower of the morning. The

amount of sweat my body could produce was startling. I supposed it was a protest at having to carry so much weight, and considered it a reminder, as if I needed one, of my marriage and, conversely, what little was left of it.

My arrival in Sri Lanka had come almost seven months to the day after Kirstin and I separated. The emptier I'd felt during the long process of losing my most precious possession, the more my body seemed to compensate by expanding. I realized, of course, that possession would seem a harsh word to describe one's life partner. Yet it was one of the milder descriptions of Kirstin that would race through my mind on the darkest days. In Sri Lanka I had hoped to avoid these emotional swoops, yet here my own body was conspiring against me.

Back outside when the first wave of hot air hit, I knew I'd waited too long. I'd planned an early morning walk to the stadium before it got bad, but the sun had already bleached the sky white. My skin began to itch.

A few plodding steps further I realized I was stooping. The cool vision I had seen from my balcony at night had vanished like a mirage. This crowded street was certainly real enough.

People moved along the sidewalks in currents. So this was what they meant by teeming. Colorful saris, pressed slacks, white shirts, bare limbs. The locals looked slim and healthy enough, and no shortage of them. In one place the human flow curved like two rows of ants around a head-high pile of split coconuts, then joined again on the other side. The smell was a blend of too many things at once: fruit going off, engine exhaust, a sewer, sweat. Although the last part may have been just me. My beard, a thick nest made for winter on the Atlantic, began to trickle.

A cluster of beggars ahead buzzed when they saw me coming. "Please, sar," moaned an old man with football-sized stumps where there should have been legs. Beside him was a woman holding a baby whose arm was bent into an impossible angle. I'd known this was coming, and still wasn't ready for it. I felt crowded already by the thick air, by my own clothes, and now by the living faces of the poor in the supposedly developing world.

I churned through the group and turned onto the main street. Traffic was a sluggish sprawl of metal and glass. Perhaps because no one had managed to paint lanes on the biggest roadway around, the result was a paralytic mass in which individual vehicles jerked forward into any opening that appeared. Many of the drivers honked, some in hysterical bursts, others in long angry wails. The noise congealed into a brassy chord that lingered in the swelter.

I stepped off the sidewalk to avoid a puddle of muck an instant before a van swerved over to troll for passengers. It screeched to a halt just inches from my calves.

"The hell you doing almost killing me like that?" I demanded. The ticket collector in the open doorway dismissed me, a non-fare, with a glance, focusing instead on a woman behind me with her hand raised. She was round, built almost on sumo lines, and wearing a blue sari that could have covered a troop of boy scouts on bivouac. At least the ticket collector didn't discriminate. He waved her in with a downward flick of his fingers. This I had to see. The van was crammed with humanity already. Would he direct her up to the roof? He gripped the door frame with one hand and swung his torso out, inviting her into the slender air space he'd opened up. Somehow she squeezed in, a limb at a time, forcing the other passengers into a new geometry of contortions, while I considered the glum irony of being fat in Third World Asia. Not for her, for me.

It was bad enough being overweight in my own country. At least at home I had the comfort of numbers. There would almost always be someone in the immediate picture with bigger gams, wider hips, a saggier belly. Here the average went from slim to wiry. Still, if the van took the sumo woman in so readily, maybe Sri Lanka wouldn't be such a bad place after all. Perhaps they considered girth, no matter how gained, a sign of stature, even something to emulate. I noted the swirl of lean people flowing around me, some staring as they went by, and thought it unlikely.

"Yes! Yes! Yes!" a voice shrieked. A motorcycle tri-shaw driver waggled his fingers in an invitation for me to climb in back. I shook my head no.

"Yes we go where you like no problem see temple. Fort? Shopping? Yes. Best price for you. My friend."

"Forget it," I muttered, looking the other way until he putted back into the traffic.

Outside an office building a slinky woman in a turquoise sari and Air Lanka chest pin caught me staring, first at the pin and then at her face with its astonishing amber smoothness. She presented me with the type of smile they use in ads to get suckers like me on the plane. At the meet-and-pass point we both started to my right, then left, then right again before ending in a stalemate.

She laughed first, an invitation to say something funny or charming or suggestive. At least something. But I fumbled it. I opened my mouth, I thought I was going to speak, and not a sound emerged. She swept by me, still laughing. I had to settle for the perfume left in her wake, more alluring than the pre-dawn smell of the city from my hotel window. Even her back look good going away.

I found the main post office, a stately colonial structure fronted by massive white pillars. Checking for mail involved a certain emotional risk. If Kirstin hadn't written it could cloud the rest of the day, even as I knew it was ridiculous to be half-way around the planet hoping for word from a woman who lived seven blocks from me. But since our separation we'd communicated best by letters. In writing we seemed to avoid the sudden malice of our personal encounters. Kirstin had known for three and a half weeks, since my last letter, that I could be reached through Poste Restante in Colombo. Maybe the distance would even help soften things between us.

The post office interior had an ornate ceiling I was admiring as I walked in until someone from behind grabbed my shoulder. I spun, not bothering to catch my falling day pack, with my fists raised and my body lowered into a protective crouch. The soldier who confronted me grinned. He was no more than a teenager, but one with a rifle strapped across his back. He pointed to my pack on the floor.

"I check," he said happily. I stared at him in confusion until he mimicked the sound of an explosion. "Bomb," he explained.

I picked up the pack and zipped it open. "Sorry," I muttered. A few customers still looked at me, but most had turned back to save their positions in line from intruders. "Don't know why that rattled me. Still getting used to everything. Trying to blend in. Find my pace. Might have known there'd be security."

The soldier, finding nothing more than a notebook, two pens and three bananas I'd lifted from a fruit basket in the hotel lobby, had already turned to the purse of a woman behind me.

The Poste Restante clerk had nothing under my name. So Kirstin hadn't bothered. She was probably glad to be free of me. In Sri Lanka there was no chance I might run into her in a movie line while she waited to go in with some other guy.

Back on the sidewalk I stopped in front of a postcard stand offering color portraits of Colombo. Some were photos of office buildings apparently shot with painstaking care from their least interesting angles. Others were not even in focus, unless they were meant to be artsy Asian mood things. I stared at the seller, a weathered women with sagging limbs and an etched scowl. I felt I knew then the real point of my trip.

I'd wanted to come not for the soccer, or to help the paper add subscribers, but to get away. From what? I was trying to escape from myself. But what was the use? I was 37 and fat. Strike one, strike two. I made a living writing about younger people who played games. Foul to the bleachers. I'd had my dreams, once, but left them behind in the wreckage when my first big newspaper break imploded. Ever since, I'd been a hanger-on, just going through motions. Wasn't it time to hit the showers myself?

I lumbered on, buffalo-shouldered, purposely avoiding the direction of the stadium. Sports could wait. Through the window of the Imperial Tea Room I saw half a dozen waiters in white sarongs loitering amid the empty tables. One at parade-rest by the door had the gray swooping mustache of the butler in an old British movie. He waved me in with a flourish that offered a choice of any seat in the place. I wasn't hungry, and I still had my bananas, but I saw the ceiling fans and went in anyway.

The squiggly Sinhalese menu included a handwritten insert in English. I ordered a plate of short eats, described as deep-fried rolls with curried fillings. I added a pot of tea. The waiter with the grand mustache wagged his head and said, "As you wish, sir."

I stared up at the slow fan and wondered: what did I wish? To go back to when Kirstin and I were first together and had everything ahead of us? I doubted it. You can't go backward in life. Sports taught me that much. The answers were always ahead. It was mostly a matter of getting the timing right. Winners knew how to use the clock as an ally, a constant reminder to advance.

The tea was excellent, a tad strong, almost edging into bitterness, but just what I needed for a pick-up. The short-eats were a solid winner. The shells offered a tasty crunch that led to soft insides just spicy enough to alert the gums without causing pain. They wouldn't sell many between innings at Fenway, but I was an instant admirer.

I searched for my waiter to order a second helping when he surprised me by being directly behind my chair. He leaned over my shoulder to whisper in my ear, "You are Mister Talls-man, no?"

"If you mean Talison, yes."

He wiped a corner of the table with an arm cloth, for no apparent reason, then straightened up and walked quickly away. Left behind was a piece of paper folded several times to the size of a matchbook.

I opened it and read the penciled message:

I HAVE THE NEWS. TURN TO THE LEFT OUTSIDE. WALK TO THE LEATHER SHOP, TURN LEFT AGAIN.

I turned around but the waiter was gone. I signaled another over. He arrived smartly and said, "Sir. How may I help you?"

"Did you just see someone give me a note?"

"Pardon me?"

"I just got a message, on paper, from another waiter. I'd like to know who it was."

"You would like another menu?" He was either genuinely confused or a gifted actor with poor career planning. I paid the bill and walked to the door, checking behind me before pushing it open.

Outside I searched the street for unusual signs, then realized I had no idea what usual would be. A shirtless man in a sarong folded up above his knees pushed a wooden-wheeled cart loaded with rebar. Two men in business suits reached over the lifeless body of an elderly man on the pavement to do a business handshake.

I turned left out the door. The leather bag store was a block away. I stopped and pretended to admire a stone Buddha the size of a baseball in a store window, while actually searching in the reflection for suspects. Our man in Colombo, I thought, feeling slightly ridiculous.

In front of the leather store I stopped again and pretended to examine the buckle on a travel bag. The proprietor emerged to explain that it was a wonderful bag, real leather, not like most other bags, this one not fall apart before you take it home, but I cut him short with a head shake. He went back inside to the air conditioning without another word.

Beyond the store was a narrow alley that curved sharply to the right. It was impossible to see where it led. I decided I wouldn't do it. I refused to walk into a turkey-shoot. If they wanted to rob me, fine, give it a shot, but don't make me do most of the work. I walked on past the entrance. Did they now expect their victims to become accomplices as well? The nerve of some petty Third World criminals.

But I found myself walking more slowly the further I went. There were easier ways to rob a person than to pass out secret notes in restaurants. I stopped beside a woman squatting beside some green coconuts the size of volleyballs. What could they take, my pens?

If they knew my name, they might also know I was hardly dripping gold and traveler's checks. Maybe it really did have something to do with news. I could only hope they didn't mean soccer.

The tournament wouldn't begin for another day anyway. And I could do all my prelim work without leaving the air-conditioned hotel. If you ask an adolescent millionaire whether he feels good, it's not hard to guess the answer. The alley offered at least the prospect of something different. Perhaps even real news, something I hadn't covered in 16 years, ever since my abrupt transfer to sports. Besides, I felt I knew how to take care of myself. I may have gone soft in places, but I hadn't forgotten everything I'd learned as a boxer. At one time I was a fairly competent one, a contender for the light heavyweight title of the state. Amateur division, but still.

I walked back towards the alley, squaring my shoulders. This time I didn't even pause at the leather store. I went in as far as the curve. Ahead the alley was empty. I continued with what felt like a powerful stride.

A stack of metal garbage cans on my left struck me as too neatly arranged. Was that the click of a door opening? I froze, listening. I heard traffic, but no footsteps. I spun around to see if I was being followed. A part of me, my legs, longed to run back out of the alley and be done with it. But I wouldn't give in. I'd interviewed countless sports stars over the years, all different types, some perceptive about their own abilities, others clearly not, but they had at least one thing in common: they weren't cowards. They knew how to treat risk as a stimulant, a way to channel energy, a catalyst to launch themselves into situations that might reveal who they were meant be, perhaps even a champion. In my own case I suspected I knew the answer too well already, but I made myself walk ahead all the same.

The sun disappeared ahead behind a four-story building on my right. A rusted steel door in the wall looked as if it hadn't been opened in years. Beyond that the alley forked. This wasn't part of the instructions, I thought, so now what was I supposed to do? I sensed the rise of an anger that would edge out the fear.

Then my arms were pressed hard against my sides. A cloth was pulled over my head and everything went black.

I pulled in hard to get free but there were four hands holding me, a person on each arm. Both had strong grips. I pivoted and dropped, lowering my center of gravity to cost them leverage. The one on my left wrist let up for an instant to try for a less sweaty hold, just the opening I needed. I whipped my hand free and swing a hook in that direction. My knuckles stung when they hit flesh. A solid throw, but not a winner. At least now I knew where my target was. I pulled my other arm free and got my legs into a right upper-cut, my knockout punch. It hit air.

Frantic jabbering from all directions told me there were three of them, at least. I spun to fire a jab at a thick voice behind me but it glanced off a shoulder. I took two steps sideways, bobbing to avoid incoming blows, and snatched the cloth off my head. I was still holding it when my arms were jerked back behind me again.

Holding my right wrist was a lineman-sized hulk with a hooked nose dripping blood into a black goatee. Beside him, forcing my other arm up in a painful twist, was a short, squat man with an oddly serene expression. Although the hulk and I were both sucking in air, he seemed unaffected by the struggle.

"Whatever the fuck you guys want," I seethed between gasps, "you got a bad way of taking it. My wallet's in my back pocket."

"Oh, Mister Talison," the third man spoke at my back. "I am very-very sorry."

I recognized the voice even before he came around front. It was Manik, the boy from the Moonstone Hotel.

2

Manik made a small ceremony of dusting off my shoulders. A useless gesture but I let him. The bigger guy with the goatee pulled the back of his hand away from his nostrils. He frowned at the blood. My one good punch.

"This wasn't supposed to happen," Manik scolded the pair. I assumed the English and disapproving tone were for my benefit. They didn't reply.

"Please accept my full apology," he said. He held his hand out but I ignored him so he used it instead to remove his yellow glasses. "I am very-very sorry," he continued. "I should say, we are sorry."

I jerked my thumb at the short one. His cropped hair emphasized the bullet shape of his skull. "He doesn't look too choked up."

The corners of his lips slid into a joyless smirk. He smoothed unseen creases from the black cotton bag and began folding it into prim squares.

"This is all my fault," Manik continued, his thin mustache squirming. "It was my idea to blindfold you. For your own protection, you see. But how could you know that when we had no chance to tell you yet? We were to explain, of course, but then you fought back and, oh my. Thank goodness no one was injured."

I flexed the fingers on my left hand. The knuckles were scuffed but I had no jams or breaks. My arms were surprisingly unaffected considering the shapes they'd been twisted into. A new layer of sweat made my clothes cling, but in a way that now felt good. I'd held my own. The exertion left me with a flush, something I was more used to seeing in others during post-game interviews.

"Suppose you tell me what's going on," I said, slowing my breathing back to normal.

Manik's brown eyes glistened with sincerity. "You must understand it is very-very important for us to be careful. I requested the blindfold for the security of our party, but also for you."

"You mean because the police might get me before the JVP could kill me?"

The two bruisers glanced at each other but said nothing. Manik alone seemed put out.

"Mister Talison," he protested. "Why would we want to harm you? We have come this way to request – in international solidarity – your assistance."

"By solidarity you mean you'd throw a bag over anybody's head?"

"Even if you do not support our cause," he went on quickly, "this is not our concern. We are not asking for your allegiance. We simply mean for you to continue your usual duties. We in turn will do our part to help you." He made it sound like opening a franchise. When I said nothing, he continued, "You will get the news."

I will still trying to digest that when he added, "Remember the words of your own brilliant Malcolm X: 'If you do not stand for something, you will fall for anything.'"

"What news?"

The tall one grunted something in Sinhalese. Manik answered him with a head wag. To me he said, "We must go."

"No. Why should I?" I asked. "You haven't told me a thing about this news."

Manik chewed his lips in a way that made the mustache dance. He spoke a few words in Sinhalese, opening the sluice on a verbal dam in the bigger guy. He and Manik argued in a back-and-forth that showed no sign of ending, until they turned to the squat one. He seemed to enjoy the role of arbiter, granting each the time to present his case by stopping interruptions from the other, asking questions for clarification, and at last holding up a hand to end the discussion. He stroked his stubble, fluttered his lips, looked at me and then up at the sky. Finally he snapped his fingers and announced the decision. It didn't help. Now there were three people shouting instead of two. They were like pro wrestlers hyping next Saturday's bout. They couldn't even spirit me away in secrecy without turning the whole enterprise into a dog's breakfast. I didn't try to hide my disappointment.

"And you guys were worried about getting caught?" I said, shaking my head. "See you later. Much later."

Even the squat one's face fell. He looked to Manik for an explanation.

"You heard me, no-neck," I said. "I'm leaving."

"But Mister Talison," Manik pleaded in a squeezed voice. "You are a reporter. And this is news."

"No. I'm a hack. I write about sports. Not politics, not movements, not anything important. I cover games. Hockey. Football. Soccer."

He started to speak but I interrupted with an upright forefinger. It was my turn to quote, from a radio call-in host I used to like: "'Because in the store of human affairs, sports is, after all, the toy department.' Now unless you've got an inside line on who's going to win the Continental Cup, why should we even waste our time?" I puffed out my shirt to dry the sweat.

Manik's tone turned earnest. "Mister Talison, I know you have an important position as a member of the international press. You write for the *Boston Post*, a very-very well known newspaper."

I felt a flutter in my gut. I hadn't mentioned where I worked, to anybody, since I'd arrived.

"And just how might you know that?" I asked, trying to sound more irritated than afraid. How far back did this set-up go?

"At the hotel you sent a cable to your editor in America. I happened to catch the name and address. That is all. I meant no harm. You must believe me. We understand you are a sports reporter. This is a prestigious position, no? Cultural work is but one part of the people's right to determine their own form of self-expression. As Karl Marx himself said, 'One may be a worker in the morning and a poet in the afternoon.'"

"I thought that was a philosopher in the afternoon."

"Splendid! You know your Marx better than I do!"

"I majored in poli sci. Big deal."

"Yes. Very-very big. It means you will have the proper understanding of our situation. And because you are a member of the international press, you may tell the world!" He clapped his hands like a child who just placed the final piece in a jigsaw puzzle.

I shrugged, a non-answer. I didn't have the heart to tell him my stories went no further than the bottoms of bird cages in the greater Boston area.

"If you should happen to discover news when no other journalist is there, your newspaper would expect you to send a report, no?"

I didn't answer.

"If you did not, who would?"

"'Who cares?' is the real question."

He clicked his gums in sympathy. "I must explain."

The hulk opened his mouth but his partner touched his elbow before he could speak.

"Last night," Manik said, then stopped to check the alley behind him for spies. He went on in a whisper. "Last night some of our members were attacked near the road to the airport."

"I knew it! It was late, wasn't it? Around 3 in the morning?"

"I was not told the time."

"Did it go on for 30 minutes, maybe longer?"

"I can't say. I know only that our people fought bravely against a larger force, and that is why they were able to retreat successfully. The army is afraid to pursue us because they know well our determination. We believe in something more important than any one person. We are willing to die for our country. But what are they fighting for? Three thousand rupees a month?"

"Right. The point is, an anonymous shoot-out at Podunk Farm, Sri Lanka, is not going to make headlines in America. Especially now that it's over. I mean, first there's the verification, which I doubt the government would give me."

"Mister Talison, you do not understand. The story has yet to take place. This is why I have brought the blindfold. So we can bring you there."

"There?"

He checked the alley again before going on. "Last night a member of our party was shot. Let me just say a very-very important member. High ranking. He is wounded, gravely. He has been treated, but without the best facilities, what can be done?"

"I'm hardly a doctor."

"He accepts his fate in service to the people. But first he wishes to talk to a member of the international press. Normally, you see, our party does not trust the capitalist media. We have been cheated so many times before, no? But this is a special case. He has little time."

"Get someone local."

"It was an option. He might even have asked me. I have been published twice already in Colombo newspapers. Yet he has specifically requested a member of the international press."

"Why?"

"I asked myself the same question. So many foreign elements are trying to destroy our country, no?"

"If you say so."

"Not only I, many people say this. It is also common knowledge the press here is controlled by the government. Even the so-called opposition newspapers are restricted in what they may print. Perhaps a member of the international press would be more free. Also more trusted."

"Call one of the wire services. They reach a lot further than my paper. Or the radio. Maybe the BBC has someone in Colombo."

"He lacks a basic political understanding of the situation. Even after we informed him of his error he continues to refer to us in broadcasts as Sinhalese extremists."

"And you hoped to get something better out of me? Hell, Manik, maybe you should just write the piece and I'll sign my name to it."

"No, never, sir. What you write is your affair, absolutely. We would not wish to interfere with your work. The truth is, I was not told why I should find a visiting member of the international press. I can only guess. Perhaps someone not living in Sri Lanka would be less tied up in the complications here. He would be safe to write the truth."

"Safe?"

The big man cut in, speaking slowly, in constructed prose: "We are asking for you, helping us, like friend, a human man. Do not think about, for party, for you, for newspaper. This for human man. He die soon. So, this his last, you know, wanting."

It might be comforting to believe that compassion for the dying played a part in my decision, but the truth is less flattering. I was attracted by the prospect of a story, a hard news article. Maybe even a scoop. The surge of energy that ran through me was unmistakable. Like a hunter whose senses become sharper when spotting the game, I felt more alive, more in tune with who I really was. It also took me back.

Once it had become clear my main contribution in the boxing ring would be better delivered directly to the Red Cross, journalism was all I wanted to do. I started out in political reporting, on the city news desk, and immediately felt at home.

One day I got a lucky tip, which led to the biggest exclusive our paper had seen in years. For almost a week I was the star, the brightest firmament on the staff list. But like any falling star I came down in a flash. They sent me to the sports desk as a crisis management dodge, but it turned into a career. After nearly two decades in press boxes and reeking locker rooms, my threats to demand a transfer back to something important were one of the stock office jokes. If I still envied my colleagues who wrote on subjects that mattered, it was only in private. I never admitted it to anyone, not even Kirstin.

"You understand that I have no control over what goes in the paper?" I asked. "That the editors decide what gets printed?"

Manik looked relieved for the first time since they'd jumped me. "It is a capitalist enterprise, no?"

"And you also understand that it may not even be a story? Most of our readers couldn't find Sri Lanka on a map. And the editors are worse. All they want to know about now is Nicaragua. Next week it'll be somewhere else. Probably not here."

"As you say," Manik answered with an accommodating smile. "You are the reporter. Now if you don't mind." He motioned to the bullet-head, who smiled as he unfolded the black bag.

"No way," I said. "I'll go, but not like that."

"It is necessary," Manik insisted. "For all of us." He put on the earnest expression again. Behind the yellow frames his eyes were practically teary.

"Make it quick," I grumbled. "It's hot enough already."

A heavy hand steadied my shoulder while the bag was slipped over my eyes. Being sightless again immediately brought the fear twinges back to my stomach.

A metal door creaked open behind me. A hand at my elbow guided me in that direction. No one spoke as we entered the building. The air inside was thick and warm. There was a faint smell of chilies in frying oil.

I kept my hands in front of me as we walked. Even with guides on both sides I couldn't shake the image of a steep cliff just a step ahead. I shuffled mummy-like through four or five rooms, each with its own floor surface, its own air pressures and odors, and then we were back outside. It was noisier than in the alley, but the main traffic still sounded a block or more away.

Manik had a rapid-fire conversation in Sinhalese with a voice that came from neither of the tough guys. Five or six steps across what might have been cobblestone brought us into another building, this one air-conditioned. I could hear voices from another room, but not clearly enough to know whether they were speaking English.

A chair was wheeled up noisily from my left. A hand on my shoulder eased me down. "Please, Mister Talison," Manik said. "I will return presently."

Two sets of footsteps faded out, leaving only the buzz of a ceiling light. The conversation in the other room was gone. I was apparently alone. I thought about pulling the bag off to confirm it, and would have, if I didn't suspect they were still in front of me, testing.

Time passed, adding to my discomfort. Finally I called out in a soft voice, "Hello?"

No answer. I tried again. "Manik?"

The darkness was making me claustrophobic. Why had I let myself get in this deep? I realized I could still drop out. Snatch off the bag, get up, walk out the nearest exit. They couldn't do anything to me out in a crowd. I might lose a story, but so what? It wasn't my job. Manik and his buddies might complain, but what more could they do? I would explain how I had someone waiting for me, a coach at the stadium, couldn't be late, had to go at once, so sorry about their friend, but that's –

A male voice purring directly into my ear startled me. "Our apologies, Mister Talison," it said. "Arrangements had to be made."

He cupped a hand under my left elbow. Another hand slid under my right. They half-lifted me, as if my legs would be too weak to make it on their own. I was led from the room into another that was carpeted, then down a long corridor that echoed our footsteps. We stopped in a doorway leading outside. A car directly in front of us waited with its engine idling.

"Mind your head," the new voice said as I was eased into the back seat. I started to sit, but the hand nudged me further into a half-lying position.

"Must not be seen," the voice explained.

"If you find it terribly uncomfortable," Manik added from the front passenger seat, "we can remove the blindfold. But you must agree not to lift your head to look up."

"Fine," I said. The bag was pulled off.

Being able to see again was a relief, even though it meant staring at the bony brown feet of the man sitting beside me. He wore blue rubber sandals worn into wedges at the heels. The half-moons on his craggy toenails were pink and his second toes were longer than the first. I imagined a police line-up from the knees down. I might recognize him.

The car swung left and we merged into the jerky Colombo traffic. A boom box just beyond the closed window on my side blasted a song by Wham.

We drove for 20 minutes or more, some of that time spent going over the same ground. At two different points I heard an identical buzz-voiced vendor call out for customers.

The radio clicked on and a beep signaled the hour. It was followed by a powerful whacking of hand drums that sounded like a signal for mass panic. Next came the professional cadence of a newscaster speaking Sinhalese. The driver said something that made everyone laugh.

"A joke?" I whispered hopefully from the back.

There was more laughter, then talking in Sinhalese. "You would not understand," Manik explained at last.

This round of laughter was louder, perhaps over my failure to get any of it. A merry bunch.

The radio dial was spun until the controlled squeak of a female singer came through. Between verses, the backing band of sitars and drums played what sounded like the soundtrack to a Hindi movie. Someone in the front seat tapped out a rhythm on the dash. Despite the vocals, the tune was almost catchy.

Next came a gloomy number sung by a man, its glutinous keening bringing to mind the possibility of a less than pleasant ending to the day. I warned myself not to be lulled by my companions' civility. The driver began to accompany the singer in a maliciously off-key voice. Thankfully, before it could go any further the car turned and the engine was shut off.

"For security," Manik apologized as the bag was slipped back over my head. I was helped from the car and led along a soft expanse of grass that dipped in the middle. Up a three-step landing I heard a muffled voice ask something. Manik answered and a bolt clicked. I was led inside, and then the bag was taken off.

The interior of the home had the luster of wealth. Dark wood paneling covered the walls and track lighting pointed at potted plants or abstract wall paintings. Manik shook hands with a hollow-cheeked boy about his age. They exchanged a look I couldn't decipher, but said nothing. The driver and the passenger with the bony feet had not come in.

"If you please," the boy said to me, motioning with his palm towards the back of the house. "We were concerned you would not arrive in time."

We walked through the kitchen to the back, crossing a trimmed lawn to a small bungalow that might have been a servant's quarters.

The boy tapped three times in slow succession on the blackened glass of the door. It was opened by a tall woman with the puffy eyes of a person who had been crying. She managed a weak smile in our direction, then formed her lips into the soundless words, "Thank you for coming."

The room inside held a single bed against the far wall, a cane chair and a dresser with a mirror holding snapshots in three of its corners. The woman leaned against the dresser with one shoulder to shove it aside.

Manik and his accomplice hurried to replace her. Together they slid the dresser across the floor, revealing a waist-high opening in the wall behind. First the woman and then the rest of us crouched through and into the other side, emerging into a dim, narrow room that smelled of rubbing alcohol.

"You have come," a quiet voice spoke from the dark. It took a moment for my eyes to pick out a low single bed and the shape of a man lying on it. "It was. . . good of you," he went on, the sentence broken by a pause while he took in a raspy breath. His accent seemed posh, more British than Sri Lankan.

The woman knelt by the bed to stroke his forehead. He murmured something in Sinhalese that made her nod. She squeezed his hand and got up. From the darkness she produced a rattan chair which she slid so close to the bed it touched the sheet.

"Please," she said to me with another effort at a smile. Courtesy must have been so much a part of her it worked on automatic pilot.

Sitting there put me directly over the man's head. He had the oversized features of a stage actor's high-bridged nose and fleshy mouth, but the color had drained from his face. His eyes fluttered for a moment as if unable to choose between open and shut. Sickbed scenes are bad enough when you know the patient. Here I felt all the more absent from any clues on how to act. I hoped he wouldn't seize up or die while I was there. What would I do then? What was I supposed to say to the woman if it was obvious he was gone?

"I must. . . thank you for coming," he said in a rhythm clipped by a wince. "I am forever being surprised by the capacity of our species for kindness. All my life I've. . . been lucky to have met such kind people. Even those I never properly knew. This is what gives me hope." He chuckled faintly. "Hope," he said again.

"You're going to be fine," I answered, and immediately felt stupid for it. The sheet covering him had splotches of red where the bandages were leaking.

There was a pause in which no one spoke. The two young men stood in the background with the woman. The room's only light filtered in through blinds at a single window high on the wall. Dust drifted in the rays.

"Why don't we get a doctor?" I said. "Surely something can be done. I can ask for one, say it's for me, tell them there's – "

"No. No thank you. I have a doctor. One of the best in the country, actually. A dear friend. From our. . . We went to school together. I trust him thoroughly."

"But no good doctor would just give up. You don't look like you're going to, whatever. Anyway, get another opinion. These people aren't perfect just because they studied medicine."

"Precisely what I tell him," he said, smiling thinly. "We would go on about it." He coughed in a way that made a snorkeling sound in his chest. A spot of blood appeared on his lips.

The woman rushed in to wipe it away. She was crying again. He cleared his throat with a tiny gurgle, then spit into the handkerchief she held under his chin. After several slow breaths he said, "I am paralyzed. A bullet in the spine. An operation would not help. And it is rather unlikely I would, would survive a stay in jail. Even some of our healthiest young comrades do not make it through. . . ah, what they call interrogation."

He murmured to the woman. She reached beneath the bed for a tin cup which she held to his lips. He took a small amount in his mouth before swallowing with an effort that made him grit his teeth.

"What can I do to help?" I asked.

"Thank you," he answered. "You were kind to come. Now. I should like to explain something about our party. So much rot has been written about us. It doesn't help. . . we refuse interviews. . . a policy I argued against, incidentally. Some of our leaders are not so trusting."

His eyes widened, perhaps at the irony of my presence, before returning to a distant stare.

"In any event, I should like to use what energy I have left. . . to advance our cause. I must break party discipline to do so, hmm, but then it would not be the first time."

He seemed to savor the thought with his eyes closed. I watched the sheet rise and lower over his chest.

His eyes opened again, then found me. "My name is Commander Dapila. Not my real name. A nom de guerre." He laughed silently. "I will not deny we have some romantic notions of how to conduct a revolution. Silly, you might think."

I wrote the name Commander Dapila in my notebook. "Of course it's up to you," I said, "but we could include your real name. For authenticity."

"Naturally I myself would have no objection. But I would ask you not to, for my family's sake. The authorities could be harder on them even after. If you don't mind."

"No problem."

"In any event, my assumed name will serve better. Now. My rank is called commander, because for a time. . . I led a group in the Anuradhapura area. But you might say more properly that I am a member of the Politburo."

I pictured dour Russians in blocky suits glaring at each other around a conference table. "That means you're one of the top, how many can I say?"

"Fourteen. At present. Below this, the Central Committee has about 50. The numbers change. Then there is the party membership. Say 1,500 full-time. Then supporters and part-time members. I don't know the actual count. It works by cells, secret cells. One may know the comrades in one's own. . . ah, cell, but not those in another. Then we have sympathizers. Many. Some say one million, some say two. I doubt it. But at any rate, Sri Lankans are searching. Water please."

I held the cup. He drank half the contents this time.

"Better, that's better," he said. "Excuse me. Where was I?"

I looked at my notebook. "Sympathizers one million, maybe two. But probably not."

"Now. The point is what happens from here. Not what we've done up to – "

His eyes darted about in several directions, as if he intended to panic but wasn't sure how to begin. The woman kneeled beside him, speaking softly and quickly.

He swallowed twice, murmuring something I couldn't understand, and the spell passed. He nodded and she got up, moving this time to the foot of the bed. She watched him with her lips moving in what might have been a prayer.

"More important is how the struggle advances. Which is why I have asked –"

From outside came the sound of a helicopter, growing louder. I looked up to the rafters in alarm, as if they might spot us through cracks in the ceiling.

"No cause for worry," the woman told me in a whisper. "They fly often here. Most of the MPs live nearby."

The man went on. "Sri Lanka is at a critical stage. Historical. At present, near anarchy. The ruling party has been in place too long. They know this, they do, yet it is not within their capacity to change. Corruption. . . this is the road they have chosen and from which they cannot depart. Personal wealth is now the only source of honor, even while more than half our children suffer, are malnourished."

He was speaking faster now. I had to abbreviate my notes to keep up.

"The Tamil struggle continues in the north, and, and, the Indian army has arrived to keep a so-called peace where no peace exists. Government goons are killing the best of our youth, our future. Two tires and one gallon of petrol and then a match. This is the reward for a young patriot today. Why? When will it end? Hmm. Now the problem. . . the problem is the center. A gap, a vacuum, in the power structure. This is what we must fill. In a time of chaos, only the most organized can lead. The JVP."

Sweat appeared in beads on his forehead. I wondered whether to wipe them off. The woman leaned in to dab his face with her sleeve. All the while she spoke softly in Sinhalese.

"Just a little more," he answered. "Now. The news I must tell you. It concerns the leadership of our party, but more importantly, for you, the government."

I nodded and flipped to a blank page.

"There is something nobody else in the party knows," he said. "Not even the Politburo."

He called the woman nearer and murmured into her ear. She stood to talk to the two against the wall. They left the room.

"I discovered this only two days ago," he went on in a quieter voice. "I have a friend. . . in a senior position in the government. Very senior. Naturally I cannot tell you his name."

"I understand."

"You may know already the leader of our party is Aruna Rajit-purna. Of course all decisions are. . . made by the cadres through the Central Committee and so on. But for various reasons, we consider one man to be the leader. Comrade Rajitpurna. Now. When he is absent, the meeting is chaired by a man named Gamanaya Perera. Perera. Remember him. He is a snake. I suspected it earlier, but now I have proof. Perera is a traitor. To the party and to the country. Our No. 2 man is working undercover. As a foreign agent for India. He is being bribed."

He breathed several times with effort, then went on. "Perera was once a good man. I know this to be true. We were imprisoned together. For some time, we shared a cell."

His voice cracked, perhaps from emotion. "I promise you, Comrade Perera was a true revolutionary. Something, however. . . I can't say. Who can say? They tortured everyone, of course. In any event, he is no longer one of us."

He said something in Sinhalese. The woman half-turned towards the wall and reached into the front of her blouse. She took out a square of paper and unfolded it slowly, to avoid tearing, before offering it to me with both hands.

The top was stamped in red: DESTROY UPON READING. The letterhead was from the Ministry of Home Affairs of the

Government of India. It was addressed to a name that was blackened out.

"Now. Your story," he said. "It is not simply that Comrade Perera is an infiltrator. That can happen. The key is how. Read this paper. It explains that Perera is being paid by the Indian intelligence authorities. Moreover –"

His voice cracked again. He raked his throat feebly before going on. "This paper is not a photocopy. It is a government document from New Delhi dated –"

"Two days ago," I noted.

"My friend, of course, has seen it. Perhaps one or two others. But that is all. The list of names you see there, with Perera? Government officials, top politicians of the ruling party. That. . . that will be of primary interest to your readers. It means our political leaders are selling themselves, and selling their country. One government is actually buying off another, in secret. Secret until now. This is news. Major news."

"Yes."

"Now. At the time you report this, you would naturally include mention of our JVP traitor. And our purpose will be served as well. But, I must advise you. . . be extremely careful for yourself, so long as you have this document."

"Why me?"

"What better way. . . than a foreign newspaper? Which must then be picked up by the local media? Perera" – he paused, aiming his eyes at me with effort – "would otherwise deny the allegations. Accuse his accuser of treachery, expel the source from the party with few ever knowing why. News from abroad, however, it reaches everyone in Sri Lanka at once. And then? He will have no option. He will have to answer for his own actions. This may be a setback for our party, of course."

He coughed again, roughly, but there was no blood.

"We will lose a veteran fighter, a key man, highly respected among the cadres. But this will not stop us. The revolution will progress. Who will notice. . . once the government of Sri Lanka is proved to be run by traitors? A ruling party corrupted by bribery from another country? How could it possibly survive?"

His eyes opened wide, straining after some dim, receding vista, then closed again.

3

I picked up my room key at the front desk and explained that I was not to be disturbed, for anybody. At the stairs I turned back to say, perhaps out of habit, "Unless my wife calls."

The manager displayed the overbite that turned even his neutral expressions into a smile. "Certainly, sir," he said. I must have looked hungry because he added, "Only allow me to inform you the restaurant will be closing in less than one hour. I must let the cook go at 9."

I took the stairs up two at a time. In my room I slid the chain bolt shut. It seemed secure. I looked out the window. An intruder would need grappling hooks and the arm of Joe Montana to reach me on the third floor. Lean and wiry as some of these people were, it was hard to picture them scaling walls. I pulled the document out from my underwear and set it on the desk. On the ridiculous notion that it might somehow be seen by someone looking in through a distant window, I slipped it instead into a book I found in the desk drawer. It was a collection of sutras, the Buddhist answer to Gideon's Bible, and if they read their scriptures here as much as people I knew did back home, a reasonable hiding place.

I stood under a cold-water shower just long enough to wash away the sweat. Back at the desk I sat naked, water dripping from my beard.

Lifting the cover to my laptop made me giddy. I drummed the

desk while waiting for it to boot up. I remembered my early days on the paper landing my first bylined assignments. There's nothing like your rookie season.

The computer issued a beep and the screen glowed white. There was a purity in the blank space I used to find mesmerizing. It meant anything could happen, perhaps even an article that would make a difference, something to change things for the better. Inevitably the optimism begins to fade and then somehow disappears. The reality just came sooner for me than for most.

The cursor blinked sky-blue in the screen's upper left corner, an invitation to create. The plastic keys were surprisingly cool. I watched the cursor jerk across the screen as my fingers popped: "A just-discovered confidential document issued by the Ministry of Home Affairs of India reveals the government in New Delhi is paying off high-ranking government officials in Colombo."

I stopped, got rid of "just-discovered," and read again. I pictured a yawning "whatevah" from a Celtics fan tiptoeing through the hard news on his way to Question the Coach. I put my middle finger on the delete button and swept the screen clean. The scoreboard was still empty. As long as I had the ball, I may as well go for the net.

"The government of India has been revealed through a top secret document to be paying off members of the Sri Lankan government." Government this, government that. Blocked by the tenacious defense of my imaginary fans' boredom, I deleted that too.

"India is bribing" I wrote, and sensed I was getting somewhere. Moving down the court.

"India is bribing leading members of the Sri Lankan government, according to a secret document from its Ministry of Home Affairs obtained in Colombo by the *Boston Post*."

Now I was in the game. I took out "Ministry of Home Affairs." Who cares what bureaucrat pushed the papers around? I changed "leading members of the Sri Lankan government" to "top politicians in Sri Lanka." I added, "The scandal may threaten the survival of the party which has ruled Sri Lanka for 10 years."

I read it through twice, then leaned back, fingers locked behind my head. For someone who hadn't written a real news lead in 16 years, I felt I'd done well. Maybe even nailed it. It had the right combination of heat and light. It might not lift hockey fans out of their seats, but it should hook at least some of the general public. On a personal level they may not care whether Sri Lanka was taken over by trained apes, but a "scandal" that could "threaten" the "survival" of a government should appeal to any reader's fondness for mayhem.

I scanned the document again, wondering where to include the names of the dirty politicians. Some of the names were Sinhalese wonders as long as my leg. The first six were each followed by "MP" and the district they served. The list ended with the seventh name, Gamanaya Perera, identified only by the letters JVP. The great vice-leader, about to be knocked plenty more rungs down his own ladder.

I added some background, mentioning that the Sri Lankan government was weakened already by the war against Tamil Tigers fighting for their own country in the north and east, while Sinhalese radicals were now mounting an insurrection in the south.

That might have led smoothly into a rogue's list of the corrupt officials along with the faux rebel Perera, but I needed to run the names by someone who knew local politics. If I printed it without including something obvious – maybe one of the MPs was the front-runner to succeed RJ – it would be like air-balling the winning foul shot with one second left.

The clock said 8:23 p.m. Breakfast time in Boston, too late for the three-star edition anyway. It would be easy enough to crank out the rest in the morning once I had the answers to a few simple questions I could put to some embassy flunky. All I needed was to alert my editors. They would want to search the files for photos of Sri Lankan politicians, maybe work up a map or some basic country info for a side-box. And of course prepare space on the front page for what would be, after all, a global scoop. I grinned at my own face in the table mirror. Maybe the government really would fall. With my byline over the story that did it. An article that actually uncovered the truth and changed people's lives. They give out prizes for that kind of thing.

I added a short explanation to the editor, promising the rest in time for the next day's early edition, then took the print-out downstairs.

The bored receptionist looked annoyed when I offered to type it in myself on her telex. I didn't help my case by asking whether she realized the rest of the world had moved on to something called fax machines. But when I boasted I could type faster than she could, and offered 100 rupees just for the opportunity to prove it, she stood up and held the chair for me.

It was a monster of a contraption but I got on a roll and whacked out the whole thing in less than 10 minutes. Still "remarkably slow" by her account.

"Visiting field disadvantage," I said, but she didn't care. She pocketed the money and wanted to know when I might care to try again.

I found the cook in the kitchen folding his apron. He pointed at the clock and said he was sorry, try him for breakfast, then picked up his bag. I got his attention back by slapping two 100 rupee notes on the cutting board.

"And there's another 100 in it for you if it tastes good," I promised. By that point I cared less about taste than volume, but I was feeling generous.

He served up a steaming hill of rice with three different curries, one fiery enough to make me hang my tongue out for air. He even produced a frosty beer before I could ask for it. I added an extra 200 rupees to the money pile and we parted happy men.

I dreamed I was back home. Kirstin was with me again. We were dressing to go to a party. She asked me how she looked, pivoting in a shimmering red dress that left her back bare. I wasn't lying when

I told her she was ravishing. In the car, however, it was not Kirstin in the passenger seat but a woman I didn't know saying something in a language I couldn't understand. "But we're already late," I argued, and then the car hit a bad patch of road and started knocking. I woke up to the sound of a door being rattled. My door.

I tiptoed to the desk. I searched for the book in the orange-tinted light coming through the window. Before I could grab it, the door knob began to turn, but very slowly. There was a soft click and the door eased open. It stopped when the chain bolt caught.

A voice from the other side hissed like a snake with a rat trapped in its throat. Another voice whispered back in rapid Sinhalese and the door quietly closed. My heartbeat flooded my ears like surf. I felt absurdly exposed, a spectator to my own fear.

A crack from beyond the door made me snap to attention. I hurried to my dufflebag for the waterproof pouch holding my passport and air ticket home. I pulled everything out and slipped the document inside.

The loud rap startled me more than I expected. "Mmmph?" I said, leaning my head near the bed, trying to sound sleepy. I ran to the bathroom, lifted the cover on the toilet tank and eased the document inside. I considered it another kind of passport, an irreplaceable one. It could get me into the big leagues after all. If I lost it or gave it up, I might forever remain another minor leaguer with a sad tale to tell about how close he came to having it all.

The rap on the door came again, followed this time by thumps. Someone was beating on it with both fists.

"Open this room!" a voice commanded. I had just enough time to leap back under the covers when the door came crashing in off its hinges.

Three Sri Lankan men in olive green uniforms followed as if glued to it, the first landing flat on the door while the other two stumbled over him. A grey-haired officer sauntered in a moment later, pouting his lower lip at the impromptu gymnastics. As the director of this cast, he seemed distinctly unimpressed.

"Huh?!" I blurted from the bed, trying to squint the way a man half-asleep might.

The first soldier scrambled to regain his feet. He was a wisp of a guy in a uniform that hung on him like a sack. Yet as I swung my feet to the floor he grabbed me by the throat and squeezed hard enough to make me gasp. It was absurd. If I'd been standing he wouldn't have come up to my shoulders. I swatted him with the back of my hand, sending him to the floor again in a heap.

He hopped up, this time with his face contorted. The superior snarled something that made him spin and march to the open doorway where he stood, glowering. The officer, seeming to repress a sigh of resignation, said, "You will forgive my men here. A little too eager to please, sometimes. Now come along with us and there won't be any need for trouble, hmm?"

"Trouble?" I echoed, staring meaningfully at the dislocated door. Somehow we had attracted no interest from the other guests. I considered that a bad sign.

The other two had already picked up my passport. They were now going through my bag. The superior tapped the side of his leg with a baton. He seemed bored.

"Do you mind telling me what this is all about?" I asked, trying to sound appropriately indignant. "Is it a custom in your country to attack visiting members of the international media in their hotel rooms? Because I think a representative from my embassy will be quite interested to hear about this."

He rolled his eyes up to the ceiling, as if it was a custom in his country to ignore appropriate indignation. He checked his fingernails for flaws. The two soldiers finished their search and said something. The leader tilted his head slightly. He turned to me. "You may put your clothes on."

They had the decency to avert their eyes while I went through my bag for underwear. When dressed I announced, "I'm not going anywhere until I can place a phone call directly to the ambassador. Furthermore – "

The officer snorted in disgust. "Oh, shut up, will you?" he said as the others shuffled me through the door frame.

Instead of the jeep I expected, a white Mercedes was parked in the driveway. I searched the lobby and the corridors, hoping for the manager or anyone else to appear. I wanted witnesses. But the place was deserted. No doubt another custom.

"I protest this – " I began in a voice loud enough to wake people, but a shove at my back sent me out the hotel door. Two of the soldiers helped me into the back seat, one on either side. The disconsolate munchkin drove.

No one spoke as we pulled out of the parking lot onto the gravel driveway. We drove through deserted Colombo streets, the jumble of my thoughts in contradiction to the leisurely pace we kept. I was still mentally preparing my denials and alibis when we arrived at a brick fence topped with rolls of barbed wire, the entrance to a military base. It might have been the air force, judging from two camouflage helicopters parked on the lawn.

The guard at the entrance gate wore a tan uniform. He stepped out of his booth to approach our car at a stroll, saw the grey-haired officer in the front seat and stiffened upright to salute us through.

The soldiers stayed at my elbows as we walked into a sprawling red-brick building. The air inside was unpleasantly warm. Every light seemed to be on, although the reception desk was empty. A wall clock said 3:42.

We marched through a bare-walled corridor and then down a flight of red metal steps, their boots clattering. The basement had the same type of corridor, only here the doors leading off it were made of steel instead of wood.

One door was open already. The cement walls held a room the size of single-car garage. In the center was the only furniture, a bare wooden table with two chairs. A fluorescent bulb on the ceiling cast the soldiers with me in a sickly tint.

They sat me in the chair nearest the door, then took up position behind me, talking in Sinhalese. One told a joke that made the others chuckle, an encouraging sign. It was followed by a long stretch of silence.

After several minutes one of the soldiers took the empty chair and set it at an angle facing me on the same side of the table. He sat down with a shy smile, then glanced at the soldiers behind me. The short one had put on a disapproving scowl, but it had no effect.

"From which part of America you are coming?" the seated one asked.

"Boston."

He smiled wider. "My cousin, he live in California."

He translated that much of the conversation to the others, then asked me, "You playing cricket?" He curled his fingers around an imaginary ball and mimicked the straight-armed overhead delivery of a bowler.

"No, not much of that in the US. We're more into baseball."

He nodded knowingly, and was about to speak when the sound of the door opening made him snap up to attention. Two Sinhalese men in civilian clothes came in. The first was a stoop-shouldered man with jowly cheeks. His wavy hair, slicked back with oil, had long grey streaks at the temples that gave him a scholarly air. He nodded curtly to the soldiers.

They saluted and left, passing a tall, long-nosed man with a patchy beard that failed to hide a weak chin. He lowered his chin to his chest, folded his arms and leaned back against the door, looking as if he might fall asleep on his feet.

The first man moved the empty chair to the opposite side of the table. He sat down with a sigh, then tossed a thick manila folder onto the table before me. Inside I could see my passport and notebook along with other papers that weren't mine, some written in Sinhalese.

He pulled a pair of black-framed plastic glasses from the pocket of his white shirt, let out a slow puff of air and began reading something I couldn't see. He murmured to himself as he went along. I watched his small brown eyes, magnified by the lenses, as they followed the words across the page. I resisted the temptation to turn back to check on the man behind me. Would he be the bad cop?

The reader stopped half-way through a third paper, his finger marking the spot. He looked up at me. "Oh, this shouldn't take long," he apologized. The tone was reassuring. Maybe he wanted to get back to bed as much as I did.

He initialed the top of the page and replaced it in the folder, then took out my passport and went through the visa pages. I hadn't been abroad much in the past three years. Just to cover Wimbledon each summer and once to Sweden to meet Kirstin's family. He flipped back to the photo page and held it up to take me in with the same gaze.

"You are Mister Gordon Talison?" he asked.

"Yes."

"Is my pronunciation correct? TA-li-son? I wondered whether it might not be Ta-LEE-son."

"No, you were right. Talison."

"I see. And have you any another names, aliases we call them? Perhaps a pen name?"

"No, just my own."

"Have you visited Sri Lanka before?"

"This is my first time."

"You arrived yesterday, Air Lanka, flight 810. And you plan to stay the week. At least this is what your visa application states."

"That's right. I'm a sportswriter. The Continental Cup is an important lead-up to the World Cup, as you probably know, so my newspaper – "

"Yes, yes, I'm aware of all that," he said with slight irritation. "I played rather avidly, in my time. Left back for our junior national team." He patted his belt and winked. "Of course it was some time ago."

I managed a smile in return. "Me too," I answered with an understanding nod, patting my own stomach. Maybe we had a lot in common.

From outside the door I could hear the shuffling steps of a group passing by. There seemed to be some confusion. Angry voices broke out and then cut off when they moved away.

I raised my eyebrows questioningly, but he seemed to notice neither the disturbance nor my reaction to it. He set my passport down so that it was facing me but still on his half of the table, then picked up a copy of my telex. He read it quietly to himself, tapping some of the words with a covered fountain pen. At one point he cast a concerned expression over my shoulder towards his partner. The long pause that followed may have been calculated to add to my discomfort. I tried to settle my mind by thinking of what sport this reminded me of, but could come up with only a childhood game: kick the can. I was deep in the other team's enemy territory.

Finally he said, with a friendly smile that seemed to mean that everything was going to work out, "Maybe you'd simply better tell us everything, Mister Talison. From the beginning."

"Fine," I answered, clearing my throat. "I'm here, and, well, I don't know if I approve of this kind of questioning, to begin with. I mean, crashing in on me late at night. I really should have legal counsel here if there's some problem with something I know nothing about, and a representative from my embassy. I have nothing to hide. I'm a journalist and I'm just doing my job. There can't be any law against that, even here."

He closed his eyes and let out a breath that made his nostrils flare. It was a moment before the relaxed expression found its way back to his face.

"You are here. . . you claim you are here to report on the tournament."

"That's right. That's exactly what I came for. And that's what I intend – "

"And yet. Not 24 hours after you arrive, you are engaged in secret meetings with members of a subversive guerrilla organization. Animals."

Truth or Dare. There was no point denying what they already

knew.

"That's not my fault. I mean, yes. I did. I met the JVP. What else was I to do? I had an interview. Someone offers an interview to a journalist and what would you have him do? Turn it down?"

"Where did this meeting take place?"

"I don't know. I was taken there in a blindfold. A dark room was all I got to see."

"Who took you?"

"Who? Well. Actually, at this time, I don't wish to state my sources."

He slapped the table with his palm hard enough to make the manila folder jump. I swallowed and tried to look unimpressed, the type who couldn't be bullied with theatrics.

He stared at me for a long moment. Finally he shook his head from side to side. In a subdued voice, he said, "We know all about your meeting with Commander Dapila."

He removed my notebook from the folder and opened it to the page where the interview began. He jabbed it five or six times with his finger, as if pointing to the proof of my guilt. "You're in serious trouble. Do you understand that, Mister Talison? Very serious trouble. Now where is Dapila?"

"I couldn't see through the blindfold. I just did what they said. I went for an interview. Read it. It's not like I was joining them or anything. Dapila, sure, he told me things, news, and I wrote them down. Suppose you tell me exactly what crime I'm supposed to have committed?"

"In the past year alone more than 200 members of the United National Party have been killed by these thugs. Elected officials of the government of Sri Lanka shot down in the street or even in their own homes. For what? For serving their country."

"So they're a guerrilla mob who kill people. What's it got to do with me?"

He glared at me. "You think this is some sort of game, don't you Talison? You think you can come here to our poor little country, write up your articles, then go home to your happy life with your wife and children and two cars. Right? As long as your career is helped, what does it matter if you get a few facts wrong?"

"I never said that. That's not how it is."

"Perhaps these young terrorists even appeal to you, hmm? When they talk about Marxism. Nicaragua. The new Cuba? Come now, Mister Talison. You're an intelligent man, a journalist. You've studied these things, I'm sure. You must have some insight into the oppressive nature of the capitalist system. The alienation of hired labor and all that. It would be perfectly understandable."

"My personal views would have nothing to do with it. I interviewed someone. They happened to be in the JVP. If I interview you, does that make me one of the Sri Lankan. . . are you army or what? You never told me."

"Your Commander Dapila," he went on, sneering at the word commander. "You know he was involved with criminal activities in Anuradhapura. He told you himself. But he didn't say exactly how, did he? A more perceptive journalist might have thought to ask, but then you're a sportswriter, you say?"

I let it slide. If that's the best he could do. He had to rummage through the folder before pulling out the paper he wanted.

"Twelve July, 1987," he read. "Mihintale. You don't know it, but it's a village east of Anuradhapura. The MP from that district has his home there. A family, a wife, seven children. Or had, shall I say, until Commander Dapila and his brave boys – and girls no doubt, they use them too – went to work. The man was killed in his own bedroom, his throat sliced from ear to ear."

He reached across the table and started to trace a line on my throat with his finger. I rocked back before he could touch my Adam's apple.

"In front of his wife, his mother and of course the children. They were made to watch, you see."

I said nothing. Wiping the sweat off my forehead would have only made me look nervous, so I let it go. He looked at me, not blinking, then went back to his paper.

"Twenty-four August, 1987. Anuradhapura. A newspaper seller, 52 years old. Shot twice. Once in each eye. The reason? He sold newspapers your subversives don't like. Oh, did I mention he had eight children? This is the work of Commander Dapila. Your revolutionary hero."

"Oh, come off it. I never called him that and you know it. I'm sure both sides have stories to tell. It's hardly any business of mine. I'm here to do a job and that's it. If my job happened to change in the process, so it goes. Right now my editors in Boston are expecting an article detailing how the Indian government is bribing Sri Lanka's politicians. Are you going to explain to them what happened if I don't make the deadline? Because I would imagine that could make an even better story, how the Sri Lankan government officially prevented – "

He snorted. "The telex wasn't sent."

"But. . . shit. I typed it in myself."

"Give us some credit, Talison. We may be a developing country, not rich or advanced like yours, but must we be thoroughly stupid as well? We know only too well how foreign elements are working to destroy our democratically elected government. You couldn't imagine we were smart enough to monitor international communications?"

"Okay, good, actually, because that's what the story was about, don't you see? Foreign elements. You should be happy to have me get that kind of news out. Think about it. You can clean out the ranks. There was even a JVP leader on the list. Can you get more fair than that?"

"It was Commander Dapila himself who told you this information, correct?"

"Yes. You have my notes."

"And exactly what proof did he offer?"

I may have paused for half a second, but no longer. "He said he would get it to me."

While he narrowed his eyes into another gut-check stare, I thought back to my notes. I couldn't recall writing anything about the document itself. Not when I had it in my hand already.

"And just how was he to get it to you? Perhaps through the same people who brought you there?"

"No, I wouldn't know. He didn't tell me that. He said it would be safer not to know."

"Safer not to know, he said?"

"Yes."

"Were those the words he used, the exact words?"

"I can't say exact or not. That's how I remember it."

"Yet this does not appear in your notes. Your rather detailed notes of the conversation."

"What's it got to do with the story? My notes are what I need to write up an article."

He thought that through, then flipped through my notebook. "'M + boy leave.' This comes just before Dapila explains that he has news for you. What does this mean?"

I looked back at him, unsure of how to answer.

"'W cries,'" he quoted. "We may assume this is Dapila's wife, correct? Does W stand for wife?"

"I wouldn't know who was his wife and who wasn't."

"Tall, slender, long hair, some say attractive?"

"It was dark in that room, you know, and – "

"Look. You will tell us where we can find Dapila. You will also tell us who was in the room with you when you met him. Do you understand? You will tell us tonight."

"I don't have to reveal the sources of my information. That is between – "

I was interrupted by a violent jerk of my chair from behind. It twisted sideways, dropping me to the cement floor. Beneath the table was a metal drain circled by a dark stain. It was the color of dried blood. I felt my stomach begin to rise. The man who dumped me asked something in Sinhalese. His voice was agitated.

"Now, now, we won't be needing any of that," the superior said.

The other one put my chair back in place at the table. He barked, "Sit."

My expression must have changed. The inquisitor became almost apologetic.

"Really, this doesn't have to be such a nuisance for either of us, you know." I could feel his partner's breath on the back of my neck.

"It is quite late after all," he continued. He checked his watch and lifted his eyebrows in mild surprise. "My goodness. Even later than I thought. It's only to be expected that we're all tired and a little irritable. Now Mister Talison." He was smiling again. "As I see it, you've gotten involved in something larger than you ever expected. I don't believe this is entirely your fault. You simply got mixed in with a group of bad fellows. It's not so uncommon for outsiders here, you know. When it comes to handling visitors, sometimes we Sri Lankans are a little too clever for our own good. One of the legacies of colonization, I suspect."

He laughed in a way that invited me to join in. I managed a tiny smile.

"It's really quite simple. Tell us where we can find Dapila. And anyone with him. Take care of that, fill in a few minor details about your meeting, or interview, let us say, and that should be it. You'll be free to go. Wash your hands of the whole affair. Go back to your hotel, get a good night's sleep. Leave the rebel-catching to us. You'll be back in the swing of things by tomorrow, plenty of time to get to the preliminaries. I'm hoping to get to a few matches myself, you know."

In the stuffy room, the memory of the scented night air came back to me like an interrupted dream. I avoided it with a long, deep breath. I told myself to keep sharp. Danger can easily come smiling.

"I'd like to help," I said, "but how can I tell you the names of people I don't know? They didn't tell me. Why would they? What could they possibly gain? And I don't know the location. Like I said, I was blindfolded when they brought me there."

The helpful look drained from his face. He pressed his lips together as if in effort to hold back an outburst, then jerked his chin up. The latch on the door behind me clacked open.

I kept my expression neutral, but the sweat soaking the front of my shirt must have been telling. The superior shoved my passport and notebook back into the folder. He walked around the table to stand behind me.

I waited, staring at the empty wall for a minute or more. It was a game of chicken. How far were they prepared to go with an American citizen, especially one linked to a major news organization? Finally, bracing myself for a punch, I turned around to look.

The superior was staring down at me with a skewed attempt at a smile. "Come," he said. The other one pulled the door open and, when I didn't move, motioned with his eyes for me to step into the corridor.

I walked to the right, the way we'd come in, but a hand on my back directed me the other way. The superior draped his left arm around my shoulder. He turned his head so he could whisper into my ear.

"I want you to know. This is important so you must listen closely. I want you to know that whatever happens from here is entirely up to you. In a manner of speaking, you are in control. Not me. The choice is yours. Do we stop or do we go on? When you wish to stop, we stop. Simply tap me on the elbow." He took his arm off my shoulder. "Like this," he said, patting my elbow twice. He put his arm back, this time tighter around my neck.

I could feel sweat trickling down my belly, yet I seemed to be both hot and cold at the same time. I wasn't sure I could trust my legs, the bones feeling less than solid. I stopped in a way that made the one behind me bump into my back.

"Look," I said, "I'm – "

"Come come now," the leader soothed, as if to a child. He

tightened the pressure on the back of my neck with his arm. "We can talk as we go."

I considered jumping them. I had the weight advantage over either one alone. Together they might be hard to beat. Military guys, they probably had training. But so had I. And I'd lost fights before. Taking a beating in a corridor seemed a better prospect than whatever else they had in mind.

We stopped at one of the closed steel doors. The tall man slid the metal cover off a view hole. He looked in, then turned around with a frown. He said something in Sinhalese.

The superior arched back to look at the door number, 31B, and seemed confused as well. He kept his arm behind my head as he led me to the next room, 30B. With his free hand he took off his glasses to look through the view hole, then put them back on to focus on me.

"This will do," he said, grinning. "Even better."

He motioned for me to look. When I didn't move he pushed my face towards the door. He slid the cover open.

Lying on the table was a teen or younger boy, naked, his wrists handcuffed behind his back. Blood dripped from the table into a large oval on the floor. I hadn't realized there could be so much.

The cover slid shut. The superior's eyes gleamed behind his thick glasses, almost as if he were happy. He tapped my elbow twice. "Maybe now there is something you would like to tell me?" he asked, smiling.

"Listen. I said I'd tell you what I know." I was breathing fast, the words coming out in spurts. "But they put a blindfold on me. There wasn't – "

He shot a hand up to cover my mouth. "We're going inside," he said, raising his eyebrows. "Yes. We're going inside."

The tall one held the door open. The superior walked in ahead of me, leaving the other time to shoot me an anxious look and hiss into my ear, "Best if you say everything now."

A burnt smell was mixed with the iron scent of blood. I walked behind the superior in shuffling steps, my mind stuck on the calculus of my next move, when I felt handcuffs snap onto my wrists. Everything seemed to speed up as a wave of panic flushed through me. I jumped to clear some space between me and the pair, putting my back against a wall.

"Don't fucking try," I growled. "First one to touch me is a dead man."

I banged back against the cement with my shoulder as if I might knock the wall down. I heard myself hyperventilate in a way that had to waste energy, but I couldn't avoid it. I stretched my lips back to bare my teeth, ready to bite.

It was easy for them to reach me on either side. I aimed a kick at the crotch of the superior but missed when he calmly stepped back. I had to hop onto my other leg just to keep upright.

They muscled me, writhing, closer to the table. I tried to drop down, but they held me up. My feet dragged behind me on the floor.

The superior grabbed my hair and forced my head closer to the table. I strained back with my neck and shoulders, my whole body shaking with effort, until we reached a standoff with my nose inches from the boy's face.

The eyes were open but only the white parts showed. An open pink gash ran from his right temple to his chin. There was a circular scorch mark on the other side of his neck, maybe a cigarette burn. It seemed too small to produce the acrid smell that crowded the room, but then I saw the bigger mark at his groin.

"Tell me," the man hissed, his breath hot in my ear. "Where is Dapila? Who is M?"

"I. . . listen to me, goddamn it. . . let me out of here."

"Where did you meet?"

The hand on the back of my head pushed more. I strained back harder, then they suddenly let go. My head snapped up and I toppled backward to the floor. It was sticky with blood.

I rolled onto my stomach and tried to rise up on one elbow, but a shoe on the back of my neck forced me down.

"Where?" the tall man shouted down.

"A house," I blurted. "Goddammit! A rich house. In a rich neighborhood. I don't know where it was. I swear. I don't even know where I am now."

The foot left my neck. I curled, expecting a kick, but was instead lifted up by my arms. A chair was placed beneath me and I sank into it. The boy's blood soaked me from my knees to my chest.

"How did you get there?"

"A car. I don't know what kind. It was big. Maybe a Mercedes. It was clean inside but not new. There were three of them besides me. But I didn't see them, I'm telling you. They made me wear a blindfold."

"You can't take notes with a blindfold."

"They took it off for the interview. Dapila didn't care. He knew he was going to die. He was shot up bad."

"Who is M?"

"He's the one who took me there. M is shorthand, stands for man. He didn't give me a name. He seemed older, at least by his voice. Another guy with him sounded young, around college student age, that's why I wrote down boy. M + boy leave, that means the two of them, when they left the room. They both spoke good English, better than most people here, so maybe they're college students. But I didn't get a good look so I can't be sure."

"Lies. All lies."

"No! They were in the dark, I'm telling you. The interview was with Dapila. The others had nothing to say. Look at my notebook."

"Who else was there?"

"The man and the boy, like I said, but they stayed in the back. And there was the woman. W is for woman. I wasn't told her name."

"Describe her."

"Like you said. She stayed in the dark too. But I could see she had long hair, black and long. I saw it from behind. And she was kind of tall, tall for a woman anyway. She seemed to be the one taking care of him. She probably was his wife. She seemed like a wife."

"How were you contacted?"

"A note came to me while I sitting in a restaurant downtown. The Colonial, or Imperial, something like that. Around the corner from the post office. I was just sitting there drinking tea by myself, and then the note was there on my table."

"Where is this note?"

"I don't know. I can't remember if I threw it away or not. If you didn't find it in my things, I must have."

"What exactly did this note say?"

"It had my name, spelled wrong, on the outside of the paper. When I unfolded it there was something like, 'I can tell you news. Meet me in the alley around the corner near the leather bag store.'"

"What time was this?"

"Before noon. Maybe 11 or so."

"Who gave you the note?"

"A waiter left it on my table."

"Describe him."

"He did it from behind me, so I couldn't be sure, but I think he was one of the older waiters there. I'm fairly sure he had grey hair. He disappeared right after giving me the note. I tried to look for him in the kitchen, but he wasn't there. Anyway I don't think he was JVP."

"Now you are the expert. Why not?"

"I don't know. Just a feeling. I figured at the time someone probably gave him a few rupees to leave the note. I mean, he wouldn't know me from any other customer."

"Go on."

"So I went to the alley by the leather shop, like the note said. Why not? Maybe it really would be news. When I got there a bag was slipped over my head from behind and they told me, 'We aren't going to harm you. We will show you the news. Come with us.' We walked through a building, came out and got into the car, then we drove for, I don't know, 30 minutes or so to the house for the interview. When it was over they brought me back. They took the blindfold off and left me near my hotel, but they told me not to turn around while they drove away, so I didn't."

They lowered their voices and spoke to each other in Sinhalese. The tall one went into a long explanation, flipping his palms up to punctuate. Finally his superior wagged his head in what seemed like reluctant agreement.

The blood soaking my shirt oozed against the skin on my chest. I looked again at the boy's bloated face and felt dizzy. I wondered whether throwing up would help my case.

The leader looked at me blankly before speaking. "Now about this silly Indian bribery story. No journalist would accept it simply because a terrorist said it was so. Yet you promised your newspaper the story."

"Yes, like I told you. He said there was a document, a government document, that they were going to give me. That's why I couldn't write the complete story yet. I didn't have the document."

"Give you? How?"

"He didn't want to tell me. He said it would be safer not to know." I hoped that was the same way I'd put it before. I would have to keep track of my lies if this was going to go on.

"When was he to give it to you?"

"I told him my deadline. He said I'd have it for sure by early morning. That's why I could promise my paper I'd have the story by tomorrow. I expected an envelope or something left for me at the hotel. I told them where I was staying. It wouldn't be hard to get someone like the waiter in the tea room to deliver it to the front desk for a few rupees."

The tall man started for the door but the other brought him back with two words in Sinhalese.

"I'm pleased you are cooperating with us now, Mister Talison," he said, smiling to prove it. "You see how much easier everything goes when you don't oppose us?"

I looked towards the table. It was impossible to tell by the face, but the gangly body looked like a boy of no more than 14, maybe less. I shuddered.

"Oh, you needn't be alarmed by that," the man said in a friendly tone. "In point of fact he's a victim of the subversives himself. A member of the party, we suspect, who went against their rules. They have so many strict regulations, you know. You see now how they deal with their own."

I hung my head. The oval of blood continued to drip into the drain.

"And we simply brought you here," he went on, "as part of our investigation into this homicide. To see whether you could help identify the body, based on your recent unfortunate experience with the subversives. Clear?"

I looked at him, but I didn't say no.

"Now you needn't bother any more with this lot. Of course we'll be pleased to help, if they try to approach you again with this absurd document business."

"You suppose they'd deliver anything now that your goons kicked down my door?"

"Indeed," he said. He shrugged as if it didn't matter. "Then you won't have to worry about writing any silly bribery articles."

"Without the proof, I guess I can't. You might have just cost me a great story."

"That's the spirit," he said happily. "You'll get right back into proper trim soon as the tournament begins, I'm sure. This so-called document is probably a ruse they cooked up to harm the good name of the government. Or maybe just a way to get something out of you. I shouldn't be at all surprised if they planned to show up at your door asking for money for some damn reason or another before it could be delivered."

I nodded lamely.

"Of course, if they do try to contact you again, with or without any supposedly secret documents, you'll call us immediately."

"Except that I don't know who you are."

He laughed as if I'd made a joke. A nod brought his partner over to unlock the handcuffs.

"I knew we would get along, Mister Talison," he said, patting me on the back while avoiding the bloody splotches.

At the doorway I made myself look back. I wanted to mark the details in my memory. The air in the corridor was cooler. I took in a deep breath to clear my lungs, but the smell of the blood on my own shirt defeated me. I followed the pair down the corridor back to the stairs, noting the steel doors all along the way.

"I hope you'll accept my apologies for troubling you to come here at such a late hour," the superior said at the building entrance. To judge by his expression, he even meant it.

His colleague wrote a phone number on a piece of paper and pressed it into my hand. He added that I should "call this number pronto if any subversives try to disturb you again."

Together they walked me to the Mercedes. A soldier I hadn't seen before waited in the driver's seat. I got in the back alone.

"It should be a marvelous tournament," the superior said after the engine started. He waved good-bye.

At the hotel a small crowd was gathered in the corridor by my empty doorway. The manager steered me aside for a closer look. His winced. "Is everything all right, sir?" he whispered.

I nodded.

"But you're bleeding."

"It's not my blood."

He waited for more.

"It's nobody's," I said.

"Will there be any other. . . problems?"

I took it that he was asking about Manik. "No," I said. "Nothing you need to worry about." We had both been vague enough to deny any deeper meaning if it came to that.

He smiled his overbite and said in a louder voice, "I shall have your room in order in no time."

Three men in sarongs had already hung a new door on the frame and were screwing in the hinges. I sidestepped them and walked in. My clothes had been tossed to every part of the room and the mattresses were upside down on the floor. The soldiers must have come back looking for evidence, for the document.

Later, alone behind my new bolted door, I sat on the bed and pressed my palms into my eyes. I tried to picture the boy's face staring past the ceiling with empty white eyes. All I could see was red. It could have been 30 seconds or half an hour I sat that way. I thought I heard birds outside, but they may have been just a memory of some distant dawn back home. It was still dark out. I opened the window. The same orange lights curved to the black sea beyond.

I could put it off no longer. I made myself walk to the bathroom. The medicine chest was open and the towels were on the floor, but that was all. I lifted the cover to the toilet tank. The document floated in its waterproof pouch like a message in a bottle.

4

The van door slid open and a warm rush of cinnamon air flowed in. Next came the aroma of coconut and curry, and then a salty tang off the sea. A row of palms marked the start of a white-sand beach. The shallow water nearby glowed turquoise, sun reflecting off the surface in dazzling sparkles. Further out the deeper water was bluer than the sky. The driver stared at the scene, then murmured, "Here Hikkaduwa." That's where I got out.

I stood in the filtered shade of a palm tree until the van was out of sight. Gummy reggae played from further down the coast road. I hoisted my dufflebag bag over my shoulder and started towards the music, trying to match my steps to the rhythm. The pace was comforting, an antidote to my frenetic urban ordeal. Slow, steady, looping. Too slow for walking, but it would get me somewhere.

During the entire two-hour ride south I'd watched the other passengers more than the scenery. They looked bored enough to be legitimate travelers, but what did that prove? At one place beside a towering white statue of a meditating Buddha, the van slowed to a crawl. Some of the passengers rose from their seats to press their palms together. I considered matching them, but kept my ass down. A spiritual intrusion might draw attention. But I took the gesture as a sign I was among decent people again, moving away from danger, out of the corrupt city. At the same time I warned myself against complacency. Christians surely did not have a monopoly on killing the neighbors they're supposed to love. And looks were deceiving. I had learned already how Manik's preppy facade could mask a practiced player in the shadow world of political intrigue.

Hikkaduwa looked like a postcard town, the beach resort of snow-bound fantasies. A good place to recuperate. All the better that it seemed oddly forlorn for a tourist season. Outdoor restaurants lining the sand on the ocean side of the road were unoccupied. Across the road where the jungle began were a row of shops selling batiks and garish wooden masks and T-shirts, but none with any buyers in sight. There were more tourist shops here than tourists. When a pink-skinned man with a pony-tail materialized to flip through a rack of sarongs in front of one shop, the head of a rival store owner next door popped out to watch.

The music grew louder as I walked on. Bob Marley and the Wailers playing Stir It Up. "C'mon baby," I started to sing along, but when a bicycle bell chimed behind me I jumped to the sand like a startled kangaroo. The bicycle could have been a locomotive to judge by my over-reaction. A lanky young man steered, or at least tried to with the burden of another man riding side-saddle in front of him on the crossbar. The bike wobbled, corrected, then weaved so violently the peddler threw up his hands. It fell, dumping the two to the pavement.

The passenger stood up. He pointed to his partner lying under the spinning rear wheel. My brain raced with proper emergency procedures. Would they realize CPR was not some excitable foreigner's attempt to end a man's suffering by crushing his heart? Was it five breaths to one pump or 15 pumps to something else? Did they even have ambulances here?

The passenger nudged the other's belly with his toe, getting no response. He lowered his head and planted a field-goal-worthy kick that, to my amazement, worked. The victim emitted a weak moan, lifted one hand off the pavement like a drowning victim waving for rescue and said something that made his partner laugh so hard he had to hold his own stomach.

Still sputtering, he noticed me for the first time, standing beside him. "Oh! Hello! You wanting brown sugar?" He nodded his head to show me the correct answer. "Very cheap."

I didn't get it. "Do I look like I need more sugar?" I asked back.

He grabbed his stomach to laugh again. His partner, now standing, righted the bike, sat down and began pushing the pedals. The passenger took off in laughing pursuit, catching it just in time to correct a wobble by jumping back onto the crossbar. What is it about the beach that lures them out of the woodwork? Drifters and wingnuts and psycho-refugees. They get as far as the coast and then they have to stop and deal with people.

In front of a used-book shop I spun a revolving stand of postcards. The top card showed a frowning white woman on top of a mottled elephant. Neither looked too happy with the deal.

"Ride elephant 100 rupees," announced a boy in ragged brown shorts. His head came up to my belt. I hoped he wasn't the elephant handler.

"I don't think so," I said. "It might bend under my weight."

"Visit Ratnagama gem capital of Sri Lanka."

"I just got here."

"Hotel you looking?"

"Not right now." No point telling him I intended to search the area well for government thugs before checking in anywhere.

He showed me his palm and said, "School pen."

"Ask your teacher."

He repeated the request. When it clearly wasn't going to produce a pen, he shoved his fists into his pockets and skipped away into the jungle.

The Blue Heaven restaurant was playing Natural Mystic, another Bob Marley song. Speakers the size of broom closets pounded out lyrics that rumbled in my chest:

There's a natural mystic flowing through the air
If you listen carefully now you will hear.

I tried to, but it was impossible. The volume hurt my eardrums. I walked on.

The Swell had customers at two separate tables, a promising sign. I chose a spot where the cement floor ended at the sand, angling my chair so I could scan both the beach and the coast road. The Marley song was still audible:

This could be the first trumpet
Might as well be the last
Many more will have to suffer
Many more will have to die
Don't ask me why.

Don't ask me why. Right. That much I understood. But not the more immediate question. Why me? I had seen torture, so I was a witness. I was implicated. Maybe they already regretted that part of their escapade. Maybe they were already plotting how to correct it. Maybe they had discovered the secret document was indeed real. If it actually could open the floodgates on the government, and take out its henchmen, what wouldn't they do to get it back?

A bang made me throw my arms up around my ears – another over-reaction, I immediately realized, to what had been nothing but a crackle of speaker static. More evidence of how unsuited I was for all this. Even a glimpse of war was enough to give me shell-shock. I should have been able to leave the basement horror behind, but my nervous system was evidently not wired that way. How infinitely worse it all would have been for the boy. His white eyes looking at nothing. Would they haunt me? Then I wondered, for how long?

I told myself the danger was over. When they sent no more than an apologetic pair of teenage soldiers to "help with any problem" as I checked out, it showed how little they considered my case. Of course no one arrived to deliver the document, so it would have looked all the more like I'd been hoaxed. I was a rookie on a foreign trip, a dupe to rope in with a scandal. The authorities probably saw me as a hack they'd helped rescue. I refused to dwell on how much they may have been right.

I didn't care. I'd seen enough of the island's politics to know I wasn't interested. I'd simply stumbled across a local fight, an undercard bout to the main event of the Tamil war for independence. Anyone would be curious enough to watch a drama unfold with its tactical choices and surges and emotional arcs towards winning or losing. But once things got out of hand and the fight spread, only a fool would stick around to get hurt.

When the song ended I closed my eyes to listen to the waves. They were lulling. Orange sunlight flickered through my eyelids. And then I was back at the interrogation scene. The gleam in the superior's eye as he made me look though the peep-hole. An odd detail, when I should have been keeping the memory of the boy intact. But how? His face was bloated beyond any photograph I might recognize. And keep the memory for whom? His parents? The rest of his family? School mates? Beyond that? The ripples of the tragedy would certainly spread further. There would be grandparents, a favorite cousin, the neighbors who had watched him grow up. He was too young for a wife and family of his own. Probably even for a girlfriend. Or so I hoped.

The teenage waitress dropped the menu onto my table with a plop. I opened my eyes to see her pouting. When I began to read rather than order, she shuffled back behind her counter to slump onto a stool.

Food, that was the ticket. A tangible. Something I could digest. I decided on the crab spaghetti: comfort food with a quirk. It might end up being pollock dyed pink, but the pasta would work. Just the thought of a bulging mouthful was enough to make me drool.

The waitress had hidden herself behind a Sinhalese newspaper. On the back was a double-page ad for a Japanese TV with the text written into the white squares of a soccer ball. A tie-in to the tournament. The first round would kick off that afternoon. Brazil was scheduled for the opener against South Korea. Probably a rout, although you never knew when those feisty Koreans would surprise you.

So I was back to sports. And why not? Games weren't such a terrible thing to put your life into, considering some of the alternatives. All I needed now was a little psychological distance between me and what had happened in Colombo and I'd be back in the press box, fully fit. It would be easy enough to wire my editor with an excuse for missing a few matches. I could say I caught some kind of Third World bug. It was practically true.

I angled my chair away from the road to face the sea. To hell with whatever might come down from Colombo. I was on vacation.

A shaggy blonde surfer jogged past my table with a board under his arm. He didn't stop when he reached the water, using the momentum to leap onto the board just as an incoming wave was about to break on his chest. He pivoted to turn across the face, then crouched as the top of the wave fell around him in a shimmering barrel. It collapsed and he tumbled into the froth, his board skimming up to the sand. That seemed an awkward ending to such a graceful start but he did a somersault in the next wave that landed him on his feet, beside the board, which he slid under his torso to start a languid paddle out to where the bigger waves were breaking.

Now that was blending in. I wondered if I could too. Someone must have rental boards. The locals might laugh at the pasty bear-in-water, flailing to get upright, but so what? Looking ridiculous was all part of the tourist experience.

The buildings thinned out the further I walked, leaving open spaces of sand on the right and jungle on the left. Quieter was better. Fewer people, less worry.

A honk from the road made me stiffen. Again I spun my head in all directions to check for escape routes. When the source turned out to be nothing more than a boxy green schoolbus filled with yapping kids in white uniforms, I promised myself to stop searching for enemies.

A grey-haired woman offered to sell me an orange-colored coconut. When I declined, not knowing what to do with it, she wished me a good day anyway and smiled like she meant it. A barefoot boy approached on a bicycle too big for him to pedal sitting down. She said something that made them both laugh before he turned onto a dirt road shaded by the jungle canopy. Now we were getting somewhere. They hadn't laughed like that in Colombo. I put a bounce into my gait. My get-going stride. I may be a big man and slow off the blocks, but once I hit my pace you don't want to be in front of me.

But the exertion seemed to draw the heat to me. By the time I reached a small corner store called the Rhino Eye, I was parched.

The proprietor, a sullen man with one arm wrapped in bandages from the elbow to the unseen fingers, looked at me for an uncomfortable moment before saying his cooler was broken. He made it sound like it was my fault. Whatever.

Back on the road a wide-load truck appeared from the south, roaring closer. From behind me came a van squealing its tires against the curve. The pavement appeared too narrow to accommodate both vehicles and me, but I was blocked from stepping further off the shoulder by the low stone wall of a small home's verandah. The truck downshifted and revved up to add speed. The van stopped honking long enough to emit the sound of its own engine accelerating. I was stunned. They were going faster? Wouldn't that make it pre-meditated? I pressed my quads flat against the wall and leaned my upper body forward. My torso was out of harm but I cringed at the prospect of my padded butt taking the brunt of the collision and carrying the rest of me with it.

That position put me almost nose-to-nose with a man on the verandah in a high-backed wicker chair. He winced in sympathy as the truck whooshed by close enough to scrape my back pocket.

He was 50, or maybe a little more. Swirls of grey on his bare chest matched the hair left on the perimeter of his otherwise smooth skull, but his brown cheeks were wrinkle-free. He removed a pair of round wire glasses and added, "Too close for comfort."

"Time is money," I replied. I gestured to the palms swaying overhead, then past their trunks to where the sea shone in eight shades of blue. White flecks of waves completed the living portrait of paradise. "Although you'd think if there was one place people might slow down to enjoy the moment," I added.

"Life is suffering," he said with a head wag, and we both smiled to signify an end to the platitudes. He folded a newspaper and set it on a wooden stand next to his chair. The English headline read: "Subversives Hit Army Depot."

"You have come down from Colombo," he guessed.

"Just now. I'm looking for a place to stay."

"Ah."

"Is there anywhere nearby you might recommend?"

"There are so many hotels and lodges back in Hikkaduwa, no?" He motioned to the tourist area where I'd left the van.

"I was thinking of something quieter." When he did nothing more than nod in understanding, I added, "I don't need to be around a lot of other people."

"There are a few guest houses in this village," he said. "Some better equipped than others, of course."

"I don't need fancy. Just quiet."

A motorcycle obliterated the beginning of his next sentence. He waited with a look of strained patience until it was gone.

"My brother-in-law has taken in guests before. There." He pointed across the road to a two-story house with a new Japanese pickup in the paved driveway. "He has electricity, flush toilet, hot bath. If you wish, I could ask."

It wasn't on the ocean side of the road, but from the front door I could still reach the water in eight seconds. Maybe a few more if I stopped in the coconut grove beside the beach to talk to the lone cow tethered to a stake. "If it's no trouble," I said.

He called over his shoulder into his own house, a grey crumbling structure that, had it been on his brother-in-law's land, might have been used as a cow shed. A boy in red school uniform shorts appeared in the doorway. He eyed me eagerly while listening to his father's instructions, then tore off across the road.

"Won't you sit?" the man said, sliding the verandah's other wicker chair closer to his. He called again into the house.

"That's very kind," I answered but he didn't acknowledge the compliment. We watched the empty road in silence. He glanced down at his newspaper but was too polite to pick it up.

"You are a tourist?" he asked at last.

"Yes," I said. "Exactly."

"Travel must be a wonderful thing," he offered.

"It can be. I guess."

A thin woman in a faded green summer dress came from the house carrying two mugs on a tray. Her silver hair was tied into a bun. She murmured to him in Sinhalese, then smiled for me. With her high, angled cheekbones and his softly hooked nose, they must have made a dashing couple in their time. She placed the tea mugs, mine first, on either side of the newspaper, pressed her palms together in a prayer-like gesture as if I were the visiting god of Boston, then returned inside. Her feet were bare.

I was about to confirm it was his wife and add a comment on how her hospitality was matched only by her beauty, when he said, "How long do you intend to stay?"

"Only a couple of days. Maybe a little more. Certainly not a week. It all depends."

I took an exploratory sip of tea. It hit my tongue with a faint nip of tannin that was immediately covered by a rush of sweet velvet smoothness. Even better than the brew I'd had at the Moonstone Inn, an accomplishment I hadn't considered possible. I took a bigger sip, swirling to engage every part of my mouth before I swallowed, and announced, "This is the best tea I have ever tried.

Maybe I should stay the whole week. Already I like it here better than Colombo."

He looked into his own cup for a moment before drinking. "I still visit the capital from time to time, though I'm supposed to be retired. My favorite time on any trip is inevitably the return. I bathe, I change my trousers for a sarong and I sit for a delicious meal, my family around me. And then I know I am home. And where else would any man want to be? I know I don't have electricity and plumbing and what-not, but I can't say I envy the wealthy in places like Colombo."

I masked my surprise. The neighbors had wires running into their homes from the utility poles. If the infrastructure was there, how much could it cost to get hooked up?

"What work were you in?" I asked.

"I was a civil servant, chiefly for the government employee's union. I helped with litigation, although I was never a lawyer." I imagined him being one of the few working parts in a bureaucratic clog. "And you?" he asked.

"I'm a reporter, a sportswriter. I work for a newspaper in Boston."

"You are American then?"

"That's right."

"I thought so. There is an American chap living in Hikkaduwa, near the Coral Gardens. He married a local girl and now they own a hotel. I understand they're not doing so badly, considering."

The boy came back at a run. His rubber sandals slid to a stop on the verandah's cement floor and he panted something in Sinhalese. His father frowned, asked a question and got a shrug.

"My brother-in-law's home is not available."

"Aw," I said.

"There is another possibility. I know the man who owns that house there."

He pointed down the road to a white bungalow on the ocean side behind two papaya trees. "He had guests last year. I can't say whether he is willing to do so again, but I could inquire."

The boy ran off.

"How do you litigate against the government?" I asked. "You know the saying, 'You can't beat City Hall.'"

He chuckled in a genial rumble that must have sounded like confidence in court. "Actually, I won the majority of my cases. It's not so difficult. When you have the evidence on your side it's a simple matter to present it in a way that will convince any reasonable man. The problem – " he paused to let the noise of a car rush by – "The problem is when your own case appears weak. Say an employee has been fired for stealing on the job, and the police have caught him with the stolen items in his home."

I shrugged to say: what can you do? But I was wrong.

"The result may seem obvious, but so many things must be done before a decision can be reached. If the other side has not followed proper procedure, for example, you may have an opening to challenge their version of the facts."

"How about a claim against the government when they do something bad, something terrible?"

He looked at me for more.

"I read this thing in the paper the other day about a boy who was killed. It sounded as if the army did it because he was a member of something called the JVP."

"Oh," he said, waving the idea away with the back of his hand. "Not my field." A line of cars was stuck behind a slow, oil-smoking Mercedes. They honked at it to no effect.

"But if you did, for whatever reason, get a case like that," I tried again. "Could you win?"

"Some people are beyond the law."

"And the government allows it?"

He tsk-tsked. "They are the government."

"I thought you had elections here."

"We used to. The last one was canceled. We haven't had a real vote in eight years."

The boy came back. He shook his head no.

"I must apologize," the man said. "I've made you wait for nothing."

"Not at all. I enjoyed the company."

I swallowed the last of my tea and stood up. I looked in the doorway to thank his wife but the room was dark. The only light came from a flickering candle before a fist-sized Buddha high up in one corner on a small altar. There was no furniture beyond a cabinet, a scratched wooden dining table and four wooden chairs. A tiny add-on room was also near-empty with just a single iron-framed bed. And that was it. The opposite door opened onto the coconut grove that led to the beach, the blue water luminous beyond the swaying grey trunks. If you took a vow of poverty, this could be a dream house.

"Please thank your wife for the tea," I said. "It was superb."

He closed his eyes to accept or dismiss the compliment, I wasn't sure. He stood up with me. I didn't know the local take on handshakes, but felt drawn to offer one anyway. I wiped my palm on my pants and was half-way there when I saw his own hands busy at his groin retying the sarong. I picked up my bag instead. He may have noticed my reluctance to go.

"There is one more possibility," he said. "I have a cabana of sorts out back. It's small, very basic, but if you were interested."

"By the water?" I asked, my hopes rising even as I mouthed the words. "Can I see it?"

We walked through the tiny house to the back porch, a covered space that held what must have been the kitchen. A stone mortar and pestle lay on the clay floor beside the faintly glowing embers of a fire.

The green tops of the coconut trees rustled over our heads. Below them the shade was dappled. A breeze off the water made the area surprisingly cool. If the cabana was just big enough to sleep in I could spend my days reading under the trees. I wondered whether the hammock had reached this part of Asia.

The cabana's thatch roof and walls were built over a concrete floor half the size of a handball court. Inside was a wooden bed with a straw mattress, and under a small wooden window, a writing desk and chair. An oil lantern hung on a nail from the ceiling beam. Conrad might have admired the set-up, gazing out at the waves between paragraphs. The Indian Ocean was a pitching wedge away.

"As I say, it isn't much."

"It's perfect," I protested, pressing my palm on the bed. The mattress was firm. I was about to test the breaking point by sitting down when I noticed a shirt and pants folded over the back of the chair. "But someone is already staying here."

"No. Only my son. Rohan," he answered, saying the name as if he had swallowed something sour. "He has a place to sleep in the house as well, if he comes home. Most nights I have no idea where he is. My eldest," he added, flipping a palm up in a gesture of hopelessness.

I imagined waking up and rolling into the sea. I might even take up swimming. For exercise, no less.

"To wash, we have our bathing well here or you could use the well across the road," Vijaya explained. "The water there is fresher. As for the toilet, you can see we have only that."

He pointed through the trees to a thatch hut the size of a phone booth. "It's the local style, I'm afraid."

"No problem," I answered. I could blend in with that too. But I cautioned myself not to sound keen. He might have been playing me like a trout from the start. Now would be time to reel me in. "I suppose it might do," I said. "But just how much would you charge?"

He pursed his lips, calculating, chuckled in a way that may have been from embarrassment, then shrugged. "Would 20 rupees per night be asking too much?"

Twenty rupees was a dollar. "I'll take it," I said quickly.

"Splendid. Then we'll have the chance to talk more."

"Of course, I was looking forward – " but he interrupted before

I could go on. "Now you would enjoy a rest after your trip, no? I'll send your key out at once."

I pulled the swimsuit up past my quivering white thighs with a grimace. Satisfied no one was watching, I thundered into the surf. The water was cool enough to be invigorating. I breast-stroked parallel to the shore for a good 50 yards, watching the cabana door the whole time, then floated on my back. I gazed up at the cloudless blue sky and felt grand. Water, my favorite element, the great equalizer, the one milieu that didn't hold my weight against me. I flipped onto my stomach and did the crawl all the way to shore. Gordie Talison, hitting the final stretch, churning home, for the Olympic. . . gold. . . med-aaaaaal.

I staggered up to the sand, heaving in great draughts of air but still not ready to quit. I continued in a bouncing jog as far as a fishing boat turned upside down. It was a long outrigger canoe with the main hull marred by a basketball-sized hole. I was about to run my fingers over the damage when a man's head popped up from the other side of the boat. He stood up quickly, brushing sand off a dingy white sarong, then looked sadly at the craft. He dragged his fingers over and again down a greying mustache.

"My boat," he said with a droopy expression.

"Nasty hole."

"Yes, very bad." His accent was thick enough to make it come out veddy bahd. He pouted while wringing his hands. "Because of this? I cannot fish."

"Why don't you fix it?"

He looked at me with one eyebrow raised. "You are perhaps 40 years old? Or 42?"

I laughed and said, "Thirty-seven. It's the beard."

"And you have children? You are married?"

"Married. . . sort of. No children."

"I have eight. Eight children! Six girls and two boys." He held his hand waist-high above the sand, perhaps to average their heights.

"My. Congratulations."

"No," he answered. "Very bad. More boys is good. Girls cost money. Boys work. Boys can fish."

I nodded in sympathy.

"In Sri Lanka now, very hard to feed a family," he continued. "So many bad things. Bad politics. Bad business. Foreign elements." He looked out to sea with a disgusted curl of his upper lip, as if more foreign elements were there on the horizon. "A kilo of rice now costs double," he said. "Two times!"

"I'm sure it's rough." I waited for him to get to the point, the touch.

"But I will not beg," he said, narrowing his eyes as if I'd misjudged him. "I have no money, this is true, but I have my pride." He patted his chest with his palm.

"Absolutely," I answered. To fill in the silence that followed, I added, "You're a fisherman."

"Exactly!" He smoothed his fingers along the gunwales.

"So why don't you fix the hole?"

"I am a fisherman," he said. "I do not do the work in wood. That is the other man's job, no? He is the expert. But he doesn't work for free. How can I give him money when my babies cry for food? First thing I am hearing every morning. Because I do not have enough."

"Listen," I said. "Why don't you let me help?" It couldn't cost much to hire a Sri Lankan carpenter for a one-shot job. And wasn't this exactly what foreign aid should be all about? A man needs a hand to fix his boat, he gets it, and the next day he's feeding his family again. Surely this was better than a million dollars the politicians and executives would siphon away anyway. With a little common sense and a bit of heart you could probably work wonders with a fraction of our aid budget.

"Now how much do you estimate it would cost?" I asked. "I'm not rich man myself, you understand, but I know – "

A finger tapped my shoulder. I turned to see a skinny, dark, handsome man in his late 20s. His teeth were a brilliant gleam of white against the contrast of his skin, and his eyes stuck out with a slight bulge.

"If you don't mind," I said shortly, turning back, but the fisherman's look of disgust was pronounced. When the young man said something in Sinhalese, it became a scowl.

"Sir," I said. "I was just about to ask you – " but he made a "phht" noise and walked away. He turned from a distance to shoot the new arrival a sour glare.

I spun to confront him with a withering stare. He laughed, making a slushy noise like the last of a drink being sucked through a straw.

"The hell you think you're doing?" I asked.

"I am Rohan," he announced. "Vijaya is my father. Where you staying."

"Good job, Rohan, what did you say? I was going to help the guy until you came along."

"Come," he said, making the wet laugh again from deep in one cheek. "I tell you about this man."

He started back. I followed, but at a distance meant to convey displeasure. In front of the cabana he pointed back to the ruined boat.

"That man, his name is Walter. What Walter say? That he cannot fish? That he have too many children?"

"Something like that."

"How many he say?"

"Eight."

"Eight!" Rohan said happily. "Last week he have five. Some time, three. You know, Walter, he never go fishing in this life. Because he hate the sea. And that boat? It stay there now, same place, four years." He ran another laugh through his jowls, then walked away towards the house. Without turning around he called, "You come first time to Sri Lanka?

I shut the wooden window and bolted the door. I pulled the plastic folder holding the secret document out from my underwear. Just enough light seeped through spaces in the thatch to let me read the list of all the traitors I might expose. Including Perera, the rebel impostor. No one could accuse me of taking sides if both camps used my story to eat their own. Although the JVP, at least in Commander Dapila's strategy, would come out stronger. Strong enough, perhaps, to be the last ones standing when the political center imploded.

That I was still interested in the outcome came as an unwelcome surprise. I resented the way my own neck and shoulders clenched up. I read again the red-ink stamp: DESTROY UPON READING. It hadn't occurred to me the admonition could be taken another way, referring not just to the paper.

I sat on the timber bench in front of my cabana watching the sky seep from blue to pink to purple. The first stars appeared over the jungle behind me. When it was too dark to see the tree trunks, I stood up. My worries could vanish with the outgoing tide. Yet even as I took the document between my fingertips and tugged gently, I knew I wouldn't rip it up. I just didn't know why.

It could have been a stand against political repression, but I doubted it. I suspected instead a stubborn reaction to being leaned on. There has always been a bit of donkey in me. It's how I managed to keep rooting for the Red Sox.

I slipped the document back into its plastic cover and walked towards Walter's golden goose of a boat. I listened during silent lulls in the waves for intruders. I was alone.

I marked two paces from the hole in the hull and dropped to my knees. I dug a hole as deep as my elbow and buried the pouch in the sand.

5

A nearly full moon rose over Vijaya's house. It glowed white on the dark surface of the sea in front of my cabana.

"Hello, Mister Gordie?" a voice came to me through the coconut grove.

A kerosene lamp on the back porch swung in a slow arc of greeting. I recognized Rohan by the bone-like outline of his arm. The lamp bobbed through the trees towards me. He held it under his chin, giving his gaunt face the mock-ferocious look of a Halloween mask.

"My mother ask me to bring to you," he said, placing the filled lamp on the floor beside my door. He gestured to the sand. "You no mind if I sit?"

"It's your beach."

A slush-pump started and died. Rohan was amused again. "Not mine," he said. "Peoples' beach."

"I suppose. You have dinner yet?"

"I don't eat."

That might explain why you're so skinny, I resisted saying.

"You liking Sri Lanka, Mister Gordie?"

It was my turn to chuckle. "Yes. Despite everything."

"What's mean? Despite everything."

"Nothing. Sure, I like it, here at least. Colombo was a downer. But then big cities often are."

"Yes. But I can't say. I only go to Colombo, not other big city. Maybe you travel to many country?"

"Some." I watched the light of a fishing boat bobbing far out at sea.

"You have a good job, no? My father say you are a journalist."

"That's right. In a way."

"My father is very good at writing. One time he was editor and chief of a magazine. But it finish because nobody have money to buy. Too much bad business now in Sri Lanka. You know? Foreign element."

"So I hear. What do you do, Rohan?"

He lowered his head to think it through. Finally he looked at me. "Do?"

"Work. What's your job?"

"Oh. I don't work."

I didn't want to pry. I did anyway. "And you're how old?"

"I am 29. Soon 30 years old. I know, I must work. I want to. But now, impossible."

"That's too bad." I was about to explain we had an unemployment problem back home too, but wasn't sure how it would translate.

"The MP from this district, you know? He don't like me. If I say yes to support him, then no problem. He tell somebody and I get the job, good pay. But I never do that. My father understands. One time he say to this MP, 'Clean clothes cannot cover a dirty man.'"

"Is that why the JVP gets support in the villages? Corrupt politicians?"

"One reason."

"A good enough reason for you?"

He lifted his shoulders as if he didn't care. "Now I go see my friend," he said. He didn't get up.

"Okay." I caught the gleam of his teeth in the lantern light.

"We go smoke, you know?"

"Not really. Smoke what?"

He slush-laughed, perhaps to cover embarrassment, and traced a lazy circle in the sand with his finger. "Brown sugar."

I looked back to the ocean, trying to guess where the next wave might appear in the moonlight. Finally he asked, "You like?"

"No."

His smile widened. "Don't be angry. I only ask. Maybe you like, maybe you don't."

"What exactly is it?" I imagined some kind of Asian PCP.

"Heroin. But not needle. For smoking."

"Heroin," I said. "Right." He said nothing. I added, in a softer voice, "I don't do hard drugs. Everyone I've ever known who did ending up regretting it."

"I am smoking now, five years," he replied. He didn't sound proud or ashamed, just stating a fact.

So that explains why you're so skinny, I thought. But then so were a lot of Sri Lankans. Rohan's eyes bulged and his cheeks seemed drawn, but he looked nothing like the typical addict you see shuffling around Boston's war zone. Maybe addiction too was softened by the tropics. "Didn't you ever think to quit?" I asked.

"Yes. I will quit. Not tonight."

"Suit yourself," I said.

"Yes."

"Your father knows?"

"Yes. That why he is angry."

"Because you're the eldest son."

He said nothing.

"And you do nothing to help the family."

He flicked a piece of shell away with a snap of his fingers.

"Even though your father has, how many kids?"

"Seven. Three here now. One brother leave. He get married."

"Lots of luck to that one," I said, unable to think of marriage in any terms other than combative. The light of the fishing boat was joined by three others. The night shift must have been coming on.

"Heroin is not good. I understand. But brown sugar is better than this – " he jabbed his arm. "When you do like that, you need every six hours. Brown sugar you smoke one time that day, enough."

"You've smoked heroin every day for the last five years?"

He looked at the sand between his feet. "Not every day," he murmured. A dog somewhere down the beach squealed.

"Do you feel like you've wasted your life? At least as far as helping your family?" Rohan looked directly at me. I thought for one uncomfortable moment he was going turn the question back on me. Finally he shrugged as if to say he agreed, it was not good, but what could he do? He flicked another shell.

"Listen, it's got nothing to do with me if you want to get ripped every night. I've smoked some myself. Not heroin. But I've had my share of marijuana. It's just a herb, right?"

Rohan looked past me to the water. The moon glow had spread wider.

"Can you lend me 30 rupees?" he asked.

"What for?"

"I give you back tomorrow no problem."

"What's the 30 rupees for, Rohan?"

He slush-chuckled. If I said nothing more maybe he'd drop it.

We listened in silence while at least more five waves broke. But I hadn't reckoned on the practiced charm of the black sheep.

"I have to pay back money to my friend. I promise I give him tonight. Because he going to Kandy, so he need money now. I pay you tomorrow. Sure."

When I said nothing he added, "Don't worry about I take your money. I am not like that. I pay back."

"It's not the money. What do I care about 30 rupees? I don't want to give it to you for heroin."

"For my friend," he said, looking directly at me again. The pop-eyed effect added to the dubious sincerity of his plea. I studied him for signs of deceit, or at least penitence. Maybe he really did owe someone money. I doubted it, but 30 rupees was a tiny amount for a squeeze.

"You understand what I think about heroin?" I asked. He wagged his head yes, my final consolation, and I gave him the money. He slid the bills into the fold of his sarong, flashed a grin as a parting gesture and walked quickly away towards Hikkaduwa. I went to bed thinking that if Walter ever needed a business partner, he wouldn't have to go far.

In the morning Vijaya was standing outside my cabana as I staggered up from the longest swim I'd attempted since school. If only my hack buddies could have seen me.

"I gather you slept well," he said.

I nodded, too breathless to speak.

"If you like, please join me for a cup of tea. My wife is now preparing some." He walked back to the house, wearing the same sarong as the day before, again with no shirt. And I thought I knew how to keep clothes shopping to a minimum.

We walked through the outdoor kitchen into the two-room house. A stick of incense burned before the small Buddha in the corner. A think line of white smoke curled out the front door to the verandah where we went to sit.

"Nice place you have," I tried, searching for something to praise. "Is that incense? Smells good."

"My wife insists," he explained. "Sometimes it's easier to just go along."

"That about sums up my view on religion."

He chuckled. I sipped my tea.

"Everyone is on a path, no?" he said. "Whether they know it or not. So it only makes sense to inquire from time to time whether you're moving in the right direction."

"Who's going to tell us if we are or not?"

"Ah. There are so many teachings on the Triple Gem."

I nodded politely.

"Ultimately," he continued, "it has to be you. The last words Buddha spoke were, 'Be a lamp unto yourself.'"

"Right." I watched a bullock cart roll by. "Deep."

He nodded in agreement. "For myself whenever I face a difficult choice I judge according to two things: my motivation and the result."

"Now you're getting somewhere. In my work it's the final score that matters. So where are you heading? What's the finish line?"

He removed his glasses. I took it as a sign of reticence, but the kind that would disappear with a little prodding.

"If it's a secret," I offered.

"No, not that. It's just that we rarely discuss our own spiritual progress. Perhaps to avoid competition. But I don't mind. I can tell you my goal is to eliminate suffering. That's from the First Noble Truth, that unenlightened life is inseparable from suffering. Which leads to the Second Noble Truth, that this suffering has causes."

"I see," I said, even though I didn't. "Well. Good for you." I supposed it was one of those unexplainable obsessions, the way another man might wish to visit all the baseball stadiums in the Major League.

"We have so many opportunities here to understand suffering, no?" he said, putting the glasses back on.

"I learned that much in Colombo."

"Oh?" He studied me over the top of the glasses.

I chastised myself for almost squawking to a man I'd met a day before. "Did you just hear something?"

It was Rohan, tapping his thigh with the flat blade of a machete as he stepped off the back porch. He stopped under a coconut tree to look up in appraisal. Not that one. When he found the tree he wanted, he wrapped a loop of twine around his feet for a brace and began hopping up the trunk.

Far up at the top, high enough that he appeared smaller, he tapped a green coconut bigger than my head. He twisted it in circles until the stem snapped. From that height it hit the sand with a thud.

He did the same with another, then began hopping down in

jumps broken by the twine. Halfway down he saw us and stopped to say something to his father. Vijaya's one-word response sent him again to the top where he twisted off a third coconut.

Back on the ground Rohan chose the biggest of the three. He chopped a half-dollar-sized hole out of the top and handed it to me. I held it until he motioned for me to drink. I tried a tiny sip in case it was awful. The liquid inside was deliciously sweet and surprisingly cool. The trees could have been refrigerated. I didn't know how they did it, and didn't ask. I was absorbed by the taste, the first word coming to mind being "nectar."

I drained it in five or six long glugging tilts, some of the liquid running through my beard and onto my chest. I was about to rub my belly in satisfaction when Rohan took my empty shell and sliced the top clean off, then cut a small wedge from the green side to use as a spoon.

"Some people like to eat the inside portion as well," Vijaya explained.

Rohan still hadn't said a word to him. They drank their coconuts with their backs to each other.

The part lining the inner walls was as soft as ice cream and even sweeter than the liquid. I scooped the interior clean, peered inside to make sure I hadn't left a trace, then pretend-staggered as if overwhelmed by sensory delight.

Vijaya held up a correcting finger. "You haven't had king coconut yet." He pointed to a tree with smaller, orange nuts. "I have three others like that one. We prefer them to young coconuts. More cooling."

He said something in Sinhalese to Rohan. When Rohan answered with no more than a mumble to his own feet, Vijaya smirked.

"He has no will," Vijaya explained to me in English. "I understand if he has fallen on hard luck. Life is suffering, no? But suffering has a cause. Eh, Rohan? Every effect has its cause, no?" He waited for a moment, just long enough to ensure there was no response, then walked back to the house.

From the shade of the cabana bench I spotted Rohan walking back from Hikkaduwa. Beside him was a young man with pressed slacks and a brilliant white shirt, clothes that seemed out of place for a hot afternoon on the beach.

"My friend," Rohan explained when they were near. He didn't mention either of our names. Maybe the same word fit for both of us. The visitor's face bore an expression of such solemn intensity he could have come to ask for a root canal. His narrow eyes darted endlessly between Rohan, me and the beach. I took him for one of Rohan's heroin-smoking pals, someone with a reason to be paranoid. Whatever, he wasn't worth my time. I began to resent the fact he was intruding, even if it was the people's beach.

"He is important person for this area," Rohan explained. The man placed a paper shopping bag down beside his shoes, away from me.

"No doubt," I answered in a flat tone.

"He ask me, can I take his bag. Only until tomorrow." Inside were four rolls of paper bound with elastics.

"So?"

"If no problem, I put in your room?" Rohan asked. "He take back tomorrow, sure."

Rohan's friend looked at me with his mouth drawn in a straight line. It was an awfully grim expression for a village dope peddler. Maybe I'd pegged him wrong. Maybe he was a college friend, the kind of perpetual grad student who studied all the time and never had fun.

"What is it?"

"Just posters."

"That's all?"

"Yes," Rohan answered. "For his business."

I reached for the bag and lifted the rolls one at a time. There was nothing else, no plastic-wrapped bags of powder.

"Leave them in the cabana as long as you want. It's your place, not mine."

At the translation the young man's tense expression broke into a quick smile. He moved towards me with a suddenness that made me lurch, but it was only to take my hand and launch into rapid-fire Sinhalese. He held my hand for an uncomfortably long time. Finally Rohan translated the extended message. "He say, 'Thanks.'" The friend hurried off as if glad just to get away.

"You play one game chess?" Rohan asked.

"I'm not much of a chess player."

"You don't know how to play chess?"

"I do but I don't have the patience. I like games with action."

"You play one game carom?"

"You mean like this?" I flicked the air with my index finger.

He tilted his head yes. On the back porch we passed his mother squatting beside the kitchen fire on the ground. Crouched beside her was a gangly girl about 12 years old. Rohan introduced her with the single word "sister." Both mother and daughter smiled at me over their shoulders before turning back to the fire. The girl pressed her palms together.

Inside I told him, "If you built a stand for that fire they wouldn't have to bend over like that every time they cooked."

He turned back with a puzzled expression, then said something in Sinhalese that made the two laugh. The girl giggled just like her mother.

"Seriously," I said in the main room. "You could make it out of the same clay as the floor and walls. With an open space in the bottom for the wood? They could at least stand up to cook instead of hunching over like that. Like a barbecue."

He chuckled at what he took for a joke, then searched in the cabinet for the carom board. For the home's only piece of furniture beside the table set and the single bed, the cabinet was surprisingly empty. Where did they keep their things?

"Come," he said, walking back out to the verandah with the board under his arm.

He moved the two wicker chairs facing together and we sat first so he could set the board between us on the arm rests. He sprinkled the surface with talcum powder, then opened a small box to empty out the round black and red wooden disks. He passed the single white one to me for the first shot. When I declined he lined it up with surgical precision and flicked hard with his middle finger, scattering everything with a clack.

An older foreign man with a shiny pink head approached on the coast road at a slow march. Rohan called, "Hey Papa!" But the man was either deaf or purposely not looking. Even as he walked right beside us, and Rohan laughingly asked, "Papa, how you feeling today, hey?" the man carried on without a word.

He was still in earshot when Rohan explained. "He come from West Germany, every year this time. His name is Becker, but we call him Papa. He hate it."

"Leave him alone then," I whispered. "Poor geezer."

"Not poor. He have money. A lot of money, to buy boys, little boys for fucking. Any age, he don't care, but younger better. I tell him one time, 'If you talk to any of my brother, you even say hello, I cut off your pecker, sure. That time also he don't answer back, but he hear me. You shoot."

I aimed to put a red disk in the corner near Rohan's right elbow but missed, the cue banking off three sides of the board without touching a thing. Rohan pocketed a red one on my side.

"Now you shoot for black," he said, lining up his shot with one eye closed.

After he'd put in five or six red disks to my none, and I flicked the cue at yet another apparently random angle, he said, "You must think and shoot."

He spread three fingers out on the board for a base and poised his index finger before the cue. "See? This way it go straight." He made three or four practice flicks in slow-motion for my benefit, then hit the cue. It knocked a red disk into the left side pocket.

On my next turn I was about to aim for a long shot in the corner when he said, "Think and shoot," pointing to an easier target in the side pocket.

"Maybe I have a strategy," I said, lining up the long shot anyway. It missed. "Of course it may not show up right away, but that's because it's a secret strategy."

A jeep came roaring towards us from the north. We heard the wheels screech before it came into view. To give it space a motorcycle heading south drifted far over to the right, but the jeep slowed anyway as it swung in next to the verandah. The soldier in the passenger seat looked at me, blinked once in surprise, and the jeep sped away.

"Goddammit!" I blurted out. "He saw me!"

Rohan stopped in the middle of his shot.

"I know that guy," I explained.

"Yes?"

"One of the soldiers I met in Colombo. I remember him because we talked about sports. He said he likes cricket. Fuck! Now they know where I'm staying."

"They do?"

"I could be wrong. Maybe it just looked like him. But did you see the way he looked at me? His eyes blinked. Why else would someone do that?"

Rohan's expression suggested he wouldn't know. Then he brightened. "Because you so handsome?" He made the slush sound.

"He knew who I was."

"Your friend?"

"No. I shouldn't even care. Let's play."

Rohan missed a complicated bank shot. He stacked the disks he had already pocketed while waiting for me to go. I looked down the road for a long time in case the jeep was coming back, then missed a shot and turned back to Rohan. He muffed an easy side-pocket shot. That made two in a row. When he blew his next one, I stopped to look at him.

"You nervous about something, Rohan?"

"I don't know what's mean, nervous."

"It means worried, tense, a – "

"I know this word. I only say I don't know because I am never nervous."

"All right. Just asking. Forget it." But I immediately countered my own advice. "I'm just wondering why, as soon as that soldier drove by, all of sudden you can't make a shot. You also started stacking disks that you had stacked already."

"Yes?"

"Look, Rohan, don't bullshit me. If you told them I'm here I'd like to know right now." I stiffened when I heard an approaching car, but it turned out to be a Honda.

"Why you asking this way?"

"Because I don't know if I can trust you. Who knows what you would do for money?"

He nodded slowly, as if to consider what his own moral boundaries might be. I silently conceded he didn't seem as nervous as I'd thought. Certainly not as much as I was.

"All right, just tell me this. Did you see anything strange on the beach lately? Somebody leaving something behind, maybe?"

Rohan's bewildered expression suggested he could use an explanation. I forced out a smile. "I'm probably just being paranoid. It might not have been the same soldier after all."

"Your turn," he said, smiling back. He hadn't taken my little tirade personally. That was one advantage to hanging out with druggies: they were used to random wig-outs.

But I couldn't follow the game. Rohan had to tell me several times when I was supposed to shoot. He won four games in a row without being challenged. I said I believed I'd let him build up enough overconfidence for one day.

"Maybe you go back to chess," he suggested.

I went into the house to sit at the table where I could still see the coast road. No more jeeps appeared.

When Rohan came in I lowered my voice so no one on the back

porch would hear. "You don't happen to have my 30 rupees, do you?"

He looked surprised.

"The money you were going to pay back today no problem?"

He looked straight at me, still without an answer.

"I knew you wouldn't," I said. I wasn't angry. The 30 rupees were nothing. I was more disappointed at myself for giving him such an easy chance to let me down. I should have just given him the money outright.

"I don't have it now," he said, his gaze still steady on me, "because I am thinking, maybe Mister Gordie want something else." He produced from the waist-fold of his sarong a crumpled wad of newspaper. He looked once over his shoulder to the verandah before slipping it to me under the table.

I started to push his hand back but he whispered, "Just look."

I checked the road, then unwrapped the paper. Inside was a palmful of dull-green buds giving off the rangy smell of marijuana. I closed the paper and shoved it into my pocket before anyone could walk in.

"So this is what you bought with my 30 rupees?"

"If you no like," he offered, holding his hand out over the table.

"I didn't exactly ask for it. But it has been a while. And I am on vacation." I wondered how smoothly one of those tree-chilled coconut drinks would cut through cotton-mouth. "As long as nobody knows," I concluded.

Rohan tilted his head slightly, then said, "I go and come." He left without saying where.

I took the *Daily Gazette* back out to the verandah. It was less slavish in its coverage of the government than the paper I'd read in Colombo. At least it balanced the day's cruel-subversive stories with a few accounts of "vigilantes" killing JVP rebels. There was no mention of a boy discovered dead at a military base in Colombo, but three teenagers, one of them a girl, were found shot to death while roped to lampposts. The only clue was a sign left behind reading, "Death to JVP."

A feature writer took a quarter page to plop out an almost psychological exploration of the life of Gamanaya Perera. Typically, some sub-editor missed the point by heading it: "The Wayward Path of a Wicked Man." Which was actually apt, for a traitor masquerading as a rebel, but nothing in the text describing him as the lone source of rational political thought in the JVP suggested it. If the article was a plant by Perera or one of his government pals, the headline writer must not have been in on the plan.

The sports section had three stories on the first games of the tournament. I hesitated, but the guilt faded as I read on. No upsets, no great goals, not much in the way of drama. I hadn't missed anything.

The rest of the news was bad, even terrible. The war in the north and east against Tamil separatists continued even though thousands of Indian soldiers had arrived to keep the peace. For some reason, the peacekeepers seemed to be shooting it up just like any other army, and getting nowhere for it. In the rest of the country it was Sinhalese killing each other, with some innocent Muslim villagers being slaughtered to round things out.

Many more will have to suffer, I mouthed to myself.

A columnist on the op-ed page began a pretty good piece with, "This is how low we have dropped, fellow Sri Lankans: terrorist sadism has reached the point of murdering funeral assistants and mourners."

Many more will have to die. I flipped to the comics page. Don't ask me why.

A thin voice from the road distracted me. I curled down one corner of the paper to look. A rickety beggar with dirt-black creases in his cheeks looked back at me with leaky eyes. He held a shaking hand out, palm up, and said something I couldn't understand.

I shook my head. "Sorry," I said. "No."

But his reaction was odd. He seemed almost happy for it. It was not a smile to induce pity. More like he was pleased simply to have made the contact. I had the unsettling feeling that I was now the one being judged, by him, the wiser of us two, with his hand still out.

I might have given him a little money just to end the charade, but ruled it out. It wouldn't do to encourage begging on someone else's property. He might come back the next day, and then every day. Word might get out and the verandah would be filled with them, a colony of beggars all looking for their payday. I wouldn't want them showing up even after I'd gone, bothering Vijaya's family on my account.

"No. Nothing," I said, then enunciated the words again along with, "I'm sorry." I shook my head with a scowl, international language for no, then turned back to the paper. I heard him murmur what might have been the Sinhalese word for "please," but I refused to lower the page.

We reached a stalemate. He waited and I pretended to read, my embarrassment mounting. I was afraid to peek again around the edge of the paper. How long before our little drama drew a crowd? The beggar must have known and decided he could wait me out. I began to resent him for it.

He went on speaking in elliptical Sinhalese until Vijaya's wife appeared behind me on the verandah. She said a few words that made his smile widen more, then dropped a coin into his palm. He brought it to his forehead with an expression of gratitude that he turned to include me in as well. As if I had anything to do with it. I felt, not for the first time in dealing with those less fortunate, miserly.

"I should have done that," I apologized to her. "I wasn't quite sure . . . I didn't want to have anyone bothering anybody, you see." The beggar turned into the Rhino Eye store up the road.

Vijaya's wife kept a patient smile on her face throughout my clumsy attempts to explain. I realized after sputtering for some time that she wouldn't understand anyway. I'd never heard her speak

English, and she had shown no interest in my conversations with Vijaya or Rohan. I shrugged in defeat, knowing the gesture would not be adequate to convey a feeling I didn't understand myself.

"Poor man," she said, surprising me. With her accent it came out, poo-er mahn. She giggled at the sound of English on her own lips. I heard her bare feet pad into the kitchen out back. "Poor man," she murmured again, to herself.

6

Rohan waved from a polite distance beyond the cabana's open window, waiting until I nodded before coming nearer.

"What you write?" he asked from the doorway.

"Nothing. Just a letter."

"Just a letter. To who?"

"Nobody. Just my wife." I sounded to myself as if I'd been caught in a lie. I covered it up with a smile.

"You write a funny joke?" he asked, poised for the punch line.

"That's one way to look at it."

His smile faded. "Yes. You like the ganja? Good, no?"

"I don't know. I haven't tried it."

His eyebrows went up in surprise. After a whole day? Was there something wrong with me?

"I didn't have a pipe. Or papers."

He nodded, then turned to look at the ocean. The water in front of the descending sun was just beginning to turn orange.

"Now is a good time?" he asked. When I nodded, he said, "I go and come."

Three boys in shorts tried to push each other into the water, squealing at the horror of getting their bare feet wet. Two lines of men 30 yards apart dragged a massive net up from the sea. It looked big enough to haul an acre of fish.

"Mister Gordie," Rohan called from the coconut trees. I could tell from his voice he was smiling.

"You don't have to call me mister," I said when his face appeared again in the doorway. "I'm not much older than you."

"I know. I don't mean mister for age."

"Anyway, Gordie will do fine."

"Gordie," he agreed, looking at the desk where I was no longer writing. "I sit here?" I got up and sat on the bed.

He shut the door and latched the wooden window. He took a sheet of rough brown paper out from his sarong.

"Now I make spliff," he announced, holding his hand out for the ganja.

He unraveled the newspaper with care, then sifted a little between his thumb and forefingers. "Good," he murmured in approval. He placed the sheet of paper over the edge of the desk and tore off two sections. With flicks of his tongue he wet the edges and stuck them together to form a broad T.

A sprinkle of pot for the long stem of the T, now some into the head, a little more for the stem, yes? He eyed it like a sculptor. No, more for the head. Yes. His fingers spun to produce a joint the size of a young carrot. He held it up by the tip so I might admire his craftsmanship.

"I knew you had some talent in you, Rohan. We just had to find it."

He handed me the joint and a box of Elephant Brand matches. The cover announced they were "Ultrasafe" in flaming red letters. I placed the joint between my lips, paused, and tried to recall the last time I had smoked.

"Figures," I said at last, "short-term memory loss." Rohan didn't bother to ask.

I pushed a breath out through my nose to empty my lungs, stopped, and added, "Or is that long-term?" before striking the match. It sparked once and sputtered out. So did the next three.

"Jesus, no wonder they're ultrasafe," I grumbled. Rohan took the box, put two matches together and swiped them into a flame he held out for me. I touched it with the end of the joint, smelling the tang of the paper followed by the thick, skunky herb. I sucked in a long, deep breath. Smooth, not too hot, no rasp. I studied the joint with my eyes squinted against smoke. The hit seemed to waft up into my skull, bump softly against the perimeter and flow all around. Good. I exhaled a heavy blue stream. Still soothing on the way out. Very good. A fine crop. My estimation of Rohan and his country went up a notch. I passed him the joint.

He closed his eyes for a slow drag. His skin seemed darker than usual in the unlit room. He opened one eye to examine the burning tip of his handiwork, then smiled at it.

I looked up to find him staring at the joint between my fingertips. Oh, right, I still had it. I took a quick hit and exhaled at a pink gecko sidling in slow motion across the thatch wall.

Rohan tapped a poly-rhythm on the desktop with his fingertips, the bottom of his palm delivering the bass. He began singing in a voice that was higher and silkier than when he spoke.

After a few lines, he stopped. "This song, you know, it's mean, the boy love the girl, but the father of the girl is too rich. He don't let her marry to any poor man, you understand? So he sing this song for her. The boy say he don't care even if she marry to another, even if she never come and he get sick and old and die by himself. If he can sing this song for her one time? Enough."

He tapped out the rhythm again, this time singing with his eyes closed while swaying to the beat. I tried closing my eyes too, but couldn't picture the scene. When I opened them, the gecko was still on the wall, frozen. Now it wouldn't even blink. I might have paralyzed it.

"So what happens to the boy?" I asked.

"Boy?"

"The boy in the song. Does the girl's father let her marry him in the end?"

Rohan had to think for a moment. "No. Maybe. I can't say. He is still singing at the end."

"A better ending than most couples get."

Suddenly the haunting image of Juanita Velasquez scrambling through the newsroom came to me. Her cheeks streaked black with mascara, her finger pointing as she spilled desk trays, knocked over the water bottle, closed the distance between us, but to do what? Not get her husband back. Nothing I could do or say would help there.

I blocked the image of the grief-mad Juanita by turning back to Rohan. "All couples, if you think about it," I said.

"Sure," he said, which might have meant, "Whatever."

I heard the waves again. "Mister Rohan," I said. "What are we doing in the dark? Let's go out and enjoy the sunset."

"Yes," he answered. "If you say mister."

He stood up in slow motion and re-tied his sarong, then pulled open the door. The grey thatch behind me turned red. The sun was about to touch the water. It made a ribbon of gold that shimmered from the horizon all the way to the end of the wet sand before us.

We walked a short distance before sitting. Rohan chose a spot not two yards from where I'd buried the document. It seemed co-incidental, but how many coincidences does it take? He pointed his chin at three local women strolling along the tide line, their heads lowered in conversation. "My father say before the tourist come? No one in the village come out to watch the sunset."

A white-haired woman in a peach sari walked slowly with her hands behind her back as she looked out to sea. In front of the big hotels in the distance I could just make out a few people sitting on the sand or at restaurant tables. Everyone faced the sun. Only the fishermen were removed from the pageant, crowded around their catch instead.

The ribbon of light on the water bent each time a swell rose, then shattered as it broke into a wave. The sound of the water was hypnotic, a shush I felt as much as heard, oozing over my pinging thoughts like honey. I wanted to stretch the moment, to slow it into a reverie, but when the sky dimmed and the sea darkened I decided that was equally beautiful. The change inherent in all things, something Vijaya had said. "It's good to be in Sri Lanka," I announced.

Rohan answered, "Yes. Also I like. Now we have so much trouble. Tamil Tiger, bad business. Green Tiger. Still I like."

I went back to doodling in the sand with a broken shell. The sun dipped below the water, crimson melting into blue. The overture to a celestial show. Next it would be stars.

The voice of Rohan's young brother came to me like the soundtrack from another movie filtering through multiplex walls. He was standing by the bench in front of the cabana. He said something that made Rohan get up.

Appearing beside the boy was a wide-shouldered man twice his height with a long two-headed drum strapped across his chest. It was only when Rohan jogged over and took him by the elbow, leading him back across the sand, that I realized he was blind.

The man said something in Sinhalese which Rohan translated. "He ask if he can sit."

"Yes, of course. Definitely. Tell him to make himself at home." I stifled a laugh. I was the only person there who wasn't at home.

The man sat, tilted his head and began speaking in a quiet voice, his milk-white eyes aimed somewhere over Rohan's shoulder. Someone should tell him about dark sunglasses, I thought, then just as quickly decided I was wrong. Why cover up for appearances? Some things in the Third World made more sense. He was blind, and he looked like he was blind. Why pretend otherwise? To please other people? To fit into their picture? The blind might be just the people to teach us all a lesson on vanity. In any case, even the best sunglasses would not have turned him into a handsome man. His blunt nose was too wide for his long, angular face, and his sunken cheeks were pockmarked.

By the constant murmuring of assent, I took it that Rohan was agreeing with whatever the man said. I imagined I could understand Sinhalese. I began to construct the dialogue. The man was telling Rohan of his revelation, that he now understood the truth, that he had been awakened, that the mysteries of where we come from and where we go after we die had been revealed.

So this is what an enlightened being looks like, I thought, wondering whether Vijaya would be delighted or jealous that I'd found him first. I imagined the man telling Rohan he was happy being blind because it helped him realize how others were not seeing the truth, that sickness and death were the way of all flesh, yet there was something that endures beyond the inevitable chemical catastrophe.

Rohan nodded as if to say, Yes, I understand now, and from this day forth I shall end my wicked ways, and quit smoking heroin, and make something positive of my life. I shall be good.

The man continued: without sight, one can see clearly into the weaknesses that destroy us. We are lost and we are alone, until we discover the path.

Yes, Rohan nodded, the path, the road to the end of all suffering. Because the truth –

"This my friend," I heard him say in English.

"Naturally," I replied to catch up. "Your friend."

"Vasudeva. He is a musician. He can't see, so he can't do a normal job. He play music, people give him money."

"Fantastic." I added dumbly, "Music is good."

"Yes. Vasudeva one time he write a song about Sri Lanka, all the beautiful places. He win first prize for the contest to go to Colombo to sing on television. Everyone here watch, maybe 50 people around the television. We all clap and yell 'Vasudeva!' when we see him."

"No kidding." I aimed a duly impressed nod to Vasudeva, then realized he wouldn't see it. "Maybe we could ask him for a song now?"

"No problem," Rohan said. "He is happy to sing."

Vasudeva didn't look happy, but he straightened his back, settled the drum in his lap and adjusted a harmonica holder hanging around his neck. It was made from a wire coat hanger and strips of black rubber. The harmonica was stamped Made in China.

He whacked the side of the drum once, producing a crack loud enough to make me jerk. Was it amplified? How could a single instrument emit a sound so huge? Then I remembered the ganja.

Vasudeva began beating an intricate rhythm on both ends of the drum. He had the *tick-ticka-tick* beat of a tabla, only the ticks were more like whacks. I struggled at first, then found the rhythm and bobbed my head, until he opened his mouth to sing. I stopped to stare. We were sitting so close I could have touched him, but he sang in a baritone that turned the head of the white-haired woman far down the beach. Yet his tone was still warm, almost as if he was whispering something intimate. Even without understanding a word, it was a stirring song.

He ended with a crack on either end of the drum that reminded me of thunder. I applauded. He tilted his head a fraction to acknowledge it and immediately began another song. This one featured a break on the harmonica, which he blew into loud enough to leave spittle bubbling on top. Rohan leaned over to explain their earlier conversation.

"Vasudeva cannot see, so he have a problem to get marry. So he come here now. He ask me to help him find a wife."

"Serious?"

"Serious," he said, nodding gravely. "But difficult. He has a good heart. But he cannot do a normal job. If I can find a girl with a bad leg, or maybe she can't hear, something like that, they can get marry and work together."

"Can you?"

"Sure." Then with a slightly less confidence, "I can try."

Vasudeva finished the song. Rohan said, "You have something you like to hear?"

"I don't know too many Sri Lankan songs."

Rohan translated, and Vasudeva began a tune on the harmonica I knew I'd hear before. I could even fill in the notes. It was obvious, but the name, it was right at the back of my mind, only my mind was – then it came to me. "Silent Night! That's right! I'd forgotten all about Christmas. What's the date today?"

Rohan didn't know. Vasudeva was too wrapped up in the harmonica, which was now coated with spit. I had to count up from the day I'd arrived, ending at December 23rd. "That means tomorrow is Christmas Eve," I announced.

"Silent Night" continued in a high and dreamy harmonica wail accompanied by the low booming of his drum. Somehow he captured it as a lullaby.

"Does he know the words?" I asked. Suddenly I wanted very much to hear it sung, all the better if it was in Sinhalese.

Rohan asked, getting a shake of the head. I closed my eyes to enjoy the instrumental version just the same, filling in the words myself in my mind. When Rohan saw my lips moving, he said, "Why you no sing?"

"Because I don't want to clear the beach."

He looked all around us. "Who will care? If you like to sing, sing," he said, as if it were obvious.

I started when the next verse came around, "Si-i-lent night . . . ho-o-ly night/Aaaall is calm . . . Aaaal is bright . . . "

The higher notes came out like squeaks from old hinges.

Rohan looked at me, shaking his head from side to side in wonder. "If you don't like to sing, don't sing," he said with a smirk.

When Vasudeva started the next song, another full-volume belter, I said to Rohan, "How much should I give him?"

"As you like."

"I know, but what do people usually give?"

"Anything is good," he said. "Some people give one rupee, some people give more. Vasudeva like to sing."

I went to the cabana and got a 20-rupee note. I handed it to Rohan. "Do you think this is all right?"

"Very good," he said. He pressed it into the fold of Vasudeva's sarong and murmured something. Vasudeva didn't smile, but said what must have meant thank you before starting on another song.

"He also ask me another thing," Rohan said, grinning. "He say he never touch a woman. So he like, just one time, to lie together. If I can find."

"Yeah?"

He slushed a laugh. "He can't see. How can he know where to look?"

"And you're going to help him?"

"That's why he come here. If he tell someone else, they tell another, and then another, and then everybody know and maybe they laugh. He say to me, he know I don't tell."

I didn't remind him he had just told the first person he had seen. Instead I asked, "Do you know someone he can, you know, lie with?"

"Sure. A whore is 100 rupees. And Vasudeva say he don't mean fucking. He only want to know what is a woman. So just touching. Maybe I can ask for less."

He laughed out loud, which struck me as rude, but Vasudeva didn't seem to notice. He continued in his booming voice as if trying to entertain the Indians we couldn't see across the ocean horizon.

"You only need 100 rupees to help him?"

"For the whore, yes. For the wife, not money."

"I can give it to you. The 100 rupees."

"As you like."

"It's for him, though. You'd better not take it. I would be extremely upset if I found out you tried to jerk him around."

He didn't look insulted. "You think I steal from Vasudeva?"

"Okay. I trust you." Or I wanted to, anyway, which was at least a start.

Rohan sang a few lines along with Vasudeva. The three boys who had been playing near the water approached shyly at the edge of our group to listen.

Rohan stopped singing. He had an idea. "Better! You come too! We go together."

"Go where?"

"To the whorehouse."

"No thanks." I checked to see whether the little boys might understand English. In a quieter voice I said, "It's not my thing."

"Not for you. For Vasudeva. You can choose for him."

I had to laugh. "All the same, I'll pass. I trust you."

"I know. But yes, you come. We go together. Just to choose." He was smiling wider now.

I didn't hide the fact I was curious. Whether it was exploiting the least fortunate or supporting their struggle through the local economy I couldn't say, but getting a prostitute for Vasudeva seemed on at least one level a good deed.

"It's practically in the Christmas spirit," I reasoned.

Rohan looked at me for an explanation. Instead I said, "We'll go together," and closed my eyes to follow the melody. Vasudeva's music was transporting. It had nothing to do with snow back in Boston, or an empty house with no Christmas tree in the window. I let it lift me above the spiraling mood that thinking of my wife could always send me into.

I opened my eyes at the closing thump of the drum, a whack to signify the show was over. The sun was gone.

All the seats on the bus we took the next day were occupied but the first. Over it was a stenciled sign that read, Reserved for Clergy. Preachers getting special seating in a country full of Buddhists? I didn't get it. Then an orange-robed monk boarded and sat there. Oh, that kind of clergy.

"Tell me something, Mister Rohan," I said, close enough to his ear that the other passengers wouldn't hear as we stood swaying with the curves. "You go to this whorehouse a lot?"

He shook his head. "Can't. No money. But I know a woman. Not from here, from the other whorehouse in Ambalangoda. You know?"

"I'm sure I don't."

"Ambalangoda, not so far from Hikkaduwa. This woman is my friend. Sometimes we fucking together because she like me. I don't pay."

"Lucky you."

"Yes. She is nice. Also one time, when Italian tourist man stay in your cabana, he ask me to find a girl. I take him to the whorehouse we go to now. He bring her back to the cabana and when he finish, he say to me, now is your turn." He made his slushy laugh. "So I get free."

"How about local girls?" I had never seen one out in the village after dark. "You can't do anything before you get married, I suppose."

"Sometimes can. But if the woman is seen, she maybe have a bad time later. Everybody talking."

"Good for you to find the woman in Al-whatever."

"Yes. Now I also have a girlfriend. She live in Matara. I want to marry. But my life right now is not good. I have no job, I smoking brown sugar. How can I marry?"

"By cleaning up your act."

"Yes." A pair of women carrying cloth shopping bags left the seat in front of us, but we didn't bother sitting down.

"So you don't see her often."

"In summer, my father give me money to buy things for, how do you call, the part of house up." He pointed to the top of the bus.

"The ceiling? The roof?"

"Yes, the roof. Rain comes in so he have to fix. My father give me 500 rupees to buy supplies in Galle. But I use the money and go to Matara."

"I don't believe it."

He shrugged. More passengers got on the bus. We were pressed closer together.

"You really spent your father's house repair money on a girl?"

He looked up at me but said nothing. With passengers piling in at each stop, I was now standing over him.

"You know your father doesn't have much."

"I know. I am thinking, my life is bad now. If I can marry, then it is not just my life. I have to think about two person. If we have a baby, three person. I must stop smoking, I must get a job. Then I can help my family. So? I go to Matara."

"Jesus, what a load you can pile when you want to."

"Yes," he agreed, perhaps not catching what kind of load I meant.

"And what happened with the girl?"

"We don't tell anything to her family yet. Maybe they don't like that I have no job."

"So you blew the 500 rupees?"

"What's mean blew?"

"Wasted. Threw away."

"If I marry, not blew. I change my life."

"What did your father say when you got back?"

"He was angry. But I don't lie. I don't say anything back. I only listen, and I move my head like this." He nodded with a look less of contrition than weary acceptance, as if his own incorrigible nature was a bother to him too. I recognized it.

"I would've kicked you out of the house."

He shrugged and looked out the window. "This stop," he said.

This village was even smaller than his. With the high tide line reaching almost to the road, the beach was too narrow for fishing boats to land.

Across the road the jungle green covered most of the view of dirt hills. Between two of the hills were a group of thatch huts that looked like my cabana.

"In Matara," Rohan said as we walked there, "I go with my girl-friend to the beach. We start holding our hands. We talking about our life. Then we start kissing. I thinking, maybe I want to do with her. The way she kissing me, I thinking, maybe she want also. But I stop. I tell her, better if we get marry first. Then I take her home. The next morning she tell me thank you, that she never do with any boy before and now she happy because she know she wait for me. Always."

"Does she know about you and other girls?"

"I tell her everything. About girls, about brown sugar. She know I don't stay this way."

A cluster of chickens ran towards us, one bumping into my ankle and protesting by clucking furiously. We passed an oozing green pond and arrived at the first hut. Rohan called out something in a quiet voice. A loud male grunt from the middle shack answered.

A man in flared blue slacks and a once-white tank-top stepped out. He wavered, scowling as if the sun hurt his eyes, before focusing on Rohan. He approached us with the exaggerated caution of someone drunk, then plopped a steadying arm around Rohan's shoulder and tugged him inside. I followed.

The shack was cramped even before we went in. With a rattan bed along one wall and a table with two chairs along its opposite, there was barely enough room for three people to stand.

The man grabbed a bottle off the table and filled a shot glass with brown liquid, spilling half as much as he poured. He started to wipe the puddle with his other hand, but it was too much to absorb. He smeared what he could on his thigh, then gave up with a hand gesture of futility. He tilted his head back and downed the liquid in a gulp. "Ah," he said, wiping his mouth with the back of his hand.

Rohan spoke in the meek voice I'd notice him use before on certain people. It made the man blurt out in a cackle. Rohan turned to me with an apologetic expression. "He say we can sit."

I took the chair nearest the door. Rohan sat on the bed.

The man lowered his head and growled something to the back wall. A woman's high-pitched voice from outside called back in a questioning tone. He looked at us, burped silently in a way that made his head jerk, then yelled again.

Two young women appeared in the doorway. I sat up straight and made myself close my mouth. I had expected something haggard for 100 rupees, but these two were startling. Sports Illustrated and swimsuits came to mind. Then the stewardess in Colombo. But here? In a village whorehouse? There had to be some cultural explanation for this I wasn't getting.

The one who sat next to Rohan on the bed, making it sag in a way that tilted his balance, had the long nose and high cheekbones of a runway model. Her dark hair, dyed with a single streak of brown down the left side, reached almost to her waist. Rohan looked at the man, at me, and then down at the floor. He was impressed.

But I couldn't help staring at the other. She was taller and darker, with a round, open, intelligent face. She sat in the chair across from mine, almost close enough to be touching knees, and gave me a tiny welcoming smile. Or maybe it was the hint of a smile that might come later, if I deserved it. I didn't see it as a come-on. Just what it meant I wasn't certain. Perhaps exactly what a clever prostitute would use to entice a wary customer. But the way her wide lips curled out at the edges, revealing the soft pink insides, made them seem too obvious for anything like guile.

The pair put their palms together in front of their faces and said in unison, "*Ayubowan.*"

Rohan said something to the woman beside him that made her laugh, a light soprano that was immediately drowned out by the pimp's cackle. The woman across from me didn't move. When she turned to look at the man, perhaps in reproach, I watched her in profile as if the thatch wall behind her was a movie screen and she was the heroine. With her hands folded in her lap and her back pressed straight against the chair, she could have been sitting for a job interview. Not with that sarong though. The dingy blue cloth patterned with tiny white flowers may once have been pretty, but now it suggested nothing beyond its own overuse. I followed it up to where she'd wrapped a knot and tucked it between her breasts. Her shoulders were bare. I wondered how her tea-colored skin would look on the beach at the sunset.

Rohan declined the offer of a drink. The man waved the glass under his nose anyway, then pivoted and shoved it to me, spilling some onto my legs.

I turned back, almost embarrassed, to the woman. The sympathy in her eyes told me she understood. I patted at the wet spot on my thigh and sniffed my fingers to see if I was going to smell like a bar rag. Instead I caught the vague scent of flowers, maybe lilacs. There was nothing like it in the room, and with her the closest to me I took it for her perfume. Unless she had been picking flowers just before we arrived, which in the circumstances seemed unlikely. But I could picture her standing in a field of lavender, miles away from any hundred-rupee whorehouses or drunken pimps.

I looked up from the floor to find her staring at me with her head at a quizzical tilt. She smiled at being caught. Even without lipstick, her lips were an almost unnatural pink. I couldn't help but study the line where the glistening border marked the wet insides. I'd never seen lips so full of themselves, almost to the point of being ugly. She could have been a painting, the way I gaped and pondered.

I realized I was gawking and looked away. When I turned back her lips flinched into the start of a smile, but again without the payoff. It was not just a whore selling herself. The same idea was reflected in her eyes. She was enjoying my discomfort. I managed a brief smile in return and turned to Rohan as if I had something to say.

He and his partner were holding hands. The man was busy trying to set the bottle upright on the table. None of them seemed to notice or care that I'd been stirred. I could look all I wanted.

I stared again as the tip of her tongue darted out twice to moisten her lips. It seemed more habit than anything contrived, but struck me as a tactical gesture nonetheless. It certainly worked. I tried to make myself look elsewhere, to take in the way her full cheeks curved in to meet her almond-tipped eyes, but now those lips were shining like beacons. The spell was broken when they parted to speak, saying something in my direction. It was in Sinhalese.

"I don't speak the language, Sinhalese, I'm afraid," I said. I passed my fingers through my hair to smooth it back and sat up straighter. Her own formal posture made me feel like a slouch. She smiled, vacantly.

"Do you speak English?" I asked slowly, pointing to her chest on the word you.

She laughed in a way that revealed the top row of her teeth. She turned to the pimp for a translation.

He grunted something in Sinhalese, drawing a "tsk" from the woman beside Rohan. The man sneered at her, then turned to me.

"Yes! Fuck! Good!" he blurted out. My hand balled into a fist that I kept hidden by my thigh. He groped for and found the head of the woman beside Rohan, then slid his fingers down the length of her hair. I could deck him with one shot. His chin was practically calling for it.

I knew I was slipping. Here of all places. I rubbed my face and shook my head the way a hockey player does to clear the cobwebs after a hard check. Steady on, son. Five minutes in their midst and I was acting like a love-struck schoolboy. If I stared at her any longer they'd double the price.

The thought that just 100 rupees separated us was enough to quicken my pulse. I pictured tracing my fingertips along the lines of those lips to feel the warmth inside, untying the knot of the sarong between her breasts, my palms racing to cover the new territory of this living work of art.

It was another of her knowing smiles that make me snap out of it. She saw into me even before I figured it out myself. She wasn't mine, she never would be. I could screw her – she might even pretend to like it – but once I got off, that would be it. The deal would be over, the money spent. I might not even want to see her, this precious thing I could never have gotten on my own terms, not for real. She would already belong to the next guy with his wallet out. And if that all sounded like a degrading exercise to me, what could it possibly mean for her?

Rohan whispered something into the other woman's ear while the pimp leered over them. I told myself to hold back, to resist no matter how compelling a case she made. I would not lose this one. Not with her. Not like this. She may have mastered the art of the sale, but I wasn't a complete idiot. It takes two to close a deal.

Inevitably I turned back, and immediately surprised myself by smiling again. Her conspiratorial glance to check on the others was another deft move, the simple act of sliding her eyes rather than turning her head pulling me back into her orbit. Rohan and the woman stared at the hand he had just placed on her tit as if it belonged to someone else. The pimp's eyes were shut into a pained squint. We turned back to each other. She mirrored my own sense of resignation. At the same time she seemed amused. Her lips again curled slightly at the corners, then spread quickly to laugh out loud at something Rohan said. When she turned to address him I noticed that her hair was black enough to shine as it fell in unfinished curls past her shoulders. She looked at me and again said something in Sinhalese.

"I'm sorry," I said, meaning it. "I really don't understand."

Rohan explained: "She ask, what your name?"

I turned back to her, wishing I could leave him out of it. "Gordie Talison."

She tried, "Gordir Tall-san."

I laughed encouragingly. "No, no. Gordie," I said. "Gor-die."

She repeated: "Gor-die?"

"Perfect," I said. "You're catching on. And what's your name?"

"Gor-die?" she said again.

"No, no, no. Your name." I pointed to my chest. "Gor-die. Gordie." Then I pointed at her, my finger almost touching the knot in her sarong.

She nodded regally. "Kumari," she said. "Ku-ma-ri."

I repeated, "Kumari."

She flashed a brilliant smile, as if hearing the sound of her own name was a joy in itself. I looked down at the dirt while I smiled myself, and vowed once again to keep my pants on.

The pimp slapped Rohan on the back hard enough to make a noise. He said something in Sinhalese and then laughed, but he was the only one. He slapped the glass down on the table and laughed again. The sound of it seemed calculated to grate on me.

"Fuck! Good!" he said, looking through half-closed lids at Kumari. I squinted at him in warning, my adrenaline starting to rise again, but he was too drunk to notice.

"Did you explain to him that this isn't for me?" I asked Rohan.

"I tell him. No problem. She come tonight."

"Fine," I said, turning back to Kumari. She tilted her head, wondering what had just been decided.

"Which one you like?" Rohan said. When I didn't answer immediately he chuckled and added, "Which one Vasudeva like?"

I pointed my chin to the one beside him. "Her," I said. "Definitely her. Vasudeva is a lucky guy."

Rohan explained it to the pimp in Sinhalese. The pimp nodded absently and picked up the bottle, waving us out with the back of his other hand.

The woman beside Rohan leaned over and kissed him on the cheek. It was a friendly peck, and almost touching for the fact. I wondered whether Kumari might do the same. But I stood up too soon and the moment was lost.

I wanted to tell her something, anything, before we left. But what? Remember me? That I wanted her too much to just fuck her? Or was there more to it I wouldn't let myself guess? It would have been impossible, even in English. Confusion was the only bilingual thing about me.

7

"I go to Rhino Eye to buy one cigarette," Rohan said. "You come?"

I followed, not to watch anyone buy a single cigarette, but because a public place included the prospect, however remote, of running into Kumari. I tucked my shirt into my stretchable-waist shorts, a wondrous invention, and pulled a little back out to hide the contour of my stomach. Loose clothing went with our tribe's fondness for black, a weak yet useful disguise. It would never make us appear svelte, but at least it wouldn't flaunt the parts we wished to cover most.

We sat at the only table. The Rhino Eye was a store for locals, but it had a few concessions for any tourist who happened to stumble in. The shelves were crowded with goods placed seemingly at random: canned soups, spices in clear plastic bags, stick brooms, school notebooks, toys, dusty boxes of what might have been flour, T-shirts, beach towels, hinges. Nothing made marketing sense. Laundry soap between the onions and a mound of padlocks? What was the connection? Would anyone looking for a notebook think to check the box behind the tinned fish? It was as if the shelves had been stocked by a crew of blind volunteers.

The proprietor said nothing to show he remembered my earlier attempt to buy a cold drink. He appeared slighter this time, with sharp, pointed eyes in a handsome face drawn down to a point by a black goatee. His manners certainly hadn't improved. He asked, in mildly accented English, "What do you want?"

Rohan placed a coin on the counter and waited for permission to remove a single cigarette from a jar on the counter. He lit it with a slow-burning rope nailed to the door frame. I ordered two lemonades and sat beside him at the table to wait.

The shopkeeper dragged himself off the stool for the four-step walk to the fridge. Glaring as if we were intruders, he withdrew two Elephant Brand soda-pops, balancing them between his left hand and the arm wrapped in bandages.

"This Leon," Rohan said. "The owner."

"How do you do," Leon said in a way that wasn't a question. Rohan spoke in Sinhalese and Leon aimed a tiny nod in my direction.

"Your first time in Sri Lanka," he noted.

"Got here a few days ago."

He returned to his counter enclave. Behind him was a smoked glass mirror that offered customers the odd option of watching themselves buy rather than him sell. He may have planned it that way to take away the attention. He sat with his back straight, making a sideways shift of his cat-eyes to the road when a fishmonger on a bicycle rode by singing about fish.

"So you're the proud owner of this fine establishment," I said.

"Pfft," he answered.

"Business not too good?"

"You can't see for yourself?" Even freighted with cynicism, his English was melodious. When I clucked in sympathy, he added, "Rohan has the right idea. Fill your head with drugs and forget everything else. Nothing is going to change, so why bother? Right?"

Rohan blew out a thin stream of smoke, then smiled absently. He sucked on the pink straw in his bottle.

"You don't seem the type to get into drugs," I told Leon.

"Oh?" He looked surprised. "What makes you say so?"

"You seem too intelligent for one thing." It was a shot at Rohan which Leon seemed to appreciate. He lifted one side of his mouth into something like a smile.

"You could be right about that," he said. "Drugs do a perfect job of making stupid people stupider. But you can't tell anybody anything. Can you Rohan?"

Rohan didn't look up. He made the liquid rise and fall in the straw a few times before extracting a gulp.

"I got into politics and look what it got me," Leon told me. He didn't point to the bandaged arm. The pause that followed seemed a challenge to my propriety.

"It's gone," he continued. "A bomb. I also tried religion. Turns out I'm not a monk. So what's left?" He waved the bandages in a weary circle to take in his shop.

"I once interviewed a guy who made bombs," I said. I didn't go into the details, how the interview was a bad idea on his part, landing him in prison. "Who did that to you?"

He stared long enough to make me feel uncomfortable for asking. At last he tilted his head. "I did," he explained dully. "It was my bomb. Went off early."

"Oh." I kept my eyes on my drink while I sipped. "Sorry to hear that."

"It was in 1971. Did Rohan not tell you? I was in the JVP. The real JVP. We controlled 75 percent of the island, for a brief time. The vanguard for the new Sri Lanka. You must have read something about us. No? The JVP?"

"I've heard of it."

Boredom may have made him loquacious. "I spent the next seven years in prison, mostly by myself. My cell was no larger than the table you're sitting at. If they had let me see a doctor, I might have saved this." He nodded at his bandages. "At least that's what the doctor now tells me. Maybe he's lying. Maybe they all were from the beginning and they still are now. I don't know. I don't even want to know. I'm through thinking about it. I've had nothing but time to think. You want to know what I discovered? Hmm?" He was goading now. Was I tough enough to swim in his sea of contempt?

"Sure," I said, the reporter's automatic answer. "If you feel like telling it."

"It doesn't make a bit of difference what you do, man. They get you in the end. They always do. The bastards win. And the 'people' you're trying to help? To uplift? They don't want it. Worse, they don't deserve it. They don't care about any workers' paradise in some glorious future. They'd rather have a bottle of arak today. So why go to all the trouble?"

He said it to me but he was staring at Rohan. If Rohan was listening, he didn't show it. He lolled in his chair like a child between shows at the cinema.

"I'm sure there's some good that comes from trying to make a better world," I said. "Even if you don't succeed at first." To cover my embarrassment in the gap that followed, I continued. "If nobody had ever tried, we'd be worse off than we are now, right?"

Leon appraised me with a glare, then turned his attention to the empty road. Apparently the issue was not worth discussing further. And he had a seven-year head start on me. Anything I might come up with was old ground to him.

"Leon was a big man in the JVP," Rohan said. "A leader."

"Really," I said. "A revolutionary hero."

Leon scoffed. When he added nothing, Rohan answered for him. "He go to Soviet Union to study. Same university as Rajitpurna. They were schoolmates."

"Seriously? You went to mother Russia with the big cheese?"

Leon shrugged. "We got scholarships to study at Patrick Lumumba University. But he wouldn't stop lecturing the professors about the great Chairman Mao, so he got kicked out. I stayed on another year eating fried cabbage. Don't ask me why. I learned enough Russian to get my face slapped by factory girls, and by the time I got back Rajitpurna was in control."

"And now?"

"Now?" he asked.

"The JVP. Are you still with them?"

"Would I be talking to you?" he sneered as if even a dolt like me should have figured that out. "They're not the JVP, not anymore. The name is the same but that's it. The people are all different."

"Rajitpurna's still there."

"Rajitpurna." He mulled over the name for a moment before going on. "He was a good man, once. He still is a great organizer. That much I grant you. To hear his speeches . . . you don't know this, but Sinhalese is a very poetic language. The way he used to speak when he asked people to join the revolution. Women would throw jewelry at his feet. But what happened next is what always happens. Power got to him. He changed. Then all he wanted was more power. It's still his problem today. He judges people solely on their strength and how he can use it. He doesn't want them to think, certainly not the masses. This bullshit about saving the fatherland from Tamil marauders and the Indian imperialist army? It's not right, man. He's appealing to their lowest instincts by using race."

"You don't support them anymore?"

"That bunch of petty criminals?"

"Not even Commander Dapila?"

He snorted. "How do you support the dead?"

"Dapila died?" I pictured his wife crying over the bed. Leon didn't appear to notice my reaction. He watched the road as he talked.

"Shot while trying to kidnap an MP right in Colombo 7. He and his wife. She was a guerrilla herself, quite famous on her own. They went out together in a blaze of guns and glory. The best way, don't you think?" His grin was malicious.

"They tried to kidnap a politician?"

"Turned out the chap wasn't even home. Typical."

"If you believe the papers."

Leon shrugged. "The government lies, the JVP lies. But Dapila's still dead."

"Was Gamanaya Perera around in your time?"

"We were allies on some of the in-fights. But he was tougher than I was. Nobody was surprised to see him rise to deputy leader. One time he and Rajitpurna got into an argument we all thought would end with bullets. Perera was the only one who would ever stand up to him. Some say he's leading the party already and just keeping Rajitpurna on as a figurehead. I wouldn't know. You probably do. I assume you're CIA?"

I snorted hard enough to inhale some of the drink through my nostrils, then coughed and sputtered to clear my sinuses. Leon must have realized it wasn't an act. No spy could be this ridiculous.

"Why all the questions then?"

"I heard a little about the JVP in Colombo. Made me curious."

"Not me. I don't care what happens to them anymore. We're not on the best terms. If I do meet them, it'll probably be because they've come to put a bullet in my head."

He slipped a rag under his bandaged hand and wiped the counter, frowning at the effort. Without looking up he said, "What do you do?"

"I'm a sportswriter."

"Sports," he said dismissively. He finished wiping and watched two laughing men in sarongs stroll by. We let the topic drop. I wondered what else would be irrelevant to a man who had spent seven years in solitary confinement for a cause he no longer believed in.

Rohan surfaced with a look of rare intensity. "The JVP, they can't drink alcohol, can't take drugs, can't smoke even one cigarette," he announced. "They live a clean life."

"Model citizens for the brave new world," Leon said sarcastically.

Rohan looked cross-eyed at him. "Like you Leon? You the better man?"

Leon sneered as if the contest was beneath him. He turned his back to fiddle with a brick-sized transistor radio, but I could see his face in the mirror. He didn't care about the radio. He would keep fiddling until we left.

It was too hot to sleep. The sea must have been calm. The only sound was the faint murmur of an occasional wave between long silent spells.

I opened the cabana door to let in cooler air. A spray of stars coated the sky down to the water line. I waited for a shooting star, realized I wouldn't know what to wish for anyway, then went back inside.

I remembered the bag under my bed. I removed a poster and slipped off the elastic. The painted words were in Sinhalese but the message was clear. There was a roughly-drawn hammer and sickle, and bigger than everything else in red letters: JVP.

In the morning I woke up feeling peppy. I marched straight into the sea and churned the water for 20 minutes like a mighty bloated Mark Spitz.

I staggered back up to the cabana feeling proud. The sun soaked into my pasty skin like balm. A tan would mean one more thing to explain back at the office, but thoughts of work hardly seemed to trouble me any more. I took that as a good sign.

Rohan found me later reading on the bench. He cleared his throat, and I invited him to sit.

"My friend say thank you to take his posters," he said.

"His JVP posters."

"Oh. You look?"

"I look."

"That's why he cannot keep. If the army find him with posters? They take him away." He snapped his fingers.

"You mean they kill him."

"Yes." This time the finger snap sent a broken shell flying. He gauged it for distance before picking up another.

"Or no," he continued. "The army, they don't know. Sometimes they take the real JVP man, that's mean he is in the party, and they let him go. Sometimes they take the man who don't care anything about politics, and next morning we find his body on the beach." He held his hands behind his back. "Or tied to the post. Or without his head. I see so many bodies." He flicked another shell. I resisted the temptation to ask whether it got easier after the first.

"So you let him keep the posters in my cabana."

"First I ask. You say yes."

"You didn't ask about JVP posters."

"You are right. I am sorry. But for you, no problem. The army don't care. They only take away Sri Lanka man. Sometime woman." He shook his head as if words would not describe it.

"So I've heard. Seen."

"Seen?"

"I met a JVP guy in Colombo, mostly by accident. He tried to set up an interview. The army found out and asked me about it. They're bastards aren't they, the army?"

"What are bastards? A bad thing, no?"

"A bad thing."

"Yes. They are bastards. But not all. My little brother now he go to army school."

"In a time like this?"

"He must do something for his life. Tamil Tigers are fighting to make their own country so the army need so many new people. They taking everybody. Many from this village. First my brother say he is going to be a soldier, but my father tell him no, he is too smart, so he go to school to be officer."

"So he's the smart one in the family." It was supposed to be a joke but Rohan didn't catch it. I added, "Not like you."

"Not like me," he agreed. "Different kind of smart."

"I don't see how that will help when they order him to shoot his own people."

"My brother would never do like that. He has a good heart."

"Not like you."

This time he laughed.

"I go find my friend. I tell him to take back the bag."

"It's no big deal."

"No, very big deal. You know, when JVP do propaganda? They show the same poster everywhere in Sri Lanka at the same time. That's mean, maybe tonight they doing a campaign. So tomorrow you go to Colombo, to Kandy, to Anuradhapura, you see the same thing. Everywhere in Sri Lanka. One message."

"Brutal efficiency."

He shrugged. I didn't explain.

"You like the JVP, Rohan?"

"Sure I like. They are dying for our country, no? They must have a good heart. But I don't like the rules. Too strict for me."

"Might be good for you."

He grinned. "Sure. Hey Gordie, today is Christmas Eve, no? I go bring the whore for Vasudeva. You come?"

I pretended to mull, then said, "I guess. Why not?"

Rohan did his cheek-ruffling laugh. "Maybe Kumari waiting just for you."

"Right," I scoffed, as if I couldn't care. I let him walk ahead so he wouldn't see me smooth back my hair with spit.

At the bus stop closest to the whorehouse, I told Rohan I had some shopping to do first.

"What you buy?" he asked. "I can help. Pay local price."

"No need. See you in front of the phone service in five minutes."

He looked closer at me to see what I was hiding, but someone called him from across the road. Two young men were leaning on a bicycle held between them. I walked away.

The store window offered a glimpse of the dingy goods inside. A pyramid of local soaps in faded yellow wrapping, a deflated red rubber ball, one plastic bottle of Head and Shoulders shampoo, three different brands of "Cream Crackers" and stacks of colored crepe paper. Dust coated everything. Somehow it added to the odd appeal of Christmas shopping in the Third World. Anything would beat the faux cheer of the Christmastime mall.

I walked between aisles, touching nothing for fear of smudging my fingers, until I found a present: a small tin music box. The lid opened to reveal a miniature carousel, its painted horses the size of raisins. Turning the arm produced the first seven notes of Greensleeves. I shut the lid and brought the box to the cashier before anything could fall off. With a piece of red crepe paper to wrap it in, the present still cost less than a dollar.

"I should do all my Christmas shopping here," I told the woman behind the corner.

"Please do," she answered with the crimson grin of a betel chewer.

Rohan was still across the street with the two men. I recognized one as the poster owner wearing the same flared slacks and bleached white shirt as the day before. The other was dressed, like Rohan, in a sarong. Did the JVP have its own dress code too?

The window ad for long distance rates from an international phone service sent my mind back home. I still hadn't contacted my editor with an excuse for not filing. She might have been worried about me. Perhaps even enough to call Kirstin.

I realized I hadn't thought of my partner once that day. Maybe she really was slipping away. I owed it to our past, and perhaps our future, to at least wish her a happy holiday. Something about Christmas the year before had briefly brought out our best sides towards each other. It was as if we'd agreed on a seasonal cease-fire. Inevitably the bickering started again by the New Year, and the endless days of love-on-the-rack were to follow.

Customers lined up to reach an elevated counter where three women high up on stools took the call orders. I stalled by pretending to read the English instructions taped to the wall so I would get served by the best-looking one. Her hair was pulled back tight against her pretty head, reappearing as a thick black rope on the front of her blouse.

I offered a jaunty smile, holding it until she had to smile in return, then said, "I'd like to call Boston please. Boston in the United

States."

"Certainly, sir," she answered in the strato-melody I was learning to appreciate. What a range of notes they could conjure up for even the simplest sentences. A single word was enough for an octave leap. It was music compared to some operators back home who droned their own boredom into you.

I kept the smile going while I explained I had two long distance calls to make. I wrote the numbers on an application form. She helped me fill in the blanks, perhaps taking more care than necessary to make sure I had everything right. I wondered if she liked me.

"Boston," she said approvingly. "I have a cousin in Toronto." I was about to joke about stopping by on her next visit when she said, "I'm going to see her in March. How far is that from where you are?" It was a lob, the ball in my court, and I felt ready for a smash, but her smile collapsed when a door opened behind her and a manager in a clip-on tie stepped out. He checked the papers on her counter while she eyed me in conspiratorial silence. He looked past me to the line of customers. "Booth number two," he snapped at me before moving on to the woman beside her.

"Thank you," I mouthed to my operator when I got there, adding a tiny wag of my head that made her smile again.

The first number I'd given was the paper's. I almost hoped for a bad connection. Something scratchy and barely functional. I could blurt out that I was recovering nicely, nothing too serious, don't worry, Merry Christmas, I'll file as soon as the medication kicks in, I'm practically better, I think I'm going to live, cough-cough, bye-bye.

The phone rang in my booth. I heard a static series of clicks and then a morose "Hul-lo" from Hal Ballard. He was point man on the graveyard shift.

"Ballard?" I asked. "What are you doing there now?"

"The crossword. What's up, Talison? Ya lucky bastid. It's 8 below here. Forget about the wind chill."

"What? Can't hear you. Hello? Are you there?"

"Unfortunately."

"Must be a bad connection. Listen. Just tell Liz I got sick. Something tropical, but I'm all right. Nobody has to worry, I'm getting better. But I can't get to the games yet. Doctor's orders. Got all that?"

"No problemo, big man, but what's wrong? You gonna be okay?"

"What? Can hardly hear you. Gotta go . . . No wait, Ballard? Let me ask you something. What do you think they'd do if I sent in a hard news story? You know, something big."

"Hey! They having one of those soccer wars?"

"Not sports. I mean something serious. A scandal. A big political thing."

I checked the operators, none of whom appeared to be listening. The manager was gone. I went on in a whisper. "Let's call it something that might even bring down the government here. If I could get you guys the document that proves it, along with the story, it would be dynamite. I'm not saying I do have it, mind you, but if I did, I mean, for example."

There was a squelch followed by silence and then a hum. Damn! They were listening! I froze. That manager. He must have assigned me this booth for that very purpose. I scanned the street for soldiers. And if I saw them? There was no back door. Maybe through the staff room? Ballard's voice came back.

" . . . or in the second round. You figure?"

"Can hardly hear you. Lousy connection. Tell Liz I'm getting better, okay?"

I hung up before I could add anything to make it worse. He'd probably tell them I was sloshed. Another long distance fumble. And that was just to the paper.

I scowled at the phone. Not good, not good at all. Even a little static was enough to rattle me? I should not have come in. Now the delay was making me more nervous. Why didn't they sell chocolate bars out of vending machines in this country, something to calm a guy down? Through the window I could see there were no soldiers outside. Of course not. What would they care? Or were they hiding? Rohan and the pair were gone. Chased off? Fuck it. The thugs would have to wait in line. I had my own domestic crisis to deal with first. Figuring out how I got there might help. So why had I wanted to call Kirstin anyway? It was pathetic, a man trying to kick his own ass. Long distance never worked, not for me, not where there was an emotional stake in the exchange. Something about reducing a person to electric pulses, maybe, or the false intimacy that evaporates at the touch of a button. I needed time to prepare, to work up my opening, something that would set the right breezy tone from the start. I stepped out of the booth, wiping sweat from the back of my neck, and started to the counter to ask for a delay. The phone rang first.

I dry-swallowed. It rang three more times. I made myself breathe slowly while I plotted. I decided to say, with as much holiday cheer as I could invent, "Meddy Chrees-mas from guess who?"

There was a click, another squelch of static, and then the connection. A male voice came on the line.

"Um, hello?" it said in the uncertain tone you use to answer someone else's phone. I could hear another voice, perhaps a woman's, in the background. The man tried to suppress a laugh. Then, "May I help you?"

"Who is this?" I demanded.

He laughed out loud this time, as if relieved I was also in on the game. "You know, I've been asking myself that question all night."

"Listen. Is this 710-1922?"

He seemed to find that funny too. "Geez, I dunno." I could hear Kirstin's faint, "Who is it?" in the background.

"Wait a sec, 710-1922," he read, "You got it, bud. But Kirstin is, ah, not exactly disposable right now."

He must have held the phone away, for his laugh this time was smaller. I covered the mouthpiece with my hand, not trusting my own lips.

He came back on. "Sorry. Um, who should I say called? I'm sure she'll call you back in the morning. Better make that the afternoon."

I pressed the hang-up button up before he had a chance to laugh again. "Bloody hell," I heard myself say out the receiver end of the phone.

Back at the counter I avoided the pretty one. I didn't even look up in case she smiled again.

"Two calls on phone number two, that will be 230 rupees please," said an older operator with a chin mole sprouting hair.

I could have spent that phone money at the whorehouse. I could have given it to the poor. I could have promised to flatten that smug jerk's face as soon as I got home. The last thought must have crept onto my expression. When I reached up to place the money on the counter, the tufted woman flinched back.

"By the way," I asked, finding a placid tone with effort, "just what time is it right now in Boston?"

"Boston? That would be . . . one moment, sir . . . 3:38. In the morning."

I produced a smile and walked out. Rohan was waiting for me, alone. We walked together in silence to the whorehouse.

At one point he turned back to me with a frown. "Something is wrong?"

"No. Why?"

He shrugged. "You looking different."

"I'm fine."

"What you buy?" He nodded to the lumpy red wrapping in my hand.

I'd forgotten I had it. It was an embarrassment now. A cheap Christmas present for a whore of similar stature.

"It's nothing. A stupid toy," I said. The shacks were in sight. "You know what, Rohan? Maybe I will take that other girl after all. Can you tell the man for me?"

He slapped his thigh in delight. "I knew you change your mind. Kumari nice. Too nice to leave alone, no?"

"Whatever."

"Good. This very good. We take two whores. I bring one to my friend hotel for Vasudeva. You can use same place. No tourist coming now, so no problem to use for free."

"Fine . . . No, not fine. Forget it. I'm not going anywhere I have to think about you watching."

"Don't worry, I don't watch you. But maybe Vasudeva need some help." He made his slushy laugh.

"Do what you want. I'm leaving with Kumari, on my own. Don't bother sticking around me."

"Yes. You do what you want too." He chuckled. "Kumari nice." He raised his eyebrows and sucked in breath through puckered lips, his signs of appreciation. "This is a good Christmas Eve, no?"

"Merry as all hell," I answered morosely. I knew that screwing Kumari wasn't likely to cheer me up, but at least part of me might feel good for a change.

Rohan called from outside the middle hut. A woman's voice, not Kumari's, answered with something that made him smile.

We waited outside, shuffling our feet in the dirt like schoolboys outside the principal's office. Patience was about to become an issue. I was ready to unload on the first person who said hello the wrong way. I needed to slow down, get back in control, blend in, but everything seemed to be picking up speed. Maybe this time I would take some of the pimp's whiskey. Anything to dull the edge.

The pimp swaggered up to the doorway where he stumbled. What a surprise. He slurred something in Sinhalese. Rohan answered with an explanation that apparently included my business.

The pimp stared at me during Rohan's explanation. His mouth made a quivering line between a smile and a sneer. He said something that made Rohan bend his head in agreement.

"He say Kumari not here. But no problem. He have another whore for you."

"The fuck is he talking about?" I seethed. I held the present behind my back. Steady, steady, don't even consider the temptation of trying to cram it up one of his nostrils. "Damn. This is one fucked-up night. Tell him I came for Kumari. Right? I don't want another one."

Rohan looked confused, but translated anyway. The man listened with his eyes closed, then opened them to stare at me as if I'd just insulted his professional integrity. Rohan translated his answer.

"He say don't worry, the other girl better looking. Not so dark."

The pimp yelled towards the hut. He placed his hands onto his hips for balance and stared up at the purple sky. We'd missed the beach sunset.

A petite women appeared in a white dress that swayed at her knees. Her skin was golden brown. With big, doll-like eyes, she was certainly pretty. Some men might even choose her over Kumari. I didn't care. I didn't want her.

The pimp said something that made her sashay up to me barefoot. She tried to kiss me but I wouldn't lower my head. I left her there straining on her tiptoes. She mock-slapped my chest, then let her hand spider-creep its way down. When she got to my belt, I spun around to keep her away. She got the message and disappeared into the hut without a word.

The pimp glowered. Was this his fighting look? Okay, good, let's go, you piece of shit. I stretched my fingers in anticipation. He said something in a loud voice to Rohan.

'What's wrong?" Rohan asked me in a whisper.

"When is Kumari going to get here?"

Rohan asked the pimp, then listened to the run-on answer while looking down at his feet. Finally he translated simply, "She not here now."

"Because she's with someone else. Of course." I looked up and blew out a slow whoosh of air. The sky was colorless now but there were no stars.

The pimp scratched clumsily at his nose and spoke again.

"He has a good idea," Rohan explained. "If you want, you pay extra, he can get Kumari."

"Good idea? No, that's a great idea. I give this fucking scumbag money so some other dipstick can shoot his wad early."

Rohan looked at me questioningly. "What's mean – "

"Forget it. Listen. Tell him I want Kumari. Tell him I want her now. You work out how much to pay. I'm not in the mood to bargain with the creep."

Rohan and the man talked. Rohan looked surprised, but wagged his head and said, "You pay 2,000 rupees, she come right now. You can have for all night."

"Oh this is too fucking much. I don't even need her all night, for one thing, and 2,000 rupees is a fucking rip-off and he fucking knows it. Here, give him – "

I yanked out my wallet and removed 200 rupees, double the usual price, then added another 200 just to get the thing over with. "Tell him you'll give him this if Kumari is here in 60 seconds. And I'm counting from now."

He took the money and started to hand it to the man.

"No!" I said, loud enough to make them look at me in alarm. "You don't give him a goddamn rupee until he understands exactly what's happening. Kumari comes here right now. She stays with me tonight. And if he so much as touches her while I'm around? I'll twist his fucking neck."

The pimp listened to Rohan's explanation, which must not have included the part about his neck, then called into the hut.

The short woman emerged, not bothering to smile this time. She heard the instructions and hurried out.

A moment later Kumari came in. When she saw me she let out a surprised yelp that sounded like delight. I had to hand it to her. It may have been a main part of her job description, but she knew how to act.

She started to run into my arms, then stopped a pace short and lowered her head. Now she was going to turn shy? What kind of routine was this? At least it saved me from having to shrug off her kisses too. I didn't feel like touching anybody, not yet, not with Rohan and the pimp watching.

She was wearing the same sarong as before. The flower print I had admired earlier now struck me as common. Surely it wasn't the only one she owned. How much could a length of cotton cost?

She ran her fingers through her hair and flipped it. The hair drifted back to cover half her face. It may have been a coquette's move, but it worked to give her the air of a starlet, one who had managed to keep some personal integrity in a world drastically short of it. The prettier short one could never have gotten away with a move like that.

"Hello, Kumari," I said.

Her lips moved into an uncertain smile. She looked at me with a question in her eyes, but didn't try to put it into words.

"*Ayubowan,*" she answered instead in a soft voice, her hands together in greeting. She had dropped the giddy part altogether, fortunately, for both of us. I was in no mood for it.

I took her long brown fingers into mine. They were warm. "Let's get out of here," I said. She looked to the others.

"Rohan, tell her that I have her for the night. She doesn't have to come back."

I watched the pimp while Rohan translated. There were no objections. She was mine. Rohan handed him the money and we turned to go.

"But . . . Gordie?" Rohan said carefully.

Of course it wouldn't be that easy. "What now?" I snapped.

"Vasudeva?"

"Oh right." I handed him another 100 rupees to give the pimp, relieved to avoid the direct contact.

I picked up Kumari's hand again and we started down the dirt path. "See you tomorrow, Rohan," I said, almost a command. "And not until then."

I could hear the smile in his voice as he called back. "Meddy Chrees-mas, Mister Gordie."

8

Kumari and I stood together by the coast road, waiting to cross.

"We've got all the time in the world," I told her as if she could understand. "No need to rush. I feel like taking it slow. I'm too, I don't know, keyed up. Wired."

I clenched my fists to show stress. She unwound my fingers and smoothed them out.

We waited as a few spaces in the traffic came and went. We hadn't established a couple's pace yet. Were we daring, the type to run laughing through a risky gap, or dazed, so wrapped up in each other that the outside world was never in more than distant focus? Finally I motioned to an opening behind a delivery van and tugged on her hand so we could jog together to the beach.

The sounds of traffic gave way to waves as we walked closer to the water. I licked my lips and tasted salt. Her hand was still in mine so I squeezed it.

"We may as well make a night of it. Call it our first date and stay out late. Somehow I don't think your dad will be waiting up."

She laughed when I did, her voice trickling. We stood at the edge of the tide and stared out to the horizon. I studied her hand, how smooth it was in my hairy paw. I couldn't help but shudder.

"You should have seen me 10, 20 years ago," I said. It was an absurd apology but I didn't care. She would get no more than the tone of it anyway.

She replied with a long string of melodic Sinhalese. It was as if she were talking to a friend, the way her face registered the depth of her words. I laughed for real this time.

"You really are a sight, you know that? I don't mean disrespect. I probably sound like a pig for saying so, but I think you're the most beautiful creature I've ever seen. I know, me saying that doesn't mean much, and anyway, lots of girls are beautiful, but it's different with you. It's not just the package. You have something else going on. A glow."

Our fingers were still entwined. We started walking along the wet sand, my heels sinking while Kumari's were light enough to stay on the surface. We came to a spot sheltered from the sight of the road by a stand of coconut trees. We leaned back against one that grew out horizontally from the grove towards the water before taking a 90-degree turn up. It was a good place to stop. Spread before us like a living mural was the sea.

"And to think that here I am, with you, alone, on a beach, under a full moon." I searched the sky. A luminescence was just emerging behind us over the jungle canopy.

"Well, not quite under the moon yet, but we will be. And you're going to look even more amazing. I'm going to take your face in my hands and hold it up to the heavens and, I don't know, feel something, better."

She said something in Sinhalese and let go of my hand. It might have been about the ocean. She lifted the hem of her sarong like a Victorian woman negotiating a muddy path and walked to it, tiptoeing into the water up to her calves. A wave made her shriek and back-pedal fast, the flowers of the sarong spreading firm against the outline of her ass. Well. Who knew? She had the legs of a sprinter. Another point in her favor.

I took off my shoes and socks, rolled up the cuffs of my pants and walked in after her. The cool water was a treat for my toes, then my feet and ankles.

"Hey look," I said, "a star. The first star." She followed where I was pointing, scanning eagerly, then said something with a pout.

I put her hand in mine and pointed our index fingers together in that direction. Her face lit up. She asked something that ended in a questioning tone.

"Star," I said. I pointed her finger for her as more examples appeared overhead. "They're all stars."

"Stars," she repeated cautiously.

"Perfect!" I clapped my hands without making a sound. "If you're catching on so fast, what's my name?"

She kicked water at me, then laughed when I lurched back to avoid it.

"Oh, so that's it? You think you're ready to take on the splash master?" I bent down to slap an armful of water at her but it fell far short. She stood in place, posing with her chin raised and her arms across her chest like a field marshal viewing the troops.

I slapped harder, this time landing a thick sheet of water that covered her from the head down.

"Aaaii!" she shrieked, covering her face with her palms. The shape of her breasts appeared through the wet sarong. I hadn't planned it that way, but couldn't help admiring my work.

"Teach you to challenge me," I said.

She kept her hands over her face. I waited but she didn't move.

"Hey, you're all right aren't you?" She still didn't move.

"C'mon, Kumari, look at me. I didn't hurt you, did I? I was just playing around. Did you get something in your eye?"

I waded nearer, but she kept her head down with her face in her palms. I started to pull her hands away just as she slid a leg behind me and pushed hard on my chest, the oldest trick in the playground. I fell like a cut tree, hitting the water with a splash.

She spread her arms wide and fell on top of me, sinking us together. We wrapped our arms around each other and play-wrestled, spinning like alligators, taking turns being on top as we pushed into deeper water. Then her lips met mine and locked, staying that way as she pulled me under. I started to lift my head for air but she kept me down to breathe into me. It worked. I was underwater but would not drown with her sweet breath swelling my lungs. When we surfaced my pants were at my ankles, another dexterous move on her part. Followed by yet another: from somewhere she produced a condom and rolled it onto my straining cock. Her legs wrapped around my back and pulled as her hand slid down to guide me in. I pushed, hard, and we moved together in a golden sheen of water lit by the full moon.

When at last we separated, me sucking in air, she sat up in the shallow water, still with that impeccable posture. Her hair was stuck in wet mats on either side of her face in a way that changed the architecture. Without the thick black frame, her high cheekbones now made her seem almost fragile.

She circled her hands around my beard and squeezed, laughing when sea water drained out.

"Ah, Kumari," I sighed.

"Ah, Gordie," she said, mimicking me.

"You do remember my name!"

On the sand we stood facing the sea again, not speaking. I sat down and Kumari sat beside me. She leaned into me as we listened to the waves. They sounded louder than in front of my cabana.

Then I began to tell her things. I'm not sure why. It may have been the pretended intimacy of strangers, the way you'll confess something on an airplane you may not tell your best friend. Or just the way she leaned on me and kept stroking my arm, as if she understood, or at least accepted.

I told her about my life, what there was of it. About meeting Kirstin while covering the women's high jump at the Worlds in Malmo. About how it felt to fall that deeply for someone, to believe in an eternity together, and then to watch as your perfect future slips through your fingers. All without the salve of having the other to blame for changing or revealing something I'd been unable to see. The fault was mine. I told her about my job, how my ambitions had been reduced to cinders. I was now a sports hack, a hanger-on, a plodder in life who wrote about the runners.

She slid her head off my shoulder and lay down on her back, but it was not a withdrawal; she smiled up at me. I lay down too. With the tips of my fingers I traced the wavy lines of her hair, touching the clear drops that collected at the tips.

"Mmm," I said. Sounds were as good as words, maybe better, but I went talking anyway. "You're right. What difference does it make here? I wish I could watch you like this forever. It doesn't matter that we can't talk. It almost makes it better. It's like being a kid again, playing for no other reason, just being who you are. It's not about what impression you're making, where your relationship is going, are they going to see through you, do you measure up. Kids don't worry about that. Not until they learn it from adults."

She responded with a monologue in Sinhalese. I didn't understand a word of it and almost didn't want to, so long as I could bask in the way she said it. I watched her full lips in motion, pressing together at the pauses while she thought, sliding up at times like she was about to tell a joke. I imagined she was giving me what I most wanted to hear, her life story. There were fond memories, I took it, as her gaze angled up to the stars, the words tripping out so fast I could not have separated one from another. Sad times too when her voice would darken and drop to a husky whisper. One time her eyes grew moist with might have been the saddest expression I've seen in anyone. It was almost too hard to watch. What depths of sorrow couldn't be reached in a beautiful young prostitute? I suppose it was then that I first wanted to hold her for real, to change her life.

She shook out of her soliloquy with a laugh, then snuggled into my shoulder.

"Kumari, I know you wouldn't even be here with me if you weren't a prostitute. I'm sorry about that. I don't know why I was born in a rich country with everything and you were born into this. Vijaya – that's the guy whose house I'm staying at – he tells me it's all about karma, that we create our own destiny with our acts and words and thoughts, even if we can't always see how because it can take more than a lifetime to work out. But how am I supposed to believe that you were ever so terrible you deserve something like this? Or that I've been good enough to never have to think about food or shelter or some sadistic goon torching me in a basement?"

She sighed and dug her big toe into the sand to slowly lift up a tiny conical pile.

"I've never done a good thing in my life, not really, not when it counted. The one chance I had, I blew it. It happened at work when I first started on the paper. I was on the city desk. I got this amazing tip thanks to a poker buddy who was going out with the sister of a guy in some political group trying to get independence for Puerto Rico. I didn't care one way or the other about Puerto Rico, but because the group was blowing up banks at the time they were big news. Of course the feds wanted them too. So when my interview ran, they came after me for the name of the guy. Naturally I refused. Journalists aren't much for being heroes, but we do have a code and one of the rules is you never rat out a source. Freedom of the press is supposed to guarantee it, but the feds don't always care. And I found out they play dirty. They sat me down in a park one Saturday to explain it. I would go to prison – they had the judge already lined up. They had my cell and even my cellmate all worked out. They showed me his file. He was an animal, ran 280, maybe more, the leader of the biggest gang in prison. Just before I got in, they were going to spread the story of what I'd done to some girl in his neighborhood. What else could I do? I sang. I gave them the name they wanted. So Juan Velasquez was the one who got locked up, not me. Twenty-five to life, which sounds like a lot, but it didn't work out that way because three weeks later they found him hanging from the bars by his bedsheets. They called it suicide."

Kumari transferred a toe-pile of sand from one foot to the other. When it held without toppling she said, "Waaaay," in a happy voice.

I had to smile. She was right. Forget that too. But I couldn't.

"Now, I only want . . . Hell, I don't even know what I want."

A shooting star burned through a quarter of the sky. I turned to see if she'd caught it just as she did the same to me. We smiled together.

She turned on her side to lean over me and stroke my forehead. My skin tingled in the places she touched.

"It's kind of funny to think that I was married," I said, "at least I thought I was, until tonight." I burst out laughing. She looked at me, concerned, then went on brushing my forehead, this time with the backs of her fingers.

"So this is how I spent my Christmas Eve, finding out for sure that my marriage was over in a stupid long distance call I never should have – wait, it's Christmas!"

I sat upright and patted the sand. I found the present and tugged on her arms for her to sit up too.

"Kumari," I announced, holding it before me in both hands. "I'm not an idiot. I know this is not real. But I wish it could be."

She eyed the little red crepe-papered box, confused.

"This is for you. I wanted to give you something because, I guess I wanted to say that, well, I like you. Okay? Merry Christmas, Kumari."

Her mouth dropped. I gathered not many customers gave her presents. Suddenly I wished I'd gotten something better.

She slowly unwrapped the crepe, careful not to tear it, until the music box emerged. Her lips spread into a smile that lit her face like the moon breaking through clouds. She held the box to her ear and turned the crank slowly, keeping her eyes shut. The tiny notes that came out were almost swallowed by the hiss of a receding wave.

When her eyes opened again they were glistening. She really did like it. I put my hands on her shoulders. "Everything is going to be fine," I promised, wondering even as I said it what I meant.

"Gordie," she said. But it wasn't right. The sound of my name on her lips startled me. Suddenly the fact of being alone with her, and congratulating myself for it, struck me as yet another measure of my failure. I was teetering, and I knew it, and yet I let myself go. It seemed a good night for a plunge. All the things I'd done wrong up to then, a lifetime of regret, flooded into me, and I let them as I savored the misery of just who I was.

"I fucked up, Kumari. I started out all right, I had my dreams, my big ideas like anyone else. They even got me into journalism. I thought if I could explain to people why things were screwed up they could do something about it instead of just getting fucked for the rest of their lives. Only it turns out that I'm as bad as any of them. Or worse. And then, I don't know. I mean look at me. I can't even – "

She stopped me with a finger on my lips. She re-wrapped the present and set it back down on the sand, then took me by the arms and eased me down. She lay on her side beside me, our bodies touching from the shoulders to the toes. She stroked my chest in lazy circles. She began singing in a soft languid voice that faded in and out of the waves. It was in Sinhalese but I loved it. One song ended and another began. I don't know how long it went on until eventually I figured it out. They were lullabies. That must have been when I fell asleep.

I woke up once in the dark. Kumari was watching me. Her eyes glowed with two tiny reflections of the moon. Maybe I dreamt it then, but I touched her cheek and she murmured something that made me warm. The ocean seemed to echo our unspoken feelings with each boom and rush of water over earth.

Later I watched her as she slept. "Kumari," I said quietly, more to myself than her. "I wish I could tell you I love you." She may have smiled in her sleep. Her lips moved, but I couldn't make out what she was trying to say.

I woke up confused, the way you do in a strange bed. Had I dreamt of birds? The sky was black and brilliant blue with stars. When I wiped my mouth sand grated on my lips. I remembered where I was.

Kumari was gone. Beside me was the impression she'd made in the sand, a woman's hips tapering down through the legs. I thought of shaping angels in the snow, a kid's game back home, and smiled. The music box was gone, and I smiled again. Now she had something to thank me for.

A shout came from down the beach, the same sound that had woken me up. Voices followed, one from a man whose laughter came out in hacks. The trailing end of it faded into the waves. They were louder than before. The surf must have gotten bigger while I slept.

The voices came back, this time talking in rapid Sinhalese. One said something that sputtered out into either sobs or laughter, I couldn't tell. Waves broke in a set of four crashes, each followed by a diminishing hiss, and then all went quiet. I lay back on the sand and closed my eyes.

When the voice came back in a scream I scrambled up. I took off in a soldier's crouch towards the closest cover, the tree we'd been leaning against earlier. The throaty laugh returned as if to mock my lumbering desperation.

I pressed myself against the trunk. I was panting hard. Two new voices joined the laughter as I tried to fit the bulk of my body behind the narrow shield of wood.

A gunshot cracked and then echoed back from the jungle in sonic waves. Bird screeches seemed to ride the sound back to the beach. A frantic gull flew almost directly over my head, heading for the safety of the open sea.

In the silence that followed my own breathing seemed about to betray me. I tried opening my mouth wider but the wheezing was obvious. I bit down on my forearm instead. The first voice came back in a pleading tone that was cut short by several men shouting at once.

I held my breath and inched my head around the trunk to look. A white circle of light illuminated three men in black uniforms, each holding a rifle as they surrounded a thin man on his knees. They were a 100-meter sprint away, give or take. The fastest would need at least 12 or 13 seconds to reach me on sand. That was enough time for me to make it across the road and into the jungle. Unless they started shooting first.

A fourth man stepped into the circle. The glare highlighted the contrast between his pressed khaki trousers and black polo shirt. On his head was a dark baseball cap. He didn't have a gun.

The captive lifted his hands back into a plea towards the new arrival, who tilted the cap back on his head, planted his feet wide and placed his fists on his hips. Without warning he spun into a back-kick that landed with a horrible crack. I thought he'd broken the man's neck, but the victim seemed unaffected. He repeated his appeal to the others.

The leader growled something that made the shortest soldier stiffen and snap his rifle up to his eye. Another command came and he aimed the gun at the prisoner's chest. He marched forward until the barrel touched his white shirt pocket.

I turned away. I didn't need to see it. I knew what was going to happen. I didn't want any part of it. Almost at once I was looking again.

The leader bent down to speak directly into the captive's ear. The answer came back in choking Sinhalese.

The leader turned his back. He walked towards the jeep, shaking his head as if disappointed. He stepped out of the circle of light.

The soldier with the raised rifle shouted something in a breaking voice. The prisoner shook his head once in defiance.

I searched the coast road for headlights, somebody walking, anything that might scare them off, but it was deserted. For the first time in my life I wished I had a gun. I could fire a warning shot, maybe ping something off the jeep. Anything to create a distraction that would make them run.

And if that didn't work? If they spotted me? And took aim? Did I have what a man needs to kill? I had never asked myself the question before, not when it counted. I shut my eyes. I still wished I had a gun.

Two soldiers circled behind the victim to grab his arms. They pulled back in a way that made him gasp. When he turned around to protest, the skinny one in front touched the barrel of the rifle to his cheek to keep him facing forward.

If the prisoner was speaking now it could only have been in whispers. His arms were tied. The soldiers stepped back to watch him squirm against the rope.

The victim tried to stand, but without his arms for leverage it was a struggle. His tormentors jeered. When got as far as a crouch, a soldier dropped a hand on his shoulder and he was back kneeling in the sand.

The soldier pointing the rifle took a step back. He jerked the barrel to warn the others away. The crack of a shot sounded again.

The front of the captive's shirt turned red. He made a sputtering sound and tried to stand but his legs would not cooperate. Another shot sounded and he toppled over.

An order from the commander sent two of them outside the spot-lit circle. They reappeared dragging a body by the hair. It was a lanky man with skin the color of blacktop and a yellow sarong that rode up his thighs as he was pulled. A soldier tugged the cloth back down before heaving him on top of the other victim.

A soldier rummaged through the back of the jeep for a red gas can. He poured the contents over the bodies, ending with the last drops into the gaping mouth of the victim in the white shirt.

But the man was not dead. I was sure I heard a sputter.

Again I shut my eyes. Again I opened them. The victim's head lifted, bobbed uncertainly, then rolled back down in a slow half-circle. The soldiers didn't seem to notice.

The engine started and revved into a growl. Anyone near the coast road would have heard it, yet still the soldiers were in no hurry. The jeep slowly backed up, then rolled closer to the pair.

The driver struck a match and tossed it in a thin red arc that landed in a fireball. The jeep continued down the beach, the circle from its spotlight growing smaller as it went away. When it reached the coast road the spot was switched off, the headlights came on and it drove away, heading north towards Colombo.

How would anybody recognize them? The grieving families they would leave behind. If I didn't do it now, no one else would ever be able to identify them. But even if I could make out the faces, and confirm their identities later through family photographs, what good what it do? What could I say about their end that might diminish a family's grief? It might be better kept as a mystery. The disappeared. Although who would choose the empty hope of not knowing over the truth? Acceptance would have to begin sometime. Did the locals get used to it? Did familiarity soften the hardest edges of a loss? How would someone like Vijaya react?

That's when it hit me, how stupid I'd been. Rohan was the one in the yellow sarong. And the man I'd seen pleading for his life must have been Rohan's JVP friend. The white shirt, the lanky body. Even the way he held his hands together to beg all seemed to fit.

I stared hard at the outline of their bodies, searching for anything that would vary from the two men I knew. But my only explanation was unconvincing. The white shirt of his friend should have meant nothing – many Sri Lankan men wore them – but his had struck me for its bleached brilliance, and here on the beach it had practically shone.

Fear began to seep back in. If they knew about Rohan and his friend, they knew about the posters and where they were kept. The soldier on the coast road who had spotted me on the verandah could have led them to the cabana. In the search for me they came across Rohan and his friend. Or else it could have all come out of my phone call to Boston. Which meant they would know, by my amateurish attempts to hide it, that I still had the document. Which also meant they would now be looking for me.

My feet wanted to run. My head knew it was futile. The army

was everywhere. It was their island. I was the outsider, the stranger alone. My only guide to moving like the locals was now dead.

The fire burned down to a reddish glow. It still illuminated the shapes of the bodies but nothing beyond.

I checked myself for the appropriate response to Rohan's death, but felt a void. I lacked a precedent. I knew tragedy mostly in its insidious, creeping form, the long slide, the daily hospital visits that gradually dulled the shock much like the nurses' rubber soles muted their steps down the long corridors. Despite a lifetime of working on a paper that thrived on it, I had no experience with the suddenness of a personal tragedy. And just what was Rohan to me anyway? I would call him a friend, but what did that mean? Here I was already wishing I had been kinder to him. How quick I had been to condemn him for his dependencies, me, a man who would eat until it hurt. I might have simply given him the money he wanted, easing at least one worry in his life. But no, it wouldn't have made a difference. My real chance to save him came and went here on the beach. This was where I let him down.

I was bound to offer Vijaya and his family whatever help they might need. Naturally he would decline. And then I could go.

I stood up to leave. I hadn't gone more than 10 meters away from the direction of the bodies when I heard an engine behind me.

It was a trap. Of course! They'd been waiting. This was how they took care of witnesses.

I dropped flat and pushed my face into the sand, waiting for the sound of shots, wondering whether I would hear or feel them first. When they didn't come, I scuttled back to the safety of the tree.

It was a car, not a jeep, that pulled up to the bodies. The engine cut off as the headlights came on to illuminate the smoking pile.

There were only two soldiers this time, both wearing olive uniforms. One went to the trunk to take out a square white board. He wedged it into the sand beside the victims, then took his hands away to test the balance.

The other leaned over the bodies, peering down. He shrugged and started to leave, but his partner had him turn back to lift one of the charred arms. He yelped and whipped his hand away, blowing air on his fingers.

The partner slid a baton under the same arm and lifted. Both leaned in for a closer look. They let the arm drop, then did the same with the other victim. When their faces were pushed almost against the man's fingers, I realized they were looking for rings.

The soldiers got back into the car. It made a squealing U-turn that sent a flying rooster-tail of sand, then sped away.

I slumped against the tree, my back to the victims. I closed my eyes and tried to picture other beaches I'd been on at other times in my life. Anywhere but here. For some reason I was no longer terrorized by the prospect of being seen.

"Let them come," I said out loud, realizing even as I spoke it was a bad idea. I was too distraught to care. They had come back looking for rings.

"Evil fucking scum," I shouted. "Come on then! Come and try me!" Anger had crowded out the fear. In the short time I'd been in Sri Lanka I'd seen three dead bodies, one of them of a friend. And I still had no idea why.

The front door to Vijaya's house was shuttered. The house was quiet. There were no soldiers, but I took a circle route around to the cabana just in case.

My door appeared locked, just as I'd left it. At Walter's boat, the sand where I'd buried the document seemed undisturbed. I considered, with a conviction that made my temples throb, digging the damn thing up and burning it for good. I went to the cabana instead.

A clatter from the house stopped me. I held my breath and slipped my head around the cabana wall.

Vijaya's wife was standing by the well, a basket of wet clothes on her hip and a metal basin at her feet. She tilted her head in puzzlement when she saw me. I tried to smile, but it must have made me look even worse. Her expression turned serious. "Gordie not fine?" she asked.

"Rohan," I said in a quiet voice. "Is he home? Did he come home last night?"

She said something in Sinhalese, then realized by my expression that I couldn't have understood. She looked to the tops of the coconut trees to think, giggled, then tried, "No come home."

Vijaya stepped out to the porch wrapping a sarong around his waist.

"Good morning, my friend," he said. "You are up early today." He rubbed his stomach with both hands, then stopped in the middle of a yawn to study me over the rims of his glasses.

"You have returned just now."

"Yes." I looked down at my feet. Somewhere I'd lost my sandals. "It's a long story."

Vijaya's wife pegged clothes to a line between two coconut trees. Rohan's yellow sarong wasn't there. I started talking fast in a low voice so she wouldn't understand.

"Vijaya, this is important, there's been some trouble. On the other side of town, on the beach, something terrible, but maybe nothing, I mean for you. I don't really know, for certain. Except that two people were shot."

Vijaya translated it for his wife anyway. She sighed and continued with the clothes.

"I saw them."

She sighed again so he didn't bother to translate. His voice was sympathetic.

"Last month we found four bodies on the sand here. In front of my own home. One of them a young woman. Practically a child." He wiped his glasses with his sarong. "There are explanations, historical causes, I know. But who could do such a thing to a fellow human being? Somebody with no daughter of his own, perhaps. But no sisters as well? No mother?" He scowled in disgust before walking back towards the house.

I called to him. "I understand Rohan isn't in?"

"He didn't come home last night. Out with his so-called friends, no doubt."

"He usually comes back in the morning, is that right?"

Vijaya answered in a small voice, "Oh." He turned to make sure his wife was out of earshot.

"You saw who was killed," he noted. His face was blank, empty of evident emotion, but his usual half-smile was gone.

"Not exactly. I did see it happen, yes. But it was too dark to make out the victims.

"Where did this happen?" he asked quietly.

"Past Hikkaduwa, on the beach. At least that's where the, well, bodies were when I left. Who knows by now?"

"They will be there. The government leaves its victims. Their idea of propaganda. We must go."

Vijaya said a few words to his wife. She tilted her head at me, perhaps in surprise, but we were out the door before she could say anything.

The bus was crammed with children in school uniforms. How many years until they were seen as weapons in their adults' brutal war? Two girls with pigtails looked up when Vijaya entered, appraised his silvery hair, then politely squirmed off their seat.

He sat and stared out the windshield while I thought of something to say.

"It didn't look all that much like Rohan," I tried at last. And then, "I would have recognized him if it was, probably."

He nodded but both times returned to the window without speaking.

"It may well be my son," he said at last.

"Not necessarily," I started to protest. "Rohan would never – "

Vijaya frowned in a way that made me stop. "We both know him."

We watched as a tourist shop owner hung a rack of batik prints up for the morning business. As if life was normal, another sunny day in paradise.

"A psychic told me once, if we weren't careful Rohan would die before me," Vijaya said. "I understood."

"Well, a psychic, I don't know. They can say anything. We all die some day," I said, and immediately realized how stupid I sounded.

Vijaya said, "These things are there. Some have particular powers. And no one escapes their karma."

"Right."

"The first issue would be my wife. How to console her." The bus stopped abruptly. A massive sway-backed cow stood in the road and bellowed. "She would have a very difficult time. Rohan being our eldest son." The driver tapped the horn twice and waited for the cow to saunter away.

"I wouldn't know what to say," I said. "If there is anything to say."

"In Buddha's time a young mother once had a baby which died. She was overcome, naturally. But even after some time, she was still unable to let go. She carried the baby to every person in the village, begging them to bring her only child back to life. But what could they do? Finally somebody told her Buddha was then visiting nearby, and that he was the only one who could help."

He stared out the window to where a bearded man with flippers and a speargun carried a string of turquoise-colored fish. The man smiled, but Vijaya didn't. When the bus went on he kept his eyes on the jungle and continued the story.

"The mother found the Buddha and laid her baby at his feet. She said, 'If you truly are the Awakened One, you'll help me. Give me back my child.'

"The Buddha said he would help, but first she must bring him a mustard seed from a home in which no one had died. So the woman hurried to the nearest home to fulfill the request. There she was told the father had died a few months earlier. In the next house it was a grandmother, and in the next an uncle, and so on, until she had been to every home in the village without collecting a single mustard seed. By the time she got back to the Buddha, she understood. She had to let her baby go."

The bus stopped to admit a tall, svelte woman in a white business suit, rare for the village. She eyed me, the foreigner, and then Vijaya as if to ask him a question. He didn't notice.

I was still searching for something helpful to say. Talking seemed to keep him occupied.

"I suppose religion helps most at a time like this," was the best I could do. "Not that I would know."

"Now with training, we can reach a place where we need never grieve again. I have long been struck by this idea. But of course to actually experience it." He nodded his head slowly, maybe a way of convincing himself.

At the bus station we got off with the chattering kids. Only when they bolted for the schoolyard did I realize how loud they'd been. Vijaya watched them for a moment before turning to me. I motioned with my chin towards the beach. He nodded and started off ahead of me.

A crowd had gathered around the victims. I let Vijaya go first, watching him for cues on how to react. He didn't hesitate, so I lined up behind him while he walked through the onlookers for a better view.

Conversations nearer the bodies were hushed. Some people stared at the victims in what might have been awe. A few scowled. One woman with a baby at her breast grimaced as if it were her own skin that had been charred. The distance they granted death, I noticed, was not much, about five yards.

A small boy near the front seemed perplexed by how one leg stuck out of the pile. He pointed to it and spoke but no one replied so he stepped closer to look. An adult hand on his shoulder yanked him back.

We worked our way through the crowd to the front. People

seemed to understand we were there as more than onlookers. They parted for us. Up close I saw that the victim who'd been wearing the yellow sarong had a square jaw and eyes that were narrow, almost Oriental. It was not Rohan.

The other was face down, his hands still balled into fists behind his back. Vijaya went no closer. He surveyed the victims and those watching with the same vacant expression. But he was also chewing his inner lip, the first sign of unease I noticed since suggesting his own son had been murdered. He looked to someone in the crowd and raised his eyebrows. The answer came in a slight head wag.

Vijaya turned back to the road. I followed, waiting for him to speak first. A woman pushed by us in a rush to reach the victims. Her eyes were wide. Her first shriek came as we stepped back onto the road. She picked up the sign and threw it to the sand. She began stomping it with her sandaled feet.

Two men from the crowd tried to console her by holding her flailing arms, each bending down to speak into an ear, but nothing would stop her from attacking the sign. The rest of the crowd watched in silence.

"The mother?" I asked.

"I suppose so. I have seen her before. She is not from my village."

One of the two holding her picked up the sign and cracked it in two over his knee. He held up the broken pieces for her to see.

"What did it say?" I asked.

"Death to rebels. Signed by the Green Tigers."

"Tamils?" I looked around to see if anyone was listening. "I'm sure they were army guys."

"Not the Tamil Tigers. Green is the color of the ruling party. Their killers call themselves Green Tigers."

We walked back to the bus stop without talking. Finally I could stand it no longer. I looked down at my shoes. "Vijaya, I am very, very sorry for putting you through all of this. I'm an idiot. Worse than an idiot. I'm – "

"Not at all. I must thank you for your concern."

I started to say more but he held up his hand. Perhaps it meant I was absolved, but I didn't feel it. We said no more until we were home.

Rohan was there at the table, eating a breakfast of curry and something white and stringy. He nodded first at his father, then grinned at me.

"Good morning," he mouthed between bites, turning the page on his newspaper to a story about cricket.

Vijaya looked at me, his eyes impossible to read. I offered a tiny shrug, unsure myself what it meant. He responded with a half-smile, then walked out to the back porch, his slumped posture reminding me of a talented football coach stuck with a team of losers.

His wife listened as he explained our trip, the whole grim experience I'd just subjected him to. She nodded once or twice while making tsk-tsk noises. When he was done she looked in at Rohan for a long moment, then sighed.

I went out to my cabana. Even as I lay down, drained, I knew sleep would not come. I got up with effort and walked into the sea. I lolled with my face in the water, animate as a jellyfish, lifting my head only to breathe.

Vijaya found me sitting on the bench, staring at the water. He handed me a tray with a cup of tea and a pair of bananas the size of my thumbs. On another day I might have found them comical.

"My wife thought you might enjoy this while she prepares your breakfast. You are hungry, no?"

I peeled a banana and downed it in a bite. "I really do want to apologize," I said. "If I hadn't been such a coward I might have gotten close enough to check the bodies. Instead I put you through all that."

He sat next to me on the bench. "Perhaps. Or you may have done exactly as you should have. The important thing is you are alive, no?"

"Yeah, but."

"Suffering is inevitable for all of us caught in the cycles of samsara. Buddha said so, but not to make us despair. The Third Noble Truth is why we may have hope. There is suffering, yes, and a cause of suffering, which is desire, but there is also an end to suffering. We can use our disillusionment to escape the cycles of pain."

We watched two outriggers down the beach launch into the water. The men inside rowed furiously through the surf. They seemed desperate to get out. The boats were halfway to the horizon before I spoke again.

"If suffering is the route to spiritual growth," I said, "my wife would be a mahatma by now."

He looked at me over his glasses. "I didn't know you were married."

"I'm not, any more. Another thing I screwed up. First work, then marriage. I'm not sure what's left to ruin."

"One time when I was meditating regularly I had a taste of something that has remained with me ever since," Vijaya said. "It was during the rainy season. I had the habit of sitting here each morning for my practice and was making good progress, I felt. One morning, I felt as if something was revealed. If you ask me what, I wouldn't know how to answer. The truth, I might say. Or if that's too grand, a deeper level of reality beneath everyday things. It comes down to where our essence is found, which I suppose I could say is where we come from, or what remains after we die. For that moment, at least, I believed I knew where to find it. Between our thoughts."

I nodded lamely. "Between our thoughts. Right."

"Everything exists in the mind, no? We create our own world, each of us, with our thoughts. Simple. But this is not the ultimate reality. Each of our worlds is only a screen, our own movie we happen to be watching. To know the real world, to look behind the screen, you must slow the thinking process, little by little, until, in my case just for a moment, something extraordinary occurs. Insight. I think that is what it was. A glimpse within, at something I had never seen before. I understood how thinking is not an endless stream. Our thoughts come and go, you see, separately. They can never overlap. The mind cannot have two simultaneous thoughts."

"Which means that there's something in between."

"Yes. Or perhaps I should say no. Because there is nothing. Only an absolute. What is it, then? I believe it's pure consciousness. The flow of all things. The pooled energy of life itself. It's difficult to picture, I know. Also impossible to describe. I only know how it felt, as if I were floating in an ocean of complete joy. To experience it, even for just that moment in my case, was stunning. I came out of my meditation and found myself shaking. My joy – no, joy is not the proper word – anyway, whatever I felt was limitless because it was no longer me feeling it. Not the same me, that is. Ah, why do I try? You can see how poor I am at trying to explain it. I could not describe it properly even to my own wife, except to say that I had seen the way things are. These things are there. And now that I know for certain it exists, naturally I am keen to go back. Back to stay. Because that is the place where we never need to grieve again." He turned to eye me directly. "Not even for ourselves."

We watched the fishermen pull their oars in unison while one stood to throw a net over the side.

"And you can do it again?" I asked.

He shrugged. "I believe so. I'm sure of it. With right effort."

"So you'll get to that place where you're beyond suffering?"

"Grief is being left alone. If you know you're inseparable from all life, how can you be alone?"

9

Under the cabana door was a waxy brown envelope. It wasn't addressed. Rohan was the permanent resident, not me, so I supposed it was for him, and probably something I should avoid. I slid the flap open anyway.

Seeing Kumari's signature on the letter sent a warm surge through my chest. I looked out towards a patch of sea where the sun glistened inside a ring of white clouds near the horizon. If Kumari was out delivering friendly letters she must have missed the army atrocities altogether. Good. I would not have wanted her to see any of it. I decided not to even bring it up. A small thing on my part, but one more way I might protect her.

My dear Gordie,

This letter is being penned for me by a friend who understands English. Despite her assistance, please do not believe it can capture any more than a portion of my true feelings.

You have told me of your life, yet know nothing of mine. I fear you have used this to create an image of someone I could never hope to equal. If you only knew, would you still give me your very best caresses?

You believe I gave you back your smile, but it was not me. The seeds of your contentment were always within. Notwithstanding

this, I shall never forget you would choose me to help them
bloom. In return for your kindness, this small poem:

> *When all of this dream has faded away*
> *Like the scent of a lotus, picked yesterday*
> *These murmurs of sorrow in a chorus of pain*
> *All to the past, until nothing remains*
> *But the soothing and endless song of the sea*
> *The voice of Gautama and the Buddha to be.*

From your forever friend,

Kumari

I read the letter again, picturing her as she dictated each line, perhaps on the beach, looking up to think. I refolded it slowly so the creases wouldn't tear over time. If it was dark, I might have been tempted to bury it with the document by Walter's boat. I may not have understood all the implications, but it was as least as valuable to me as a career scoop. I made a silent vow to myself as I slipped it into the bottom of my dufflebag inside a folded shirt. I would not screw this one up.

"You looking tired," Rohan said as we sat on the verandah. He aimed one eye at me while tilting his head back to drain a glass of water. When he lowered the glass he was grinning. "Of course! I know why. You have a fantastic night with Kumari."

"No. That's not it."

He smacked his forehead. "I tell you, no? Kumari nice. She like you."

"It's not like that."

He nodded to agree, but at the same time waggled his eyebrows suggestively while adding his slushy laugh.

I flipped through the newspaper to the sports page. I winced when I saw that Holland and West Germany had played a thriller back in Colombo. Holland had come from behind to win.

My editor in Boston would be miffed at having to run a wire service snoozer after they'd gone to the expense of sending me. But we both knew she couldn't fire me. It was no secret I'd been offered good money by a rival paper to switch teams. On the other hand, she couldn't let me set an example that might undermine her authority. If I came back completely empty she would have to put me on some cheapshit assignment to show the troops who was in command. Like the year I skipped out of a 49ers victory parade – marching bands and a three-alarm hangover do not mix – and wasn't allowed back until I'd covered a brain-leaching tractor pull in Stockton.

I wasn't worried. If I had the bribery story, evidence and all, I would go back a hero. No one at the paper had ever brought down a government. They would probably want to move me to the news section for good. It was not out of the question to suppose that some of my faithful readers from sports would move over with me. We might even get things done together. The regular news pages could certainly use something to goose things up a bit.

Rohan nodded to the front page of the paper. The banner head was "Dooleratne Assassinated."

"JVP," Rohan said with a knowing nod.

The article detailed how the No. 2 man in the ruling party had been shot dead at noon on one of Colombo's busiest streets. The assassins, two "subversives," escaped on a single motorcycle. The paper said they faced "imminent capture."

"That's mean, they get away," Rohan explained.

Above the story was a four-column picture of the blood-stained sidewalk. Beside that was a box, bordered in bold, with a presidential edict signed by RJ: motorcycle helmets were now banned.

"If that happened yesterday, maybe what they did on the beach was some kind of retaliation," I said

Rohan looked at me. "What's mean retaliation?"

"Pay back, revenge. Their guy was killed yesterday afternoon in Colombo, right? So maybe that's why they killed those guys in the next village last night."

"Killed?"

"Not so far from where I left you. Army men shot them, then set them on fire." I checked to see whether anyone was lurking on the coast road, then lowered my voice anyway. "I saw it."

"You saw them killed?"

"Yes."

"Did army man see you?" he asked, setting his glass on the wooden stand.

"It was too dark."

He exhaled with billowed cheeks. "Good," he said. He picked up the glass. "How many killed?"

"Two, both young guys. I couldn't see them well. I thought one was you. It was weird going with your father to look at your corpse."

Rohan chuckled. "I don't die yet." He called into the doorway, "*Ama.*"

There was no answer so he called again, louder. His mother came out wiping her hands on an apron. They spoke in Sinhalese. When she went back in Rohan said, "They not from this village. My father don't know."

"That's good. I guess." I wondered what the woman we saw arrive at the beach was doing just then. It had been an hour. Would it get worse as time went on? Would the loss grow deeper? Or was there a maximum level of sorrow, something that might continue and fester but could never be topped?

I flipped through the paper. The editorial asked why the misguided youth of Sri Lanka would let a few terrorists in the JVP give the generation a bad name. The writer wanted to know why they weren't challenging these subversives to uphold Sinhalese virtue and protect their once-proud race from the infiltration of foreign ideas.

I asked, "What about your guy with the posters? I thought he was coming to take them away."

"He come early. You don't see him?"

"No. His posters are still there."

He was startled. "No. He have to take to Colombo."

He thought for a moment, then called again to his mother. She answered a few questions from inside. Rohan stood up.

"She don't know," he said.

We walked to the cabana. He took the bag of posters, not bothering to unwind them, out to the sand. He touched a match to the end of one, then fed it into the others, until they were a little blaze. When it was done he stirred the ashes with his foot.

Leon leaned back on his stool with his head against the mirror. He would not deign to get up to serve just us. When Rohan dropped a coin on the counter he jabbed his bandages in the direction of the cigarette jar. Rohan withdrew a cigarette and popped it between his lips. He took up the burning rope, listening as Leon explained something in Sinhalese. The cigarette hung unlit as Leon continued. Rohan closed his eyes and let out a long, slow breath, like an angry man determined not to lose his temper. When his eyes opened again they were staring at his own stunned expression in the mirror.

Leon turned to me with his half-smirk before speaking to Rohan again. As if ordered, Rohan shuffled over to the table and sat down. He removed the cigarette and said something to himself in Sinhalese with a tone of disbelief.

"A boy from the next village got torched last night," Leon explained. "Rohan knew him."

I should have realized when I first saw the white shirt. His friend with the posters. Why hadn't I looked closer when I went back with Vijaya?

"You also knew him?" Leon asked.

"No. We met just the one time. Briefly."

"Rohan says you saw him killed."

"What? Who? Me?" I scanned the store to see whether anyone else had heard. I also checked for escape routes. There was a back door that opened to the sand, but the only other way out was to the coast road. "No, not exactly."

I glared at Rohan in a warning to keep his mouth shut, but he wasn't paying attention. Leon turned his bored expression to the road.

"What the hell you telling him that for, Rohan?" I hissed.

"Stop fretting," Leon sneered as if to a whining child. "You think the army cares if you see them kill someone? Or a whole crowd or people? What are you going to do?"

"Maybe I don't like Rohan telling people my business."

He laughed. "Secrets don't keep on an island, my friend. We can't help but talk. Everybody here has something on someone else and they can't wait to tell it. For some reason, most of it in this area goes through me." He scratched the back of his neck with his bandaged arm. "Perhaps they see I'm in no shape to do anyone any harm."

He punctuated the line with a rapid smile that left no trace. His expression reverted back to its practiced indifference.

"Anyway, I didn't see much," I said. "Four of them in an army jeep, but I couldn't make out faces. It was dark."

He lifted his shoulders to dismiss it. "Even if you could." He added something in Sinhalese that made Rohan respond with a weak grunt.

Leon brought two Elephant Brand lemon drinks to the table. He motioned with his chin for me to sit across from Rohan.

"It's the same criminals we fought in '71," he said. "What's the difference? The privates then are the colonels now. The politicians are richer and fatter. It's what we call progress." He slid a rag under his arm to wipe the table.

"How could they kill two unarmed people like that?" I asked. "It wasn't just getting rid of them. They were vicious."

Leon shrugged. "Part of the job. The JVP hit their man in

Colombo yesterday so they have to retaliate, no? What else does an army do but fight?"

"Did Rohan's friend have anything to do with the Colombo killing?"

"Maybe. Probably not."

"Nobody deserves to die like that. When they started the fire? He wasn't even dead."

Leon looked out to the road as if the details couldn't possibly interest him.

I heard an odd quiver in my own voice, but I didn't stop. "Three of them were in military uniform. They were drunk. One more was in regular clothes. With a black baseball cap. He was the leader. They took orders from him."

Rohan took the straw from his bottle and began tying it into knots, pulling the ends tighter with each new addition. I could hear his teeth grinding.

"Do you know who they are?" I asked Leon. "They left a board signed by the Green Tigers."

Leon aligned the cigarette and candy jars together on the counter. He showed no sign of having heard me.

"Well? What about it, Leon? You said you know the people around here. Do you know any of the Green Tigers?"

He smirked from one side of his mouth, a reproach for being naive. "And if I did?"

"They're guilty of murder. Somebody ought to do something about it."

"Really?" he said, feigning interest. "For example?"

"I don't know. Maybe write an article or something."

"Of course." He nodded his head with his eyes closed. "The pen is mightier than the sword."

"C'mon. I didn't say that."

"The truth will out," he continued, watching with narrowed eyes for my reaction. "Freedom will prevail."

"Look, all I'm saying – "

"Be my guest," he said, holding out his bandages in place of an offering palm. "Write your article. Write all the articles you want. What are you going to say? The Green Tigers are bad?"

"Not like that. I don't know, maybe if the news got out what was happening here – "

"News that the government of Sri Lanka kills its political opponents? You think people didn't know that in 1971? You think people don't know it now? Ask anyone in the village here if it's news to them."

"All I'm saying is the fuckers who killed Rohan's friend shouldn't be allowed to get away with it."

Rohan looked up from the twisted straw. "Yes," he said. His eyes were brimming. "The fuckers."

Leon scoffed.

"Are you saying they should get away with it?" I demanded. "And nobody should do anything about it? They should just go free?"

"There's always karma." He smirked. "If you believe that rot. I don't. Not anymore."

"Karma doesn't mean waiting for something to happen," I said. Rohan's head was down but he was listening. "That's what your dad tells me. It means action. Good actions, good results."

Leon let out a laugh that didn't reach the hard squint of his eyes. "You think his friend didn't believe that? In all of that claptrap? You know, for being such great atheists, the JVP are more devout than all the ones wasting their lives away in the temples. Scratch any communist and you'll find the worst kind of bubble-headed dreamer. Who believes more in the empty promise of paradise here on earth? In the eternal glory of the ultimate truth? That only they happen to understand? They even have their own perfect little god in Rajitpurna. And where does it get you in the end. Hmm?" He lifted his chin to cite himself as the example, first to me and then to Rohan.

We looked at him but said nothing. Suddenly he seemed embarrassed. It was a difficult emotion to watch in a man like Leon. He muttered something, then wiped the counter again.

"Anyway, Leon," I offered in a conciliatory tone, "I'm not saying the JVP are right. I wouldn't know. What I do know is that the people who did that to Rohan's friend shouldn't be allowed to get away with it. I don't care what you believe in or what your politics are. If you turn your back and pretend evil doesn't exist, it doesn't just disappear."

Leon leaned back with his head on the mirror. He'd recovered his air of superiority.

"I used to think I had the answers too," he said.

"Just because – "

Rohan slammed the table with his fist hard enough to make the pop bottles rattle. He pointed at Leon and said something in a guttural voice I had never heard him use before. Leon watched him with scientific detachment. Rohan swallowed audibly and went on, the words pouring out in a rage of Sinhalese that seemed to surprise even himself. Finally he wiped his eyes with a sweep of his palm and stared at the table.

"Fine, Rohan," Leon said. "Go ahead. You might be lucky, get further than I ever did. Just don't go to prison. That's my advice. It's not worth it."

He turned to me. "The Tamil Tigers are more clever than we were. They each carry their own cyanide pill. They know better than to surrender."

Rohan said something in Sinhalese that Leon started to interrupt, but Rohan raised his voice in a way that stopped him. When he finished, Leon spoke again in English.

"Wait until they put you on the bomb detail. What are you going to say then?"

Rohan stood up. Leon gestured to his drink. He hadn't touched it.

"I go now," Rohan said to me. He squared his bony shoulders as he walked out the door.

I followed him, catching up when he stopped to talk to a pimple-faced teenager in a New York Yankees T-shirt. They spoke in hushed voices. When the boy left, I asked Rohan who he was.

"My friend." He walked on towards the center of town. I kept a step behind. At a traffic block where three cars waited for an elderly woman to cross the road, he looked back over his shoulder.

"Yes," he said, "I think you are right."

"Right about what?"

He looked at me before going on. "My father is a smart man. I know this. Also my brothers have top marks in school. The teachers like very much. Only me in my family, I waste my life. Five years now I am smoking heroin. I don't do one thing that is good." He scowled and turned to keep walking.

A middle-aged man called out to him. Rohan nodded but said nothing. Further on he turned back again. "You are right."

"I don't know what I'm supposed to be right about."

"My friend, he die a good man. If I die tomorrow who will say this?"

"Getting yourself killed isn't going to make the world a better place."

"I don't die yet."

"Don't you think your friend thought the same thing?"

"I know the JVP. They are same as other people. Some good, some bad. But one thing is different. They are not afraid to die. Or to kill – the bigger test. My father say that."

"He might be right, but –

"I go see my friend now. She is in JVP."

"She?"

"We go to the same college. She is very smart. That time, she like me, but now not like that. Just friend. You come?"

My hands automatically went up in a blocking motion. The obvious answer was no. This was not my fight. Let them have their atrocities. I'd rather stay out of it and go home in one piece.

But then I saw myself in that cringing pose, shrinking back, the way I always did, and lowered my hands. Rohan waved down the next van heading north. It was packed with riders, but I squeezed in after him, hunching so my head would angle under the ceiling. We passed through the center of town, and then the whorehouse shacks. I didn't see Kumari. Rohan didn't even look.

We got off next to a stand selling roti. Rohan asked directions from the seller, a girl no more than 5 or 6. She peeled a scab off her wrist and said something that made him look to a cluster of buildings further down the road. A tiny trickle of blood appeared where the scab had been. She licked it clean and we walked on.

Past the buildings we turned onto a dirt path leading up into the jungle. Three matching brown bungalows, each with a white picket fence, stood out among the thatch huts like the start of a suburban subdivision that ran out of money. The path went up a hill and under a cashew tree.

On the other side of the hill was a bathing well. Two young women with sarongs wrapped above the swell of their breasts were soaping up. They looked like twins, both gorgeous. One emptied a bucket onto her face that made it wet and shiny, then beamed a smile at me. Not for the first time I had to wonder, how did this island ever manage such extremes of natural beauty and ugly violence?

Rohan walked on without a glance at the pair, leading us through a pasture of wild grass as high as my armpits. On the other side we arrived at a modern house with white stucco walls. The window spaces, instead of the more common open-air grill, held actual glass.

Rohan raised his hand to knock, then changed his mind. I followed him around to the back where he called something out. The door creaked and a little girl emerged with her thumb in her mouth. She stared up at me in wonder. I widened my eyes and whispered "Boo." It drove her in a happy squealing retreat back into the house.

The girl reappeared in the arms of an attractive woman. She was slightly on the side of plump but it worked for her, filling out her face in a way that made her seem friendly by default. She greeted Rohan with a broad smile. He smiled back, a little sheepishly, and she motioned us in to sit on a rattan couch decorated with purple cushions. She left the room and Rohan explained, "We drink tea."

The little girl came back. Rohan asked her a question in Sinhalese but she didn't answer. He waved his hand for her to come nearer. She seemed to consider it, and ventured the first step, but stopped at a safe distance to stare at me instead.

The woman returned carrying a tray with a white pot and three cups on saucers. She asked me, with an easy smile, if I was a tourist friend of Rohan's.

"Kind of," I said, and then Rohan took over in Sinhalese.

She listened to his explanation while watching me, murmuring a few times to show that she understood. When he finished she turned to me with the same smile. "You are a journalist?"

"Um, yes," I answered, wondering whether Rohan had remembered to mention sports. "I was in Colombo working on an assignment but now I'm here. It's a long story."

"It usually is, if you're with Rohan. My name is Ranya. I'm an old friend of Rohan's from college. But it has been so long." She asked him a question in Sinhalese that made him look up at the ceiling. When he came up with the answer they both shook their heads in wonder.

Rohan took a gulp of tea, then put his cup down with a dark expression that seemed unlike him. She matched it and they talked quietly for while, probably about the killing on the beach. Ranya looked at me a few times while she spoke at length in Sinhalese. Rohan pinched the skin under his chin, his thinking mode.

I let the conversation drift into the background, a Sinhalese duet without the music, his soft voice an octave or two below hers. Then I realized they were looking at me and waiting.

"Excuse me?" I said, correcting my slouch.

"So you are also interested in our party?" She was smiling politely this time.

"Well, yes." I tried to guess what Rohan could have told her. "I thought it might make a good story when I was up in Colombo. And now, apparently, here too. After what happened last night."

She nodded with her eyes closed. A moment of respect for the dearly departed. She opened them and waited for me to continue.

"You have to understand, my original assignment had nothing to do with politics. I just happened to come across some news opportunities, actually by accident."

"Is that so?" she said.

"Yes." I considered explaining then that her party's second-in-command was being bribed by the Indian government. Imagine a sports hack from half a world away knowing something about her own organization that would astound her. But I just as quickly rejected it. It was more than just gossip, it was information too valuable to simply hand out to anyone. Or too dangerous. "So you are also, yourself, a member of the . . . can I say, organization?"

She laughed. "The JVP. You can say it here. We're at home."

"Yes, of course. The JVP."

"I've been a member for three years. We've grown considerably in that time. Now Rohan tells me he is interested in joining as well. But naturally I am also curious about you. I can't say we get many examples of international solidarity in this village."

"Naturally," I said, chuckling to show that if it was a joke, I got it. "But as a journalist, of course, I'm always interested in news, wherever it happens."

She nodded and sipped. Rohan examined his fingernails.

"The struggle for freedom from oppression knows no national boundaries," she offered.

"Mmm," I offered back. "So I'm told."

"I have no authority to speak for the propaganda unit," Ranya said. The little girl crawled into her lap and whipped her head around to peek at me. "In normal circumstances we do not grant interviews to the media, I'm afraid." She began to braid the girl's hair.

"I understand that. But then I have already done interviews with some leading members. A Politburo member, as it happens."

One eyebrow went up. "Really? Who was that?"

I took a lingering sip of tea. There didn't seem to be any point in hiding it here. "Commander Dapila. In Colombo."

She was impressed. "A great man," she said, and let another moment of respect pass without words. "Then perhaps another interview would not be so difficult to arrange. As I say, it is not my decision. But if you don't mind coming with me, I can introduce you to someone. Rohan will also enjoy meeting him." The smile was sly now. "My husband."

She steered the little girl back towards the kitchen, but it was a struggle. Now she wanted to hang around. I'd gone from ogre to prime attraction in 10 minutes. An elderly woman's wavery voice called from the kitchen and the girl ran in.

We walked back on the same path. She asked me about the weather in Boston, then hugged herself with a shudder when I explained how the wind chill factor works.

At the bathing well the two beauties were gone, replaced by a middle-aged man rubbing a bar of soap onto his bald head. Ranya exchanged a few words with him that made them both smile. She led us off the path and up to a ridge that overlooked the distant sea.

We walked down the slope into a thickly wooded grove. Inside where it was almost dark the air was cooler. Following no trail I could see, she left the path to walk into the thick of the trees. Twice she stopped and held branches for me so I wouldn't get whacked.

We came to a clear spot in the canopy, picking up a trail that led a short distance to a yellow two-story Colonial-style house that could have been imported from Cape Cod. Ranya opened the front door without knocking.

A curly-bearded man in a sky-blue sarong stood up from a writing desk in the center of the main room. His shirt was open down to the last button, revealing a chest and shoulders covered in fur. He approached us at a healthy bounce across the room, shaking hands while Ranya spoke. "Rohan" was the only word I picked out.

The man was a hard-gripper. We stayed locked in the handshake while she spoke about me. He just wouldn't let my hand go. Was it a subtle challenge or some fraternal sign I was missing? Ranya came to the rescue by offering me a chair at the dining table. I sat between the hairy handshaker and Rohan, half-listening as they launched into a lengthy conversation in Sinhalese. I hoped that Ranya might help with a translation, but she left the room.

Something wasn't right. Despite the social pleasantries, I felt the jitters creeping in. I dismissed them as standard nervousness, a practical response given my proximity to subversives who were officially proscribed and unofficially hunted. Then I realized it was the house itself that had me spooked. It was like a stage set. People were here, but not to live. Maybe this was what they meant by "safe-house."

Rohan let out a snort that made me flinch. He rapid-fired questions at our host. The answers made his mouth open wider. I touched his elbow and lifted my eyebrows, a signal that if something was going wrong, I wanted to know, now. He said, "This man know my brother."

"How about that," I nodded, hiding my disappointment.

"My brother Colvin. He is in officer school."

"Interesting," I added, and smiled politely at the man.

"No. He know because my brother is also a JVP man."

"Serious?" I looked at the man again. He didn't follow.

"He's in the army and the JVP?" I asked Rohan.

Ranya came into the room carrying a bowl of cashew nuts. "So many of the army are with us already," she explained. "A number of our cadres have joined the forces. They receive military training, not to mention the pay. Then when they quit they bring us their weapons. It's helpful for our mission. But not all of them leave. Some have remained. They're waiting for the proper time."

"Wow," I said.

Ranya laughed and translated the word for the man. He nodded to show me he understood. "Wow," he said in agreement.

"Shall I ask now about your interview?" Ranya asked.

"Yes, why not?" She was a step ahead of me again. I would have to think faster if I was going to keep up with these people.

She spoke in a woman's trickling Sinhalese, gesturing with her eyes to Rohan and then me, back and forth, until the man interrupted with a question. She explained further until he finally wagged his head to show that he got it. We all watched while he tugged his right ear lobe. He had a few more questions for Rohan, seemed satisfied with the answers, and then turned to me. Ranya translated.

"He says he will bring your request to a meeting tonight. If the others also approve, you may have your interview. Of course you may request to talk with any member of the party you wish. But we assume since you've already met Commander Dapila you are interested in meeting our leader."

"The leader Rajitpurna. Yes. That would get the most press, of course. All for the cause." I hoped she hadn't noticed my surprise. I would have considered myself lucky to get anyone else in their top rank. I hadn't even thought to ask for an audience with the pope.

The three talked in Sinhalese while I considered the impact of a double scoop in the same day's paper. Or maybe I would expose the government sell-out to New Delhi first, and wait until the next day to deliver my exclusive with the most wanted man in Sri Lanka. How sharp was that? A good editor would play it up, use it for the same dominant space on the front page both days. It would be like a winning streak. I could see it going huge fast, getting picked up around the planet. There would be an immediate demand for more news as the ruling party crumbled, and wouldn't I be in the perfect place to deliver it? How odd to have everything lining up my way. By not rushing the story into print back in Colombo, I'd set myself up for a week or more of star journalism. Prize-winning work. And to think that if I'd stayed in Colombo I'd be in a reeking locker room trying to make some chiseled teenager sound coherent.

Rohan noticed me smiling to myself. He opened his mouth to ask why, but the man spoke first with a string of questions. Something about the proper way Rohan sat up, hands folded in his lap, worried me. It may have been his party interview.

Would he be sitting like this, answering questions in a deferential murmur, if I hadn't told him about the murders on the beach? Or hadn't tried to lecture Leon on political morality? How ridiculous I could get. I comforted myself with the thought that Rohan's new-found spirit of revolution would fade with his next puff of brown sugar. Otherwise the possibility that he might get hurt was undeniable. What if he ended up like his friend on the beach? Or the kid in the army base? I saw myself standing before Vijaya, for real this time, trying to find the words to explain.

Ranya's puttering noises from the kitchen were a comfort. She seemed clear-headed enough. A moment alone with her should be enough for me to issue a damning character reference on Rohan. Surely the JVP had no room for a heroin addict.

But it wouldn't be that easy. What right did I have? I didn't live under a government that burned its youth alive. Could I stop anyone from fighting that?

Rohan slid a glance to see what I was looking for in the kitchen, then focused back on the questions. Everything about his demeanor struck me as an act. The way he spoke with such deference wasn't him. I debated telling the pair all I knew about Rohan, the good and bad. Let them make the call.

Of course they would refuse him. And if the government really was teetering – I remembered the edict banning motorcycle helmets – maybe the JVP had a fighting chance to take over. Ratting on Rohan now could cost him a place on the winning team. Meanwhile, JVP discipline might be just what he needed, the local equivalent of sending your unruly kid to cadet school.

He said something that made the pair laugh, his slushy chuckle blending in quietly. Maybe he could even bring something to the party, like a sense of humor. Still I couldn't picture him fitting in for long with such strident toe-the-liners, and it was a relief when he and the man stood up at last to shake hands.

Ranya appeared to see us out the door. "We will contact you soon about your interview," she told me. "Let's hope everything works out."

As we left they stood together in the doorway, arm in arm, like a suburban couple waving good-bye after a bridge game.

I never did get his name or title, I realized, waving back. If he could secure an interview with Rajitpurna, maybe he was even in the Politburo himself. That would make two I'd met already. Not a bad catch for a hack on an undeclared holiday.

When we were alone again on the path I asked Rohan whether he knew who the man was.

He looked puzzled. "The husband of Ranya."

"I mean his name, his position."

He lifted his eyebrows. "Very important man in JVP. A big man."

Back at the coast road we sat on the grass to wait for our bus. The sun was arcing towards to the sea but we had an hour or more before sunset. I needed the time to write up my notes for the interview. And also to think.

A van approached, the window on our side a crammed mash of limbs and torsos. Rohan waved for it to stop anyway. The driver wisely ignored us.

"So Mister Rohan," I said when the road was empty again. "You really thinking of joining the JVP?"

"Sure. Why not?"

"You know how strict they are. You told me yourself they don't even let their members smoke cigarettes."

"Because they have a goal in their life."

"What do you think they'd do if they found out you smoke heroin?"

"They know now. I tell them."

"What? Why?"

"I don't lie."

"And they'll still accept you?"

"They know I have a strong mind to quit. Also I have many friend in Hikkaduwa. I can do good for them, for the country. Also for me. Right now, what is my goal?"

"But are you sure you want to do your good through the JVP? They're not the most forgiving people in the world."

"What's mean forgiving?"

"Say a newspaper guy sells a paper the JVP doesn't like. They order you to kill him. If you forgive him, you let him live. If you don't forgive him, well, you kill him."

Rohan showed me his disappointment with a sideways glance.

"I don't do like that. You know me."

Another van sped by, also filled with people. He didn't bother waving this time.

"I know you," I said. "I don't know them. They talk a good political line, but are they really Marxists if they can just kill anyone they don't like? In my book a paper-seller is a worker, not the enemy. If you don't like the paper, hell, don't buy it."

He shrugged as if to say: why buy newspapers anyway?

"And what about how the JVP is adding followers by claiming to be the only party that can save the motherland for the Sinhalese? Marxists aren't supposed to be patriotic, or racist."

Rohan scratched his chin stubble. "In Sri Lanka if you talk about the motherland and Sinhalese, everybody listen. All politicians know that. Of course this is a Tamil country too. And Muslim, and Christian. All are equal. My father say, no matter how we looking, that's mean the difference, we all suffer the same."

"Well, where do you think you'll end up if you join the JVP? Look at Leon. Look at your friend last night."

"Yes," he said. "Look at my friend."

At last a taxi-van stopped to let out a man with a basket of fish. We crowded into his space, and said nothing more among the crowd of passengers.

Back at the cabana I put my head on the pillow to rest for just a moment but fell asleep almost at once.

I woke up to a sound outside my door. The last slats of a crimson sun were filtering in through the thatch. I sat up groggily and listened. The sound came again, a soft three-tap, on the door. Why the secret? My senses were tingling as I opened it. Kumari had come.

10

She was there in the doorway with the sun in her hair. Her curves contoured in the rectangular frame. She smiled shyly and looked down. It made her seem younger, almost like a girl. But her posture was still regal

"Kumari," I said, and added dumbly, "It's you." As an opener it was weak, but I hoped it would convey delight along with my surprise.

I finger-combed my hair with one hand and smoothed my beard down with the other. I rued not having changed out my sticky Celtics jersey. My hands felt big and conspicuous. I let them fall uselessly against my thighs, then just as quickly raised them again to reach for a friendly hug.

"I'm glad you've come," I said, my throat feeling dry as I closed the distance. Something made me stop a step early and lower my arms. "I mean, I'm happy," I added, patting my shirt pocket and smiling like a simpleton. "The same way I felt at getting your letter."

She looked up at me, inquisitive, and took a tiny step inside. Yes, it was all right. She could come in. In the dim interior her cheeks turned chocolate. Her eyes still held the wide gaze of a deer in unfamiliar territory, but she was ready to smile.

I moved my arm in an elaborate sweep that took in the room to say my house is your house. She replied with a mock curtsy, then placed a hand over her own heart. I felt like she'd touched me for real.

The momentum for the hug was lost, but I reached for her elbow in consolation. "Come in, come in," I urged, tugging as if she were blind.

She took two more steps and stopped abruptly. We stared together at the single bed at our knees. She turned away first, looking back over her shoulder to the doorway. I let go of her elbow.

"One second," I said quickly, removing a shuffle of papers from the desk chair. I pointed to the chair like a magician about to make it disappear. "Chair," I explained. "For you." I held it for her as she sat down.

I took the foot of the bed, a safe distance away, then immediately stood up again to light the kerosene lantern. It wasn't dark yet but it did give me something to do. See how proficient I could be? Light, fire, master of the elements.

But once I'd replaced the lantern on the ceiling hook I realized my mistake. The light directly behind her head would shine glaringly on me and only emphasize the difference in our ages. I offered a flimsy smile and muttered, "Aw, what the hell." She raised her shoulders in a shrug that matched mine.

I got up to shut the door but changed my mind on the way there. The sudden appearance of Rohan or Vijaya in the open doorway might still make her bolt, but closing it wasn't worth the risk of giving her the wrong idea. Whatever that might be.

She said something in her liquid Sinhalese. By the rising intonation I took it for a question, but how was I to know? Instead I closed my eyes and sighed happily.

"I agree with you 100 percent," I said. "But tell me again anyway. I love hearing the way you say it."

When I opened my eyes her arms were out towards me. In her upturned palms was a small package wrapped in shiny brown wax paper.

"For me?" I said, tapping my chest. Blue plastic bracelets clicked on her wrist as she hefted the package to say yes.

"A Christmas present?"

She nodded eagerly.

"Aw," I said, feeling great. "That poem was one of the best presents I ever got. You didn't have to do this."

She looked at me and blinked, a question to a question.

"Anyway, you shouldn't have." I took the package with a formal bow. I felt a paperback beneath the wrapping. I held onto it between my palms anyway to make the moment last. Over the sea an eggplant-colored cloud drifted through the pink sky. I caught Kumari's scent on a breeze off the water. It reminded me of the row of lilac bushes in a front yard I had neither seen nor thought of since I was a boy.

She nibbled her lower lip, a gesture of nervousness I took as a compliment. "Whatever it is, I love it already," I said to assure her. I slid a finger along the slick surface of the paper.

"This really is something," I added, holding it up to the lantern so the waxy surface gleamed. "You didn't have to. But I'm glad you did. Not if it was expensive, of course. But the sentiment. The idea."

She folded her arms across her chest in mock impatience, her lips pushed out in an exaggerated pout.

I prepared for my first glimpse of a second-hand novel from one of the souvenir shops. I'd looked through all their stacks already. Odds were it would be something by Stephen King.

"Probably time I read one of those things anyway," I told her. "Everyone else seems to have. Besides, just your bringing it here makes it special. It's already a memory. You standing in my doorway like that. The way the sun glinted off your hair? It was like a vision. Jesus, listen to me. You make me talk like a real jerk sometimes. I mean it isn't your fault, but, damn. Soon as I see you I feel my knees start to go wobbly and my heart beats faster and it's like I'm 16 again."

I leaned over to plant a quick peck on her cheek. She angled her head to let me.

"This has got to be the weirdest Christmas I ever had," I continued, looking at her over the top of the package. "But you being here now makes it one of the best." She looked down, shy again.

Maybe it wasn't so stupid to feel 16 again. My life in front of me for a change. I warned myself not to lose control, not to fall so deep and fast that I ended up dragging someone else with me on the way down. I knew already how steep the slide could get. But why couldn't this time be different? Already Kumari had brought me the heady tang of a long dead lilac shrub, and with it my childhood. She had returned unknowingly a gift I had carelessly mislaid long ago. Wasn't there something I could do for her?

The wrapping had been folded with care, the corners neat and sharp. The craftsmanship seemed out of place for any of the village stores. Maybe she'd done it herself. Maybe she was clever with her hands too.

Kumari spoke again in Sinhalese, now using a mock-angry tone. She wagged a finger at the package, or maybe me, and thrust out her hand as if to take it back.

"Okay, okay," I said, "here we go."

I slid open one corner with a thumbnail, planning to unfold it with care, but then on an impulse ripped the paper off in a rush. I made a gleeful little riot of it. I removed the book and held the cover up to the lantern. At least half of my pleasure came from not having to pretend.

"A Pocket Dictionary for Sinhalese and English," I read off the cover jacket. "It's perfect!"

The corners of some pages were dog-eared, but the book was in good shape. "Really, this is just what I needed. How did you know?"

She smiled widely, pleased with her success.

"I should have bought one of these myself. I don't know why I didn't. Maybe it's because I didn't have anyone I really wanted to talk to, before I met you."

She pointed at the book.

"Okay, hang on." I flipped the pages. "This should only. . . wait a minute. H-I-J-K-LMNOP. . . Wait, let me try something from here instead. Common phrases." I found the expression for thank you very much. "*Es-thu-ti*," I said. "*Bohoma es-thu-ti.*"

She applauded with soundless hand claps, then said something back in Sinhalese.

"Don't tell me, I know it already, I'm welcome. Right?"

She rolled her eyes up, pretending impatience, and pointed at the book again.

"Nah, I guessed that one already anyway. Give me a second, I'll come up with something better." I flipped back to B and found the word for beautiful, *lassanna*. When I said it and added "Kumari," pointing at her, she tipped her head mechanically to accept. She didn't seem surprised or pleased. Beautiful girls must hear it all the time.

She held her palm out for the book. A moment later she looked at me and announced, "Hahn-soam Gordie." In her musical tone it sounded like a gypsy's curse, but I was feeling too good to let such thoughts bother me now.

"Aw g'wan," I said, feigning embarrassment. "I'll bet you say that to. . . never mind. Look up another word."

She turned to the common phrases section and said, with a beginner's caution, "I am soh-ree I do not speak Eeen-glish."

Outside the color was gone from the sky, the ocean beneath it dark. They were blank sheets, inviting us to scrawl our halting attempts at meaning on them. And the only words that would register would be those inscribed out of a love as unknowable and as mysterious as the sea and the sky. For all I cared the lantern over her head could have been the only light left on the island.

"Maybe if I was living here I could learn Sinhalese," I said. "You could be my teacher. We'd teach each other." She was quiet. Not just in words, her expression too. She stared at the floor.

I added, "And we could take care of each other."

She leaned closer towards me. Her eyes were the darkest tone of brown, giving off no reflection. I stared into them, hoping to lose myself. But I couldn't, and instead felt a familiar sadness welling up. Why did she have to be so attractive, I thought. I let my head droop under its own weight. Our hands were together on the open page.

"I wish I could speak Sinhalese right now," I murmured into her ear. I wanted to brush back the hair on her forehead, but both hands were wrapped up with hers. "And then I could tell you exactly what I think. I mean, what I feel. About you."

I looked down at the book, wondering which words I might try first to get the point across.

"I don't know if we were supposed to meet or what, but it feels that way to me now. I'd like to believe it was my destiny, or fate. Vijaya would tell me it's karma, but I can't think of anything so good I've done to deserve you."

She continued stroking my hand but said nothing.

"Not that I do have you."

She stopped stroking my hand and took it in hers. She gave it a squeeze that I decided to interpret as encouragement.

"I know you're not mine, not like that. Not yet, anyway. But I want to help you. That's how we'll start. It burns me up when I think about you working, having to, you know, whatever. I understand there are reasons, maybe you grew up in a family that couldn't care for you or it's a caste thing or something so now you have to do this to eat. The point is, you don't have to. Not any more. I'm not saying this just for your sake, to be kind. This isn't charity. I'm saying it for me too. It's for us. For whatever meaning of us you prefer. I don't ask for anything in return."

I aimed a whoosh of air up towards the ceiling. "Listen to me talk," I said, producing a laugh that must have sounded forced.

Kumari looked at me and then turned her head quickly. Was she trying not to laugh? I slid my fingers under her chin to tilt her face up. Her eyes were flooded. She blinked rapidly with her lips together in a hard line, but couldn't stop a tear that slid half-way down her cheek to leave a glistening brown trail. I wiped it off with the back of my fingers. It tasted like the sea, and dissolved whatever cynicism remained in the dark corners of my caution. What if any relatively rich American would be a prospect for a desperate Sinhalese girl? What if she were so talented she could simulate breathless passion, and mimic the effortless flowering of the sell that convinces a lover? I would never believe that a prostitute could cry a tear that tasted so much like an elixir of innocence.

She swallowed audibly, then murmured, "Gordie." She was frowning at the floor between my feet, summoning something inside. I studied the line of her jaw. It curved back towards her ear in a mahogany-smooth spread of skin that was almost an invitation for fingers to touch. At last she squeezed my hand again and said something that ended in the only Sinhalese I remembered: "*Es-thu-ti.*"

I freed my fingers and took her by the shoulders, examining her like a work of art I'd bought for reasons I didn't understand. I held her that way for a moment, unsure what I wanted to do. Finally I shook her to break the spell.

"Aaargh. If only we could talk. Anyway, Kumari, I'm the one who has to thank you. You've made me glad I came to Sri Lanka. And after some of the shit I've been through, that's saying a lot. Now give me the damn book."

She looked dejected. Maybe she wanted me to keep squeezing her shoulders, or I was supposed to kiss her. I'd lost a precious moment. Another fumble. I flipped the pages quickly to find what I needed. I put the words for "work" and "no" together to form what I thought was an obvious, "Kumari no work."

She pouted. "No Kumari work" was equally baffling. I repeated it both ways more slowly, added the English equivalent, then tried the Sinhalese again with stresses on various syllables, yet nothing would erase the distressed look on her face.

Finally I stood and slipped my wallet out of my back pocket. I removed a wad of Sinhalese bills, showed her several thousand rupees and said, "You don't have to work there any more. See? I'm going to give you the money instead."

But her reaction startled me. She was appalled.

"No, wait," I said, almost desperately. "Kumari no work. You understand that much, yes? I can support you. See? I'm rich."

I waved the bills under her chin, but she whipped her head away so she wouldn't have to see.

"Please, Kumari, you're making a mistake. You have to understand. I'm just trying to help."

I flipped furiously through the book for the Sinhalese word for mistake, but saying it didn't help. I tried to show her the printed word in case my pronunciation was the problem, but she wouldn't look. No matter what I did, the act of me standing by the bed offering money gave her the wrong idea. Perhaps we'd misunderstood each other all along. I dismissed the thought, aware of a looming sense of dread that might flood me.

"Kumari," I said, taking her hands in mine again. She pulled her fingers free and stood up. Her posture was more rigid than before.

"Wait," I said. "Please. Sit." She turned towards the door but watched me from the corners of her eyes, appraising. I put my hands together in the style of a Sinhalese greeting and said again, "Please."

I held the chair out for her, then sat further down the bed to show that I needn't be so close. She held her hand out for the book. I gave it to her, but only after she would sit.

She looked up a word, mouthed it silently a few times to herself, then looked up another. She closed the book and looked at the thatch ceiling with her lips moving. Finally she turned to me. "When go home?"

"Me?" I asked, pointing to my chest. She nodded.

My return flight was scheduled in three days. I took the dictionary from her and searched through the Ws. Wednesday wasn't listed.

"Oh, for Christ's sake," I muttered, going back a page to find the word for "three."

I said "*thuna*" while holding up three fingers. No mistake there. I showed her my palms to mean wait. I found the word for day and put it together into "three days."

She moved her head a fraction to indicate she understood, but said nothing. The lantern flared, making our shadows dance against the back wall.

"But Kumari," I said. "Don't worry about that. I can come back. I can come back anytime. I'm not that far away, not with airplanes and everything."

I looked up the word "return," then put it between Gordie and Sri Lanka. She seemed to understand. She took the book to look up something.

"Rohan friend?" she said.

"Rohan friend." I repeated. "How's that?"

"Rohan Gordie friend?"

"Rohan Gordie friend. Yes, Rohan is Gordie's friend. If that's what you mean."

"Yes Rohan friend," she said, as if to confirm it. She looked again through the book.

"Rohan honest?" she asked, aspirating the h as in "hover."

"That's a tough one," I said. "He's a good man, inside, but he's, how do I put it, not always himself. . . Just a minute."

I took the book and started to look up "depends" but found only "dependable," hardly the word I wanted.

I held up a finger to begin. "Okay," I said, pointing to myself, "Rohan." I continued by forming my hands into the shape of an imaginary person beside me. "Rohan friend."

"Rohan, Rohan friend," she said, nodding first at me and then at the empty space on the bed between us.

"Very good. Yes. Now. Rohan, Rohan friend," I said again, moving my hand between me and the imaginary person to suggest a connection. "Honest."

Kumari nodded her head.

"Excellent. Now. Rohan, Rohan no-friend, ah, just a minute, no, what's the word for no? Damn." I took the book to look through the Ns again.

"Rohan no friend," Kumari said, nodding her head and pointing to the other side of the bed away from Rohan's imaginary friend.

"Perfect! Okay, Rohan, Rohan no-friend." I waved my hand back and forth again, then said, "Honest?" and shrugged my shoulders. "Honest yes? Honest no?" I shrugged again. "I don't know. Maybe yes, maybe no."

Kumari tilted her head. Next question. "Rohan rupee?" she asked.

"Rohan rupee?" I tried. "You've got me. Rohan rupee. I don't understand."

She took the book and flipped through it quickly, then said, "Rohan rupee where?"

"Oh, where does Rohan get rupees? You mean what is his job?"

She looked back, uncomprehending.

"Job," I said, "work. You want to know what Rohan's work is?" I had to look up the word for work again. I wasn't making much of an advertisement for myself as a language partner. But once I found it the word for work served me better this time.

"Okay? So. Rohan has no work," I said. "No work, no rupees." I shook my head no to make the point. "Only sometimes, rupees from his mother. Ama. Mother. Rupees. For cigarettes." I made the motion of a person smoking. "That's as much as I know."

She nodded her head and was about to speak again when I asked, "Why?"

She raised her eyes and pointed at the book. I found the word for why and tried again.

She answered with a long explanation in Sinhalese, pointing at various times to herself, me, and the imaginary Rohan. Finally I shrugged my shoulders to show I wasn't getting it.

She chewed the inside of her lower lip while she thought, then said, "Rohan friend, Kumari friend, Gordie friend."

"Right," I said slowly. "We're all friends. You and me and Rohan. Is that it?"

"Gordie, America."

"Okay."

"Kumari, Sri Lanka."

"Right."

"Kumari – " she put her thumb and forefingers together and pretended to write. Then she took up the imaginary paper in both hands and presented it to someone. "Rohan," she said, then mimed Rohan writing.

"I get it! You'll write to me and Rohan will translate the letters. It's a great idea! Although you might have the same friend who wrote your letter do it. Her English was perfect."

She shook her head to indicate that she hadn't understood. She repeated the letter connection between the three of us.

"Fine. I can write to you through Rohan." I went through the gestures of our three-way correspondence to confirm it until she nodded. Her lips spread into a smile.

"Well, excellent might not be the best word," I continued. "Rohan's English isn't exactly great. Who knows how well he can write it. Vijaya might be better shot, come to think of it. His English is better than mine." I wondered whether he would know that Kumari was a prostitute. Maybe there was something in the way she wore her sarong, or some speech pattern, that a local would spot at once. Or maybe it wouldn't matter anyway. Vijaya seemed the type who would not discriminate, especially once he knew her. Maybe if I left him some money he could even try to help her find a job. Anything to keep her occupied until I came back for her.

The realization that I'd just considered the practicality of bringing her back to Boston surprised me, but not unpleasantly. "Kumari come America?" I said. "With Gordie? Yes?"

She flipped through the dictionary.

"Kumari busy," she announced, throwing me for a loop. Surely she couldn't mean her career opportunities prevented foreign relocation. I was about to ask through the dictionary but she startled me by standing up. I felt a jolt at the thought of her leaving.

Instead she came closer. Standing in front of me as I sat on the bed, my head was level with her chest. She looked down at me, almost sadly, then stepped forward. She put one hand on the back of my head and pulled me into her. My head turned sideways at the nudge of her palm and nestled between her breasts.

"Gordie," she said, twirling my hair in circles. Then: "Gordie, Gordie, Gordie." I wrapped my arms around her back and squeezed. She bent down, kissed the top of my head and pulled away.

She turned to walk out. "Wait," I said, "do you have to go? It's still early."

She looked at me questioningly, then said, "Gordie" again, this time adding a sigh.

"Will you come later? Tomorrow?" I asked. She held up her palm and wiggled the fingers.

"Or I'll come visit you." I said. "Just tell me when."

"Bye," she mouthed silently over her shoulder. She walked away quickly down the beach. I watched her until she was too tiny to make out from the other distant dots of people.

But we'd gotten somewhere. Further than I would have hoped. The groundwork was done. Now it was just details.

In the house I waited happily at the table for my dinner. The smells alone were intoxicating. My mouth flooded at the prospect of another culinary extravaganza borne in by the grinning females of Vijaya's family.

But the first one through the door with a plate of papadam was a young man. The officer school son. He was lighter-skinned than Rohan and just as tall, although built on more powerful lines. With a little definition, a few months in the weight room, he could have the body of a speedy cornerback.

"You haven't met my second son," Vijaya said, entering behind him.

I stood up to draw out the greeting with a hand-shake. So this is what a rebel infiltrator looked like. He took my hand with a confident clench, perhaps something they teach in officer school.

"Hello," he said, a little shyly. "I am Colvin." He added a winning smile, reminding me of the one Rohan would use to get out of a jam. I gathered he wasn't entirely comfortable with English, but also that he wouldn't let the fact bother him enough to clam up. He chuckled at the way I stared and motioned me to my chair. "You seet," he said, almost like an order.

Vijaya took one of the chairs against the wall and Colvin did the same. With his short-sleeve shirt neatly pressed and his spine flat against the chair back, I had no trouble picturing him in an officer's uniform. Colvin the guerrilla was not nearly as easy an image to conjure up.

"Why don't you have some papadam now while you wait for the rest?" Vijaya offered. "You are hungry, no?"

"It has been a long day. Hard to believe it's still Christmas."

"So it is. Well. Merry Christmas, then."

"In honor of the occasion, why don't we all eat together?" I asked.

He smiled. "You wouldn't mind if Colvin and I joined you?"

"On the contrary. And maybe the women would like to sit with us too."

They laughed politely at what they took for a joke. Once the men were seated I waited at least a full second before swooping onto the papadam. They were as thin as they were tasty, just the kind of food a hungry man can vanquish in a flash. The pair saw me and backed off, despite my crumb-spitting exhortations for them to join in. Vijaya picked up the empty plate and walked back to the kitchen. Colvin and I studied each other with unspoken grins.

"So you're the local whiz who's going to officer school," I said.

He held his hands up in front of his face, fending off the word barrage. "No good speaking English. Please more slowly."

"Sorry. You," I said pointing. "Army?" I straightened my spine and saluted.

"Yes," he answered, saluting back and smiling widely. "I am an army man soon. Now in training."

"And how do you like it? Is the army good?"

"Yes, good," he said. His father appeared with another, taller stack of papadam. Colvin said something to him in Sinhalese.

"He says he enjoys the physical training best. He was the captain of his cricket squad in school. But he is not so keen on the discipline."

"No kidding. I'd hate that myself, I'm sure. Some idiot ordering me to dig a pit for no reason."

Vijaya translated and Colvin said something with a laugh. Vijaya explained, "He says that's why he's in officer school. So he can be the idiot giving the orders."

"Seriously, though, what about having to shoot at Tamils? Or other Sinhalese? This must be an awful time to be in the Sri Lankan army. Doesn't he worry about it?"

Vijaya answered without asking him. "Of course. We discussed it many times. I myself was opposed to his joining. Colvin felt he had no choice. I worked 27 years for the civil service, yet I was powerless to find him a job without offering a bribe. Where was I to find this money? And even if I had it, why should I pay a criminal politician just so my son can work for his country?"

Colvin watched us without reaction. It was hard to tell how much he was picking up.

I licked my fingertips to collect the remaining papadam crumbs from the plate. Tasty, but no match for my hunger. Fortunately Vijaya's youngest daughter appeared carrying a steaming tray of rice. That started a gourmet parade that eventually covered the table with food. "So why don't you eat?" Vijaya said. It was like a starting gun going off in my ear.

The meal sent me into a small ecstasy. I swirled rice and small servings of curries together with my fingers, trying different color and taste combinations, delighting in a quest to find the most sublime blend. The two let me get a good head start, perhaps in deference to my appetite, but once I settled into a leisurely pace they joined in and held their own. Colvin laughed between bites and said something to his father. Vijaya translated, "He says you eat like they do in the barracks."

I chewed faster to down a cheek-puffing mound of curried fish with rice and a little dahl, then asked, "Was I going that fast?"

Colvin laughed again as he spoke to his father. "If you don't move quickly at a table of army men," Vijaya said, "you eat nothing. But he says you would have no trouble."

Vijaya's wife brought out another huge tray of rice. She took away the empty bowl of green curry and said the Sinhalese for what might have been, "We'll have to wheel him out of here."

"We will save them some food, won't we?" I asked, worried that I might be eating the household out of a month's provisions in a single night of gluttony. Vijaya assured me they would be happy only if I were to enjoy as much as I desired.

"The day I leave here, I'm going on a serious diet," I announced.

Vijaya translated this to Colvin. He raised his eyebrows in appreciation of the task. He asked his father something, the only word of which I understood being "Rohan." Vijaya's answer in Sinhalese came with a tiny frown. He asked me, "You don't know where Rohan has gone this evening?"

"Me? Why, no," I answered. If Rohan really was going to join the JVP, I supposed his brother would find out soon enough. When would Vijaya get the news?

After dinner Colvin excused himself, first to me and then to his father. Vijaya explained that he was off to visit an old school friend. When he was gone the two of us took our tea out to the verandah.

"It's chilly tonight," Vijaya said, rubbing his bare arms.

There was a soft breeze in from the jungle across the road that I found refreshing. "You must be joking," I said. "It's December, I'm wearing a short-sleeve shirt, and you're telling me it's cold?"

"I prefer the hot weather. In this season the nights can get too cold."

We sipped our tea, enjoying a quiet spell with no traffic on the coast road. "He seems like a good boy," I said.

"Who's that?"

"Colvin."

"Oh yes, of course," Vijaya said. "He never gives me trouble."

I smiled at the inference. "Imagine if all your kids were like Rohan."

He shook his head slowly. "One Rohan is enough for any family."

The Rhino Eye had three people sitting at its single table, the most I'd ever seen. "Leon," I said, "business is booming." He looked at me with practiced indifference.

One of the customers had long blonde hair matted into dread-locks. The one beside him had a buzz cut that made places on his skull gleam where the lantern glow shone through. He stopped talking when I walked in, whispered to his partner, then they both lowered their heads to hide their faces. The third one had his back to me.

"Something I said?" I asked Leon.

"Ask your friend."

The third customer turned around. It was Rohan.

"Mister Gordie has come," he announced, inviting me to the table with a palm-down wave. "This my friend," he explained to the pair. The cropped one studied me with suspicion, then mumbled something behind his hand in German. He looked ready to start a sprint for the jungle across the road.

"What's up, guys?" I asked. They eyed each other to trade some non-verbal signal I couldn't catch, then looked back at me. Neither answered. Rohan shot me a sly grin but dropped it before they noticed. His eyes appeared clear. After my last 24 hours, I probably looked worse.

"My friend," Rohan said again, this time taking in the pair with a nod. "They coming from West Germany."

"How about that Beckenbauer?" I offered. The one with dreads stared as if he'd seen me before and was trying to recall where.

"Tell us your name," he demanded.

Rohan shrugged in my direction. I could hear the start of a sheesh-sheesh laugh that he managed to keep down.

"Gordie," I answered. "And yours?" He looked at his partner and shuddered his head to mean no.

"Whatever," I said. "Listen, Rohan, don't let me get in the way of anything." The shred of curiosity I'd had to see an actual Sri Lankan drug deal was outweighed by disapproval. Being judgmental was never my favorite trait, but then he was the eldest son. I sighed as if it were a shame, yet not one worthy of my time. Back at the counter I took a candy drop from a jar Leon was filling. "And a pack of Thansher's," I said, leaving the money on the counter.

"No problem, you sit, we just talking," Rohan told me. Leon slid my mini-cigars over without looking up.

"No, thank *you*," I said to Leon, who didn't react.

Rohan addressed the Germans in a stage whisper everyone could hear. "I tell you, this man my friend, no problem. He smoking so much ganja himself. All the time." The pair looked up to confirm I was a hemp-head. Now it was my turn to get uncomfortable.

"I don't know about all the time," I muttered. The Germans stayed silent.

"Anyway, who doesn't?" I added. When they still eyed me as if I were radioactive, I realized I didn't care what a couple of scrawny tourists thought. I turned back to run my finger along Leon's over-polished counter, miming the act of someone finding a disgusting layer of dust.

Leon didn't get this one either. He busied himself by polishing the mirror at his back. Rohan's voice went on in hushed conversation with the pair but I didn't bother listening.

"Really, Leon," I said, "four customers now? At the same time?"

He grimaced with one side of his mouth pulling down, as if crowds were now his biggest problem. Or it may have been his version of a smile. I tried again. "First J.C. Penney and now this."

He turned to rearrange some biscuit tins in the window, consigning my gibe to the same empty box in which he swept whatever he couldn't use, which as far as I could tell was just about everything.

I opened my Thansher's and slid one out, picking through my pocket for the Ultrasafe matches. Four of them sparked and died in succession. Leon, exasperated more than me at my lack of success, gestured to the punk smoldering near the counter. I was about to light the cigar when an oxen cart clattered by on wooden wheels. It was trailed by a long, slow line of cars. In the front passenger seat of a battered green Volvo I saw Manik, his yellow frame glasses and wisp of a mustache unmistakable.

"Hey!" I yelled but the Volvo kept rolling. I shouted louder. "Manik!"

"Friend of yours?" Leon asked, probably surprised I would have one.

"No. Just a guy I met." I took a pull on the cigar. "In Colombo."

I ambled to the open doorway for fresh air. The others must have seen that I was checking on the car. It was parked ahead on the side of the road.

"Guess I'll just see what's new with him," I said, walking out without looking back. Manik stood by the rear bumper with his hand already out for a shake. He took my palm and pumped it.

"Mister Talison! What a splendid surprise!"

"What are you doing here?" I asked. He must have taken it as an accusation. He dropped my hand.

"We are just passing by," he said, his thin mustache working. "But how good to see you again! We had no idea you were in this area."

"You sure about that?"

"How could we? You went away so suddenly." The driver still

hadn't turned around, but when he adjusted the rear-view mirror I could see his eyes.

"Don't give me any shit, Manik. Were you sent down here to check on me?"

"No!" he protested. "Mister Talison, we have nothing but gratitude to offer you for doing your interview. And particularly in my case, for keeping my role in it a personal matter. I know the authorities can be persuasive, but thank goodness in your situation – "

"You still haven't told me what you're doing here."

He smiled. "Oh Mister Talison, you won't believe it."

"What are you doing here, Manik?"

The smile grew. "You should be pleased to know I am working!" He reached into his back pocket and produced a notebook. "As a journalist!"

"Aren't you supposed to be in school?"

He laughed. "Impossible. The universities are still on strike. We've had no classes for seven months. Not that I mind. It gives me a chance to do more important things. You understand what I mean." He dropped his voice. "For the party."

"That's what you're doing here now?"

"Not directly. I truly am working. I took the drive down to interview the fishermen near Matara who are protesting a factory for its pollution. The article is not for a major newspaper like yours, I'm afraid, so not many will ever read it, but if some do, and the news spreads, maybe the factory will have to stop the pollution." He shrugged. "All for the cause, no?"

I remembered a time when I would have said something just like that. "Sure it is." I resisted the urge to offer advice: don't let them sucker you onto the sports page.

The driver leaned his head out the window, still without turning around so I could see him. He muttered something towards the ground. Manik answered in Sinhalese.

"We are very-very late," he explained apologetically. "We are expected."

"Listen, Manik, don't tell anyone you saw me here."

"As you wish."

"I mean anyone. Not your friends, not the party, not the people at the Moonstone Hotel. I don't want the government or the army or anybody else in Colombo to know I'm here."

Even to my own ears I sounded on the verge of paranoia. Manik couldn't have known about the document buried a javelin throw away, nor how it could tilt the history of his island. If I developed the courage to dig it up. From flattering myself with the idea of being a role model it hadn't taken long to remember my true calling as a coward.

Manik nodded gravely. "I understand," he said, his eyes intense. "I will always be indebted to you."

"It was nothing."

"Mister Talison, we both know it could have been everything for me, had you given them my name."

"I might have, if I thought it would do me any good."

"Not you," he said with a smile. He replaced his notebook and we shook hands again. "Thank you, Mister Talison. From me and from my family."

Back in the car he leaned over to say something to the driver, who watched me instead of the road as the car pulled away.

At the Rhino Eye the Germans were gone. Rohan sat alone at the table. "Looks like business is good with you too," I said, offering him a cigar from my pack of Thansher's. He waved it away with a sweep of his palm.

"I no smoking," he said.

"Right. I completely forgot."

He nodded to accept my apology, then asked Leon for two lemon drinks. Leon mumbled something in Sinhalese that made Rohan snort and get up to pull the bottles himself from the fridge. I reached into my pants for the money, but he held up a hand.

"I pay," he said.

Even Leon lifted an eyebrow. Rohan took a tight roll of rupees from the fold in his sarong and unwrapped a bill. He re-wound the roll, giving it a smart flick with his fingernail before sliding it back in place.

"The West Germans?" I asked.

He chuckled. "Tonight I thinking I must do something good, not for me but for other people, and just like that – " he snapped his fingers – "a good thing happen to me! You want another food? More to drink?"

My bottle was still full. "I'm fine," I answered, then automatically offered him a cigar in return. He held up his hand again.

"Sorry," I apologized. "Do you mind if I have one?"

"Go ahead."

"If it bugs you I won't."

"You are smoking, not me, so no problem," he said.

I lit the Thansher's, blew a stream of smoke towards the entrance behind me and pointed the tip of the cigar at Rohan's money roll. I whispered so Leon couldn't hear. "Are you really going to give it to the party?"

"Sure," he said, not bothering to whisper back.

"What if they ask where it came from?"

"Why they ask? Money is money. If they can use, they use."

"But – "

"Some people are good at doing a speech, some people can make a poster. I help my way."

"What about the heroin? You really going to quit?"

"I quit. I have a strong mind. Now my body will be strong also. So I can work."

"When was the last time you smoked?"

"Brown sugar?"

"Yes."

He puckered his lips to calculate, then touched several fingertips in turn with his thumb. Finally he said, "Yesterday."

"Ah."

"But now I quit, sure."

"So you haven't smoked yet today?"

"I am telling you. I quit."

"It's that easy?"

"Not easy. Sometimes very hard. I know because I quit before. One time for two months. But this time? I don't start again."

"Whatever you say."

"Before, when I quit, my life is still the same. No job, nothing to do, only bad business in Sri Lanka. The day is long, no? What can I do? I smoke."

I may have looked unconvinced. Rohan leaned closer. "True! Tomorrow I see the doctor to get pills. Seventeen different pills. I take for four days, then no more problem and I never want to smoke again."

"Seventeen pills? It sounds scarier than the heroin. What's in them?"

"Medicine. I don't know."

Colvin walked in, his chin up and his chest out. He greeted Leon with a cordial nod, then grinned at me. He said something to his older brother in Sinhalese.

Rohan scowled but said nothing. Colvin spoke again.

Rohan looked at me this time. "He say my father want to know where I get money."

"How did he know you have it?"

Rohan shrugged. He scraped the Elephant Brand label off one of the bottles. "Not his business. This is my work."

He said the same, perhaps, in Sinhalese. Colvin answered in a tone that may have been critical.

"Why I should explain my life to my father?" Rohan asked me.

"Maybe because you're his eldest son," I offered. "And you've been ripping him off for five years."

His lips went down at the corners. "Always he talking about Buddhism, about Marxism," he said, spitting the words out. "Always talking. Now I am doing."

Colvin watched the speech uncertainly. He may not have

understood everything, but his forehead wrinkled in a way that showed he knew it wasn't good.

Rohan had apparently not told Colvin he knew about his brother's role as a JVP infiltrator. Could the rebel group have room for them both? Colvin said something in Sinhalese. This time it was Leon who answered.

"Behold the new man," he said, sneering in Rohan's direction.

Rohan looked up at him wearily.

Leon continued with something in Sinhalese that made Colvin nod in agreement. Rohan stared out the door, drumming the tabletop with his fingers.

"He won't be the first person to discover how the revolution isn't paradise after all," Leon explained. He aimed his goatee in Rohan's direction like a doctor discussing a comatose patient. "He just found out sooner than most. Exactly how many hours has it been?"

Rohan swept the bottles off the table with the back of his hand. They hit the wooden floor with a clatter, but didn't break. He stood up with his nostrils flaring. He picked up the bottles and placed them with exaggerated care on the counter under Leon's nose.

Leon aimed a malicious grin over Rohan's shoulder towards me. "And he thinks he can quit smoking just like that," he said, snapping the fingers on his good hand.

"Maybe he can," I answered.

Leon tittered, the first time I heard him utter anything resembling a laugh. If it was meant to rile me, it worked.

"Are you the expert now, Leon?" I said. "I didn't realize you knew so much about human potential."

Rohan took me in with the same sullen expression he'd used on Leon. It was if we were discussing someone he knew only vaguely.

Leon smirked. "How interesting. You believe he can quit his drug habit? Just like that?"

"Yes. If Rohan says he can quit, he can quit."

Colvin nodded, but warily.

"You're trying to be kind," Leon said in a tone that suggested it was a character flaw. "You're afraid to tell him what you really think."

"Listen. In the first place, you don't know fuck-all about what I really think. In the second place, if you're so sure of yourself, back it up. I'm willing to make a little wager on it. Are you?"

His dark eyes gleamed. "A gambling man," he said. "Fine. I would be willing to help you redistribute the wealth, as we say. How much longer will you be here?"

"I'm supposed to fly back in three days."

"That should do. If Rohan doesn't touch heroin for the next three days, you win. If not – and I know everybody around here, including the people he smokes with – I win. Fair?"

"I guess."

I realized he could rook me on the verification. One of Rohan's addict pals would probably sell him out for a cigarette from the counter jar. But even that might work if it gave him a better look at the people he considered his friends. The point was to show Rohan I believed in him. Whether I actually did or not didn't matter.

"What shall we bet, then?"

"You tell me, Leon," I said. "How much can you stand to lose?"

He rubbed the back of his neck with his bandages. "You'll have the advantage of me there. I'm hardly a rich man. Actually, the bank is threatening to foreclose."

"I never said it has to be money. How about something of equal value?"

I patted my pants, rejecting my mini-flashlight keyholder, which Kirstin had given me one Christmas, as too emotionally complicated to appraise. In my shirt pocket I found something better: a fountain pen.

"It's a good one," I said, setting it carefully on the counter. "Gold nib, silver casing. An antique."

He removed the cap and held the tip up to the light bulb.

"Sheaffer," he read, not bothering to hide the fact he was impressed.

"So what have you got?" I looked around the shop's dismal wares. "I wouldn't take your whole inventory if you gave it to me. That pen is worth at least $100."

Leon smirked to accept the point. He reached under the counter to remove a black cloth cover over a metal chest. It was padlocked, but with the key in his good hand and the bandaged arm as a brace he managed to work it open. The top drawer of the chest was empty except for a single lighter. He picked it up carefully, breathed on it once for moisture and polished it against his chest. He turned it over a few times to check for scratches, then handed it to me.

"A lighter," I said, popping the lid. The latch made a tiny chime when it flipped open. "Big deal."

"A sterling silver lighter," he corrected, "which happens to be custom-made. You'll see there's no manufacturer's stamp? It's not some factory piece. Heft it. That is a solid example of German craftsmanship."

I wouldn't have known sterling silver from tin, but it certainly felt solid. Rohan and Colvin eyed the piece with me from various angles.

"Fine," I said, setting it on the counter. "My pen against your lighter."

"Fine," he repeated. He replaced the lighter in the chest and picked up the pen to put it in too.

"Whoa, pal," I said, showing an open palm. "You haven't won a thing yet."

He feigned surprised at the challenge. "But for safekeeping," he said.

"No way. I'm not coming back in three days to find out you sold both of them."

"Very well," he said, not insulted. He placed the pen and the lighter on my side of the counter. "You hold them. In the event I win, as soon as we find out that Rohan has smoked, you agree to bring them here. Colvin is our witness. You do trust him, I'm sure. Our good little soldier cannot tell a lie."

I took it that Colvin's role in the JVP was one village secret Leon had yet to hear. Or if he had, he didn't know that I knew. Whatever hand I got dealt, I would need to play it wisely to get the best of someone like Leon.

"Colvin will do," I said. And Rohan would get another reminder of who he would let down by losing.

Rohan stood up to leave. Colvin said something but Rohan flicked it away with an impatient wave. "No," he said. "I must work."

He got to the road and turned back to glare at Leon. He seemed about to deliver a devastating parting shot. Instead he turned to me. "You come?" he asked.

I had to jog to catch up. We continued in the dark towards the busy part of Hikkaduwa. The spicy aroma of a roti stall hit us before we saw it. The chewy rolls were practically calling my name. I told Rohan we had to stop. He reached for his money roll but I got my wallet out first to buy four fish rotis, then had to eat three myself.

"My father," Rohan said after giving half his roti to a sorry-looking dog, "I know he have a difficult life. He has little money. He has me. But he don't understand everything. He don't understand me. Not now."

My mouth was too crammed to say anything. Rohan spoke again.

"And Leon is a bastard."

"True. But if you lost your hand like that, you might be mad too."

"I don't care that he is angry. But why he try to make other people angry too?"

"Maybe because he spent seven years in prison for an empty dream," I said.

Rohan shook his head. "Not a dream," he said. "Not empty."

11

I lay still, half-asleep, as morning light crept into the cabana interior. I heard the sound of something that didn't fit the constant rhythm of the sea. Was it shuffling feet? Someone breathing? The last remnant of a dream?

Through the open wooden window I saw the rise of a smooth bald head, then the top half of a teenaged monk in a bright orange robe. The eyes blinked twice, scrunching the muscles in his temples. He whispered, "Yes. I am Gamini."

"What?" I said, not whispering. I sat up with a bolt, causing him to jump back from the window. He may have been in his late teens but he was no taller than a grade school boy.

He regained his composure to nod an unsmiling hello. He said in a low, conspiratorial voice, "You are the newspaperman. Mister Talison."

"And you're a monk."

"Of course. Let me in. I mustn't be seen out here."

Inside he surveyed the corners of the shadowy room by sliding his eyes rather than turning his head, reminding me of a reptile. When the inspection brought him back to me, the difference in our sizes must have seemed striking. He took another step back for a better view.

"You're up early, Gamini."

"Yes. Every day."

I spread my arms wide in a morning stretch. He may have been surprised I could reach the opposite walls at the same time. Or he was calculating whether I could crush him with my hands.

"Well," I said at last.

"I have disturbed you. You were sleeping."

I answered with a yawn.

"I apologize. I am not based in this area, so I must use all possible precautions."

I folded my arms across my chest. "Yes?"

"Because of the party," he said.

I pictured a crowded room of people drinking beer out of bottles, but couldn't fit an adolescent monk into the scene. "There was a party," I noted.

"There is a party."

I got it. "Of course. I'm still waking up. You're in the JVP. Right. So you're not really a monk."

He looked insulted. "Why do you say this?"

"I thought a monk would spend his time meditating. Being peaceful. Looking for the answers within and all that."

"So?" he said defiantly.

"Never mind. It's never a good idea to argue religion or politics in a bar. That was my father's rule."

"But we are not in a bar."

I smiled at the thought. "I just meant that religion and politics are two hot topics that people argue enough about already, and here you are putting them together."

His sleek forehead puckered. "One cannot put together something which is already joined. Life is politics and religion is life."

"If you say so."

"Not only I say so. Many of us in the temples support the party. Most, I may say, of the younger monks. But it is true, a number of older monks have yet to accept change."

"What happened to religion being the opiate of the masses?"

He floated a hand in the air to dismiss the challenge. "If Karl

Marx had known the teachings of Lord Buddha he would not have said it that way. In point of fact, the two are perfectly compatible. Both say we must rule our own destiny without expecting help from a higher authority, do they not?"

I shrugged. "I wouldn't know."

"Both say wisdom and action are needed to end the suffering of the masses, do they not?"

"It's kind of early for a political debate, Gamini. Ask me in an hour and I might come up with something."

He looked puzzled. "But we cannot wait. We must go immediately."

"We must? I didn't say I was going anywhere."

His head tilted further back to read me more clearly. "You are Mister Talison, no?"

"Gordie Talison, yes."

"You are a member of the international press?"

"That's right."

He was relieved. "Then it is you who has requested an interview."

"Right. My interview. I just didn't connect you with, well." I lowered my voice. "The leader. So you're taking me to him?"

"We must leave before many people are about. As I say, I am not based here."

I held the door for him but he didn't immediately walk out. He poked his bald head out like a periscope, searching in all directions. When he felt it was safe, he looked back once at me and then took off in the flat-footed jog bellhops use in expensive hotels. By the time we reached Walter's boat I was panting.

He squatted behind it on the ocean side. He peeked over the bow to confirm that no one was following, then stood up to go on. I stopped him by touching his elbow. He gaped at my heaving belly with scientific curiosity before insisting, "We must go."

"Wait," I commanded. "I have to get something."

I dug in the sand while he watched in bewilderment. Was there no end to the strangeness of foreigners? When the hole came up empty, I got alarmed, and dug wider, scooping vigorously with both hands, until the plastic pouch appeared. I brushed off the sand and slid it inside my waistband.

"My things," I explained, but Gamini was more worried about being seen. I was tempted to stop him in his tracks by showing him the secret document. Which shock would be bigger, proof of government corruption or his own party's No. 2 man unearthed as a traitor?

We headed south on a path through the jungle parallel to the coast road. His rabbit pace made the orange robe flap behind his heels. He looked like a giant orchid escaping the garden. It was a relief to see him stop at last behind a row of empty oil barrels.

"We must be quiet," he admonished, but I couldn't just stop breathing.

"Where's my interview?" I asked between gasps.

He winced at the volume before answering in a reproachful whisper, "I do not know." His blinking eyes never left the road.

"Great," I whispered. "You're the one taking me and you don't even know where we're going."

He ignored me.

"I am going to meet Rajitpurna, right?"

He said nothing. Maybe he had taken a vow against lying. I asked, in a louder voice, "Before we go anywhere I need you to tell me, Gamini, are we going to see Rajitpurna?"

"Please," he begged. "I am not permitted to say. You must wait."

The absurdity of it hit me. A tiny, blinking, bald, reptilian kid in a colored robe was delivering me to the boss of the dreaded JVP.

"Gamini," I announced, "take me to your leader."

A government bus swayed down the coast road towards us from the north, but he didn't care.

"Tell me one thing," I asked in a hushed voice. "Have you met him?"

He leaned closer so he could whisper into my ear while watching the road. "Not in person," he said. "But I listen to his speeches."

"He's on the radio?"

"On cassette."

"Rajitpurna is out on cassette?"

"He records messages for all party members. The cassettes go to every part of the motherland, all on the same day. It is how we must communicate because the government has declared us illegal. Also because they are trying to kill him."

"What does he say in the cassettes?"

He thought for a moment. "He asks, why are so many hungry when we have a perfect climate to grow food, the sea for fishing, where people come from all over the world to our beautiful island and precious gems come up from the ground. He says Sri Lanka should be a paradise where everyone shares the wealth. Instead most suffer."

"I've noticed that part."

"Because capitalism is a tool used by our own exploiters as well their imperialist allies. We are no longer masters in our own land. If a poor Sri Lankan today works hard, who benefits? Not him. Not the motherland. Foreign elements. The head of the CIA today has more influence in Sri Lanka than any Sinhalese alive."

"Screw the CIA."

He blinked a few times as if he had his doubts about me. "Yes," was all he said.

"But shouldn't you be worried about Buddhism if the JVP wins? Look what happened in Tibet. The Chinese army there razed the temples. Where would guys like you be then?"

"It would never be like that in Sri Lanka. If the people want temples, temples will be there. It's under the present government that Buddhism is suffering. They are killing monks."

"That's a bit hard to believe," I said.

"Last month three monks from my own temple were taken away." He turned from the road to blink at me a few times. "They have not come back."

We watched an elderly woman walk across the road carrying a basket of mangoes. She disappeared into the jungle.

Gamini stood when a brown Toyota sedan appeared. The headlights flicked on and off. He touched my knee.

"We go," he whispered, standing up quickly and waving his hand downward for me to follow. He walked slower this time, as if out for a morning stroll.

"Do not look at the car," he ordered from one side of his mouth. It passed us at a quiet roll. The driver's thin brown arm was bent out the window to rest a hand on the roof. Beside him was a woman with shoulder-length black hair. Neither turned to look at us as the car disappeared around the next bend.

We found it ahead idling next to an empty tea stall. Gamini reached it with a sag of relief. He opened the rear left door, jerked his shiny head for me to climb in, then took off at a run. I caught the last flash of orange vanish into the green jungle. He didn't even say good-bye.

"And I was just beginning to like the kid, too," I said, getting nothing back. Neither of the two in front turned around. The driver put the car in gear and eased back onto the road, turning right.

A heady scent of flowers came to me, something familiar I couldn't place. Was it a childhood memory? My attention was drawn by how the slanting sunlight lit up places in the woman's hair. I felt my pulse quicken, then shook my head in disbelief.

She swung around to greet me, her smile brilliant. "Good morning, Gordie," Kumari said in smooth, British-accented English. "I hope you slept well?"

"Kumari?" I heard myself say back.

She laughed, the same trickling sound that had reached me before like some mysterious music. Now my throat took up the pounding of my heart. I stared at her, my head still shaking. "What is happening here?"

"I know you're surprised," she said, honey in her tone. I

shuddered to shake off the blow.

"You speak English?"

"I'm afraid I do," she said, her plump lips drooping into a brief frown to apologize. "I regret I couldn't tell you before today. My assignment."

My brain was stuck between gears, unable to grasp onto anything beyond the most glaring fact of my own stupidity. "Assignment for the JVP?"

"Yes."

"You're one of them?"

"Yes."

"And you're a prostitute?"

She laughed. "Actually, I was a teacher. But for the good of the party, we do what we must."

I stared out the window at nothing. "They actually make you do that? Some party."

She turned completely in her seat for a better look at me, then laughed again. "Nobody makes me do anything. This is a crucial region for our struggle. Intelligence from here is a top priority. Because of my appearance, it seems, I was suited to the job."

"Right." Suddenly I wanted the car ride to be over. I slid to the left and rolled down the window. I stuck my head out to get wind onto my face. The moment I got back from the interview I could start packing. I might even catch a bus back to Colombo the same day.

"There are worse assignments," she said with an odd inflection. She lowered her eyes. Was it the shy act again? "This one was my idea."

"Jesus. I hope you got lots of information." I said it with what I hoped would come across as disgust.

"Oh, but I have," she said, her almond eyes widening to emphasize the point. "More than we expected. You would be surprised to learn what men will tell a poor village prostitute."

I turned back to the window. The sea appeared in slices through a stand of trees. There were whitecaps further out beyond the last fishing boats. "Fuck this," I muttered to myself.

"No, you mustn't think that way, Gordie."

I willed myself not to look in her direction. I could still smell the blossoms, her perfume. I stuck my head out the window to clear it. When I finally pulled it back in, I didn't bother wiping the hair off my face. Kumari's delighted expression had given way to a look of pity. It did nothing to improve my mood.

"Gordie, you must understand," she said, the sincerity practically dripping off each syllable. "This is not about me or you. It's for something bigger."

She reached back to sweep the hair off my forehead but I pushed her hand away. I leaned harder against the door.

The sea appeared again after a string of hotels ended. A line of fishermen on the beach hauled in a massive net with their slow-motion chain-walk. If it weren't for the interview I could have left the car right there and caught a bus back to the cabana. I muttered a stream of silent invectives. Kumari made a sympathetic noise in her throat, the kind you might use to calm an injured pet.

I stole a quick look. The pity was gone. It was now, what, resolve? Unless that was an act too.

"Gordie," she called as if I were in a distant room. I didn't look up. If her power over me was through appearances I might counter it by keeping her out of sight. At the same time I realized, with a bitter rise in my stomach, how ridiculous I was. Me, at 37, being played by a girl. The things men do for the simple architectural genetics of a pretty face.

"Gordie," she said again, this time firmly. "I know you're hurt. I know I hurt you. But what you don't – "

"Listen, Kumari? You don't know shit about me. Okay? So why don't we just drop it? I've got an interview to think about. This is *my* work."

I pulled the notebook from my back pocket and pretended to write, angling it so she wouldn't see the furious scribbles.

The driver murmured something. Kumari answered by pointing to a schoolhouse on the right. We passed a playground of squealing boys in white uniforms chasing a ball, then turned right onto a dirt road that S-curved into the jungle. The car began to bounce and sway, but Kumari turned back again to talk to me.

"I never lied to you," she said quietly.

We passed a grove of cinnamon trees. I sucked in a long breath, trying to flood my senses. There was no good answer, I knew. But I spoke anyway. "Only because you never said a word."

Kumari said something to the driver that made him hold his hand out to the road in a gesture of protest. She said it again, this time with an edge. He nodded twice, quickly, then pulled the car into the shade of a banyan tree. He shut off the engine and stared ahead. Beside us was a vast reservoir that reflected the line of trees growing on its far bank.

Kumari got out, and when I didn't follow, came around to my side of the car to open the door. I still took my time. She was half-way towards a small grove at the furthest corner of the reservoir before I started walking.

When I reached the grove Kumari wasn't there. "Right," I blurted-ed. "So now we're going to play hide and go fucking seek."

"Over here," she said in a soft voice. She was leaning back against the trunk of a bo tree. Her bracelets jangled as her arms lifted towards me.

"No. No possible way," I said, standing my ground. "Give me some credit here. I don't care how good-looking you are. You can't always expect men to drop at your feet."

"Please Gordie?" Her voice was different, a tone I couldn't place. "Don't be bitter."

I waited, kicking at the leaves under my feet, then walked nearer. I made a point of stopping just beyond her fingertips.

She stepped forward and grabbed the back of my neck, pulling me to her. Before I had a chance to say anything her lips were on mine.

I kissed her back. Then I pushed her away.

"You can't," I said.

She leaned forward until her head was on my shoulder and she was in my arms and I was holding her up. She read me correctly. I was still angry but not enough to let her drop.

"Why didn't you admit you spoke English? At least when you came to me last night?"

"I told you, I was working," she explained. "Your friend is interested in the party. We needed to learn more about him. And about you."

"So there I was, telling you everything without even realizing it."

"I told you I was good," she said.

"Wait. This. What you're doing right now. Is this part of the assignment?"

"You're different, Gordie. I knew it when you first visited, for the blind man. And then when you came back for me. You didn't just take me out and screw me, even though you wanted to so badly."

"Was I that obvious?"

"You couldn't stop staring!" she said with a bright smile. "Anyone could tell." A flock of birds took off in a rustle of leaves above us.

"So what happens now?"

She seemed surprised. "You have an interview."

"That's not what I meant."

Her face tilted up and her eyelids fluttered closed. She let me kiss her.

We stepped out from the trees back onto the path. When Kumari let go of my hand it felt like the current had been switched off in my fingers. I was about to say so when a *pak-pak* sound of shots came from across the reservoir. Kumari tackled me, pushing me face-down into the dirt. She lay on top of me.

I lifted my head to look.

"Shh!" she hissed, pressing my head back down. "Follow me. Like this." She wriggled off and crawled on her belly back towards the trees. I stayed close behind.

We scuttled behind the biggest pair of trunks growing out of the same spot. I made myself sound calmer than I was. "What the hell was that?"

"The driver has been shot. I don't know why. I'm sure we weren't being followed. We'll have to leave on foot."

"How do you know he was hit? We couldn't see anything."

"That was a rifle. Ranjit keeps a .45 under his seat. He would have used it."

Dogs began barking from the road we'd driven up. They could have been trackers. Kumari aimed an ear in that direction. "Wait here," she whispered. "I'm going to take a look."

"No. You wait here. I'll look."

But she was already crawling away at a swift clip, limbs churning. I started to follow, but Kumari shot back a fierce look of reproach before moving on.

I stayed for a moment, then clenched my teeth and pushed ahead anyway, copying her noiseless roll at the end to land behind a sparse cover of dried bush. We waited that way, heads on the ground, for a full minute until Kumari parted a tiny viewing space in the branches.

An army jeep was parked behind our car. Our driver's body hung out the open door with his hair dangling in the dirt. A soldier in green fatigues pulled a blanket from the trunk and shook it out. Another had his head in the open window on the passenger side. When he pulled it out, I saw he was wearing a black baseball cap.

"That's him!" I hissed. "From last night! The guy who killed Rohan's friend on the beach!"

Kumari said nothing. She was surveying the trees behind us.

The soldier at the trunk walked to the front of the car with a walkie-talkie to his ear. He nodded and said something we couldn't hear. He and the man in the cap turned together to look in our direction.

"Shit!" I blurted in a whisper. "They've seen us!"

"Quiet," Kumari commanded. "They haven't. Or they would be here."

The two were still looking in our direction. The soldier pointed his walkie-talkie at something to our right, but the other shook his head. They continued scanning.

"The driver told them where we are," I said.

"No. Not Ranjit." We heard the whine of a distant engine.

"More cars coming," Kumari said. "Listen carefully, Gordie. You see the ridge back there?"

I stared in the direction she pointed to, seeing nothing but trees. "It all looks the same."

"No. There's a ridge. Walk quickly in the direction of the tallest tree you see. That one." She waited until I nodded. "From there you'll see the ridge. It's not large, the height of a man, but it's there. At the south end – that means your left – there's a gap. Go through it and follow the path on the other side until it comes to a pond. I'll meet you there."

She was vibrating energy, her eyes piercing, her body coiled, but there was no fear. She'd been here before. When I said nothing, she nodded once and crawled back out to the open dirt. I held my breath as she slithered through the sunny patch, her blue sarong such a bright target against the red clay. When she reached the trees she got up into a runner's crouch, then turned to check on me.

I held up a palm to tell her to wait. I crawled the same way, the backs of my legs tingling where the first bullet might strike. When I reached her, and could speak, my voice had an authority that surprised me.

"Listen, I've got this figured out. We'll stay together. If they catch us I'll tell them you're working with me, you're my interpreter. They can't hurt you. I won't let them."

"No. Alone you've got a better chance. If you're caught with me they'll shoot us both." She said it almost coldly. I reached for her hand but she whipped it back, stood up and ran into the jungle away from the direction of the ridge. In three strides she was gone.

I took deep breaths to build up oxygen. Why had I let myself get so out of shape? Any one of the thousands of athletes I'd covered would be better at this. I scurried past the first trees in a crouch and then, out of sight, straightened up to walk quickly, trying to establish an endurable stride.

It didn't work. The adrenaline swelled in my veins and I found myself racing towards the tall tree. Every thump of my feet seemed to land with a tell-tale crash, but it was no use. My legs charged in a panicked imitation of a real runner.

The engines grew loud enough to drown out my gasping breaths. I pictured a convoy of green trucks, each one crammed in the back with opposing rows of soldiers. I went faster, swiping madly at branches that reached out to hold me. I was making a clamor of it, I knew, but could not stop.

At the tall tree I doubled over to catch my wind. The car noises were gone. The attackers might have gone looking elsewhere.

I could see the ridge in the near distance. It was head-high and formed of clay that showed red through the foliage. I pushed on, looking only in that direction, not willing to let anything distract me from my goal.

At the ridge I crouched beside a stump to hold my gut, wondered if throwing up would be any help. I wiped sweat from my eyes and was surprised to see my palm come up red. I must have cut myself on branches without feeling it. The sight of my own blood was as good as a spur. I stood up and ran beside the length of the ridge to find the gap.

It was there as Kumari had said, a space just wide enough for me to squeeze through. I ran between two boulders and found a narrow, mostly overgrown path on the other side. It seemed no more than an animal trail, but there was nothing bigger around so I took it.

Kumari hadn't said how far it would be to the pond. I slowed to a jog to save energy. The soldiers might well have been following close behind but crossing through the gap had at least given me the relief of getting somewhere. I was over the panic. Luckily Kumari hadn't been there to see me when I was gripped and crashing through the bush like a hunted buffalo.

The path ahead disappeared. The open space before me held a pile of dried thatch. Beyond it on the left was a grove of rubber trees. To the right was a rise. Which way? Why hadn't Kumari told me about this? I stood at the spot for several nervous seconds, sensing that not deciding was the same as waiting to be caught. A pond seemed more likely to be at a lower elevation, so I went left through the trees.

I ran for several minutes more but saw nothing like a pond. In several places I picked up a path but each time it disappeared. At one point it spread disarmingly into a maze of trails between thick trees that could all have been paths. I took the closest one, but with a growing notion of being utterly lost.

When my thigh muscles started to quiver I slowed to a walk. In a small patch of mud I saw footprints that were reassuring. At last, proof of a proper trail, the first promising sign since I'd chosen the rubber tree grove. I kneeled to examine the rippled grooves. They were long and deep, the steps of a heavy man, one I would not want to meet alone in a jungle. The pattern could have come from a hiking boot, an odd thing for this area, I thought, until I looked at my own Vibram-soled topsiders. The footprints were mine. I was going in a circle, maybe one that would bring me right back to the car.

"Fuck," I hissed to myself. I dry-swallowed, tasting fear. I wanted to run again, my body aching to get away, but which way? Any miscalculation now could bring me closer to the danger.

"What a horrible fucking place," I whispered to no one. I slid back against the nearest tree to sit in the dirt. I watched my belly push and pull air as if it belonged to someone else. "The fuck am I doing here anyway?" I asked. "Running around like a rabid dog." I stared up at the canopy, thick enough to block the sun. "I don't deserve this. No one does." I could breathe slower now. "Especially not Kumari." I made a vow: I would find her and save her. So I would be the one who rescued her. Her savior. Her ticket to somewhere far away from an island where everything attractive was corrupted by cruelty.

A rustling of leaves made me freeze. It was just behind me. I slowly made myself turn, hands in front of my face as if they could stop a bullet. Through my fingers I saw the black shining scales of a snake as thick as my leg.

It was near enough to touch. One lunge and it would have been on me. My thoughts jumped to races I'd covered, how focused the competitors were in their starting blocks. They knew it was also a mental contest against their own shortcomings. The materials were there already, the body, the training, the energy, but nobody had it down to perfection, so the point was how to channel everything into a single explosive instant better than the competition. To do that, you had to be calm.

So I was. I willed myself to make the larger connection to my presence in that time and place, and what it could be. I decided I was a predator too. I could take control. I could decide which one of us would be the prey that day. Eat or be eaten. One of us makes a stand. But not there, not then, I also decided. I would rule it out. The snake would instead be my ally, a link to the natural order of things, the flow. It was the attackers who were out of sync. They were the ones trying to break the life chain. And they would not. At least not through me. I fought back an urge to reach out and touch the moving stream of scales for some kind of confirmation. The muscular curves slowly took it away.

I steadied my breath, made it deeper, slower, then took off at a brisk walking clip. Almost as quickly I caught my foot on an exposed root and was in the air. I reached out to brace for the fall with my hands open but the momentum still carried me into a belly slide that scuffed my forehead and ripped my shirt.

I climbed up on one knee, then felt a hand grab my shoulder. I was caught. And already down. Still I would not give in to a tide of panic I felt deeper within. I rapidly considered my options. I couldn't kick anyone from that position. A punch would be weight-less. My only two weapons were gone. I could still try a tackle and run.

"This way, Mister Gordie," a voice said with hushed urgency. "Dangerous here." He tugged on my armpit until I was up, then ran ahead before I could see his face. The brown vinyl strap across his shoulder was attached to a rifle he held at his chest. He wore rubber sandals.

I caught up when he stopped to swing the rifle to his back before vaulting over a fallen tree. He checked to see that I had cleared it too. He couldn't have been more than 14 years old. His eyes be-trayed his fright.

"I'm supposed to go to the pond!" I said, but he ran ahead as if he hadn't heard. When he left the path altogether to crash through the bush, it occurred to me that we were creating a trail anyone could follow. But he was too far ahead to hear. His green T-shirt moved in and out of sight between tree trunks.

Finally he stopped and squatted with his head lowered. "You go this way," he said, pointing to the right of a spreading mango tree.

"No. I'm supposed to go to the pond," I insisted. "I have to meet Kumari." He tilted his head once, meaning either yes or no, then ran away in the direction we had come.

I followed his direction with the queasy feeling of being watched. I pictured army men behind every tree around me. If a JVP grom-met could find me, trained soldiers could do no worse.

The path ended in a murky puddle that I might have tried to leap if I were a decade younger. Would anybody call that a pond? I sloshed through and spotted the ears and upper head of some-one crouched behind a granite boulder. The head raised a notch to reveal a face, another youngster. He put a finger to his lips as he stood. He had the long limbs of a still-growing teenager. The same type of rifle was slung over one of his shoulders. Over the other was a bandolier of bullets.

"Wait," I insisted, placing one hand on the rock for support while I sucked in air. "One minute."

He crouched back down to peer over my shoulder. He kept his finger on the trigger.

"Where's Kumari?" I asked. "Is she all right?"

He cringed at how loudly I'd asked. His eyes darted in several directions as if expecting soldiers to appear everywhere at once. He watched me pant with a restless stare.

I nodded for him to go ahead. The trail climbed to a flat plateau that opened onto a grassy plain where he slowed down. He turned to check on me before going on.

We came to a plowed field, marching through the middle of the empty furrows. It seemed a risk when the edge was nearer jungle cover, but he was the one with the gun. Now it was swinging behind his back.

"Kumari is okay isn't she?" I asked when we reached trees on the other side. He wagged his head but said nothing. I wondered whether he understood.

"Kumari," I said. I used my hands to shape curves. "The woman. I meet where?"

He shook his head again but said nothing. We hiked through another jungle similar to the one I'd just been in, or maybe it was the same one. We came out of it into a flatland with a few stunted shrubs growing out of sandy soil. A thatch hut was just visible against a backdrop of trees in the distance. When I pointed to it, the guide said, "Yes, yes."

Before we reached it we could see two men in front watching our advance. They stood from their wooden chairs when we got near. They were big enough to interest the scouting office of any team in the NFL. Their eyes never left me as the guide spoke to them in Sinhalese. Once I thought I heard the word Talison. Inside the hut were rows of rifles leaning against three of the walls.

One of the pair was a curly-haired man with the melon-sized biceps of a lifter. He wore a black leather holster on his hip and squatted with a grunt to pluck a long stem of grass to fit between his lips.

Something in the way the other one balanced on his feet, even though he was taller and thicker, made him seem lithe. He put me in mind of the snake I had seen. He was handsome in the rugged way of an action actor, and even resembled a bit of a ham in the way he narrowed his eyes when he growled at the guide. The boy turned to explain it to the other one, but he turned away. The actor looked back to me.

"Nobody searched you at all?"

"No. Why should they?"

He shrugged. "Security. You understand." As if it would make a difference whether I did or not.

The one with the holster lifted his beefy arms to demonstrate how I should raise mine. With a glance of annoyance at the guide for having to maneuver all that muscle into bending down, he began by patting my ankles. I felt the plastic-covered document against the skin below my navel. Would he get that close?

His hands worked swiftly up to a slide over my crotch, no guns there, and then to the soft spread of my belly. He might have pitied me, a big man who had let himself go to fat. He finished with my back, then returned with a frown to the one area that had concerned him, my right pocket. He waggled his fingers for me to produce the bulging contents. I showed him my key chain, Leon's lighter and some change.

He nodded for me to put it all back, but with a last mournful look at the lighter.

"Any cigarettes?" he tried.

"No, I don't smoke. Just cigars, once in a while. None on me now."

He dismissed it with a tiny nod.

"No need to apologize. I quit smoking when I joined the party." He winked and added, "Almost."

The other one pointed towards the hut. "Now we wait. Sit inside if you prefer."

"Where's Kumari?" I asked.

He shrugged. "Who?"

"The woman I came with. We were in the car together. Kumari. I need to find out whether she's all right."

The bigger one turned up his palms. "Why wouldn't she be?"

"She was going to meet me by the pond. I found this guy instead, so she must have told him to get me. I'd just like to know where she is now."

He asked the guide something. When the answer came, he whistled lowly and exchanged a look with his partner. They were both impressed.

The one with the holster said, "Comrade K. I didn't realize you knew her. Sorry."

"That's okay."

"Is it true? She is very beautiful?"

"Yes."

"Some of the comrades say this, even women. I should have understood when you said her name but generally she goes by the initial only. We all have separate names for party purposes."

"Of course."

"My real name is Hasitha. Not so interesting. So for party work I use the name Kohomba. It means a god. I don't necessarily believe in gods but the name is good, no?"

"It rolls off the tongue. How do you know Kumari?"

"Comrade K? She is known by everyone in the party."

"Kumari?"

He slid the holster up higher. "She comes from a wealthy family. Her father is in shipping, manufacturing, so many enterprises. A tycoon. Most of the money in Sri Lanka is owned by a few families, you know. That is why we have so much suffering. That and the foreign elements."

"So she's rich."

He thick shoulders bounced when he laughed. "She isn't, her family is. She gave her money away when she joined the people's struggle. She cares only for Sri Lanka. Comrade Rajitpurna himself has praised her."

"Do you know where I'll be doing my interview with Rajitpurna? And will Kumari – Comrade K – be meeting me there or what?"

He flipped up his palms again. "Who can say?" He held up a finger for silence. "You hear something?"

I tried to. "That bird chirping?"

The other one hawked some spit before closing his eyes to listen. He seemed unsure, so he asked the guide. The answer was a shrug. It was quiet.

Kohomba said something in Sinhalese that made the other two laugh. The cawing of a bird came out of the nearby trees, a racket in the thick warm air, and when it ended we could hear the distant chop of a helicopter. The two big guys froze.

The guide pointed to a dusky line of mountains in the distance, but there was nothing there. The bigger man pointed in the opposite direction and listened with his ear that way, but shook his head to say he couldn't tell for sure.

"What's going on?" I asked. "Somebody fill me in here."

"A helicopter is air force," Kohomba answered. "But it's strange. They don't fly here."

"They do now," I said. "It's getting closer."

The sound, still far off, seemed to come from no one direction. They three looked at each other uncertainly. Then with a suddenness that didn't seem possible, the noise became loud.

"There!" Kohomba shouted, already running. We took off after him towards the grove 50 meters away. For huge men the two were surprisingly quick, beating the guide to cover. I joined them last under the canopy an instant before the helicopter appeared just above the trees. The underside was painted in camouflage.

It roared once past the hut and then turned back in a loop to hover over it. Two men in uniform were crouched in the open doorway. The down-draft blew fronds off the roof. A loudspeaker sounded with a man speaking Sinhalese.

"What is it?" I half-yelled into Kohomba's ear.

"He says walk out with your arms up."

The helicopter rose and flew three tight circles before breaking off to head towards the mountains. We didn't move. It was almost out of sight when it turned back, the nose dipped and it headed straight for the hut at speed. A rocket screeched off the underside trailing white smoke. It hit the roof with a blast that blew the walls out in four directions. What was left of the hut burned in small fires. The helicopter swung around in another circle and came back to hover again. The two in the doorway leaned out to look down at the damage. One shook his head at the pilot and twirled his finger in a small circle. The helicopter flew off the way it had come.

The three started talking at once, angrily. The argument was interrupted when Kohomba turned to me. He took the pistol from his holster and touched it to my temple. "Who are you?" he demanded, seething. "Why did you lead them to us?"

"I didn't," I explained, trying to sound as settled as any innocent person would. I leaned away but the steel of the barrel stayed hard against my flesh. "I don't even know where we are."

"This site is secure," Kohomba said. "It has always been secure. Until now. When you came."

I pointed to the guide. "He's the one who brought me here."

The bigger one added something that made Kohomba think for a moment and then lower the gun. They both looked at the guide. He produced an expression of such confusion that I believed him.

"He didn't do it either," I said. "He would have been killed too if we hadn't run like that."

Kohomba said something to him that sounded accusatory, but put the gun back in the holster. The guide shook his head and all three began to argue again.

"Shut up! All of you," I ordered. "Blame each other later. I want to get out of here now before they come back."

The guide stood up first. We followed him single file further into the trees. The biggest one took up the rear behind me.

An hour's hike brought us up into hills covered with rows of shoulder-high tea bushes. We could have been in a maze, cutting across rows and turning so many times I suspected they were doing it just so I couldn't retrace the route. At last we came to a gazebo not far from a cobalt-blue warehouse. The air was thick with the smell of roasted tea.

"You wait," Kohomba told me. The other two started to go to the warehouse with him, but he put his hand on the guide's shoulder and said something. The guide grumbled and squatted down beside me. We didn't look at each other.

A minute later Kumari came running from the warehouse.

"Gordie!" she cried. She threw her arms around my neck and squeezed.

"You're okay," I said, holding her as if to keep her from running away. "You're not hurt."

She said something in Sinhalese that made the guide leap up and run into the warehouse.

"I was so frightened for you," she said in a breathy rush. "I just hoped if they found you they wouldn't harm a foreign journalist. They tell me you handled yourself well."

I basked in her praise. "Nah. All I did was run."

I leaned over to kiss her but she pushed me away.

"We're leaving," she said. "We're not secure here. That helicopter should not have come."

"Tell me about it. Another few seconds and I – "

"I'll return."

I started to nod but she was already half-way back to the warehouse. I listened to a grinding mechanical whir, perhaps something to do with making tea, and realized how thirsty I was.

Five young men and a woman, all carrying rifles, left the warehouse, one at a time, running hunched over into the tea bushes.

Kohomba came out next, walking. "We're going," he said, waving me over. I joined him in the open space. His expression was odd.

"The soldiers are coming here?" I asked in alarm.

He looked to the warehouse, then bent his hands back and forth to flex the wrists. The grinding sound droned on.

"No interview today," he said. "Official order." The excitement in his voice was obvious.

"Rajitpurna is here, isn't he?"

He answered with a head tilt. "One day I will tell my grandchildren."

"You met your perfect leader," I said.

"Yes. He is a visionary."

"The man who could soon run the country."

"Yes. Although many of our daily management duties are now carried out by Comrade Perera. I had never met him before either."

"The No. 2 man," I stammered.

"We don't believe in one or two. The Central Committee and the Politburo work in harmony as the vanguard of the popular will. But it's true, Comrade Perera is the only one beside our leader who can issue a decree."

Even as he kept gazing to the warehouse like a backstage groupie, Kohomba struck me as one of the good ones. A little young, and maybe a little thick, but the type I would want on my team. Would his reverence wither once he found out Perera was crooked?

Kumari came out again. Kohomba straightened into attention as she spoke in Sinhalese. When she finished he ran smartly off into the bushes.

"Kumari, listen. There's something I have to tell you."

"In the car."

"It's about Perera."

"All the better," she said. "Come." She walked rapidly into the green maze.

I called to her back, "I got this information from Commander Dapila in Colombo."

"Faster," she said over her shoulder. "We're not safe here."

We came onto a gravel driveway lined on both sides with shade trees. Kohomba stood sentry in front of a shiny Toyota Camry with three of its doors open. He nodded once to Kumari and disappeared into the bushes.

The driver's arm pointed over the roof to the front passenger seat, my spot, then pulled his door shut. Kumari got in the back beside a man with a soft, faintly lined face and ripples of oiled hair tinged grey at the temples.

He smiled at Kumari, then took me in with a polite nod. "Hello. Thank you for coming. I am Perera," he said, offering a hand. His fingers were long and tapered, the hands of an artist. He wore a gold ring that bulged with a glittering blue gem the size of pecan. It seemed extravagant for a supposed rebel. "And you must be the foreign correspondent," he said, his tone gentle, almost bemused. "How do you do?"

"Talison," I said, forcing a smile.

A wine dark Mercedes with tinted windows pulled up beside us in a gravel-spitting stop. The driver walked to our car and leaned in my window to ask Perera something. Perera answered "yes" in English and the man left.

The back door of the Mercedes opened and a tall, slightly stooped man with a beard and aviator sunglasses stepped out. He searched in all directions, a pointer sniffing the air, before coming over to us. A black beret tilted over one eye gave him a rakish air. When he neared us he nodded solemnly. I couldn't see his eyes, so I checked behind me to see who he was aiming at.

"Comrade Rajitpurna," Kumari cued me from behind. "He's come to say hello. To you."

I opened the door to get out, but he waved his hand to stop me. "I'm afraid we shall not be able to complete our interview today," he said. "Yet another change of plans." He sounded tired. Or maybe annoyed. "For now simply allow me to thank you for your effort."

He reached into the car. For a big leader he didn't have much of a grip. His hand felt soft, almost spongy. I wished I could see his eyes rather than my own reflection in his glasses. He spun on his heels and disappeared into the tea bushes without saying good-bye.

The driver made a tiny ahem noise in his throat and checked the rear-view mirror. Perera lowered his head a fraction and the car rolled forward. The driver looked over both shoulders, then hit the gas hard enough to fishtail away on the gravel.

We turned from the driveway onto a dirt road. The driver seemed to make a little show of how well he could handle the car, gripping the wheel with a racer's extended arms, narrowing his eyes to spot upcoming holes. I noticed Kumari and Perera bumped against each other on some of the bigger dips, but there was not much they could do to help that.

"So. I understand you're the No. 2 man in the JVP," I said. Kumari watched me with an expression that was hard to gauge.

"A misconception popularized by the capitalist media," Perera purred back. "We reject a hierarchical system of leadership. It is rather the party members who lead us. If you must, I am simply one member of the Politburo."

"An important member," I offered.

He accepted with a tiny sigh and an almost imperceptible bow.

"I've missed my other interview, but since we're together, perhaps a few questions for you."

He joined his fingertips in a steeple. "If it serves our struggle, please."

I pulled my notebook out. "How do you see the JVP's role in the immediate future of Sri Lanka?"

A weak opener but Perera nodded as if giving it thought before launching into a speech he must have delivered hundreds of times. I stopped writing word-for-word after he said, "Indeed, as in many formerly colonized countries, our people have discovered for themselves the true nature of both direct and indirect imperialist exploitation."

My next question about the JVP's military strategy evoked more of the same, followed by a quote from Mao about the masses being the fish the party swims through. Why was I bothering when it had nothing to do with my real story? I'd spent enough of this round feeling him out. Time to start throwing punches.

"And what role do you see foreign governments playing right now in Sri Lankan politics?"

He didn't flinch, launching into a condemnation of Indian chauvinists, American super-capitalists and European neo-imperialists. "The recent dark history of Sri Lanka is one of subservience," he said. "Only with a JVP government will the Sri Lankan people once more be masters in their own house."

"And what about rumors the Indian government is right now bribing influential Sri Lankan leaders? Both ranking officials in the government and their political opponents?"

Kumari looked at me in confusion. Perera managed a slight smile, as if amused.

"And where, may I ask, would you have heard such rumors?"

"Actually, rumors may not be the best word," I accepted, matching his forced smile. "I heard it myself. From Commander Dapila."

"A revolutionary hero," Perera said, watching me now. The driver asked something but was ignored.

"Right," I went on. "He told me some interesting things about how India is bribing political figures in Sri Lanka."

"Is that so?" Perera said. Something in his tone made the driver look back at him in the mirror. Perera opened his mouth to say more, but I interrupted. I couldn't let up now, not when I had him on the ropes.

"Could you also tell me, tell readers around the world, I should say, your reaction to Commander Dapila's charge that you, sir, are a paid agent of the Indian government? That you are included with a group of ruling party politicians now taking bribes? Which means you are a traitor twice over? To your party, and to your country?"

I pressed the tip of my pen hard on the notebook, hoping no one would notice the shaking in my hands.

Perera wiped his lip with the back of his finger. He stared at me but said nothing. It was Kumari who spoke.

"Gordie, this is not a matter for joking."

I gestured to Perera. "He knows I'm serious. Look at him."

Perera chuckled icily. "Lies are constantly being spread about our party, Mister . . . I'm sorry. Your good name again?"

"Talison. But this one happens – "

"And I'm simply trying to determine whether your lie has come from the government's black agents, as they so often do, or if began with you and your organization."

He turned to Kumari and began speaking in Sinhalese. The driver adjusted his mirror to angle it onto me.

"He is," Kumari insisted in English. "Colombo ran it through. You know that."

Perera replied with a long string of Sinhalese. Kumari nodded at points along the way. She wasn't looking at me.

"Look," I interrupted. "I have proof."

"Gordie?" Kumari asked. She didn't go on.

"Documented proof."

"Then you will kindly show us," Perera suggested.

A squelch of static came from the steering column. The driver turned in his seat to look back at Perera. When Perera said nothing, the driver asked a question. Perera looked at him in surprise, then flicked the back of his hand twice to say yes.

The driver slid aside a wooden panel in the dashboard, revealing a hand-mike with a black coil. He pressed a button on the side of the mike and spoke. The voice that came back was yelling. Screams could be heard in the background, along with the rolling grind of the tea warehouse machinery.

The driver spoke again into the mike, his voice rising. When he released the button we heard the sound of rapid shots, machine-gun fire. They crackled out of the speaker in pops. The voice on the other end raged something.

"Extraordinary," Perera murmured.

The speaker issued a blast of noise that hurt my eardrums, followed by a steady hum. The driver reached down absently to click the set off. He didn't bother to slide the panel closed.

Perera barked something that made the driver swerve to the side of the dirt road. We were in a flat plain of cropped farmland.

"But, how?" Kumari asked no one.

"Precisely," Perera answered. "I believe Mister Talison may be able to answer that question. Shall we get out?" He opened his door and swung a leg out.

"No," I said, staring straight ahead. "Take me back."

He was standing beside my door with a revolver in his hand. Out of courtesy, perhaps, he didn't point it at me. Kumari watched him with her eyes wide.

I got out but stood behind the open door, my only hope for a shield. Perera motioned with his chin for me to step away from it.

"Kumari," I said evenly.

"He won't hurt you," she said, but without confidence. She quickly added something to Perera in Sinhalese.

On Perera's command, the driver got out to pat me down. When he reached my pockets I started to pull the contents out myself but he grabbed my wrist and shook his head no. He withdrew the lighter.

"Aha!" Perera said, snatching it from him in triumph.

He opened and closed the lid a few times, then held it up to the sky as if he might be able to see through it. He shook it near his ear, was still not satisfied, and finally flicked the wheel. It lit up.

He snapped at the driver, who hurried to the field to find a stone the size of a puck. Perera placed the lighter on the ground and smashed it with the stone. When that merely produced a dent, he hit it again, harder, then peeled back one of the metal sides. Inside, next to the cylinder of fuel, was a tiny, blinking red light. No bigger than a pea, it flashed with the garish finality of a police car illuminating a suspect.

"Israeli-made," Perera explained to Kumari. To me he added, "But easy enough to find on the black market. Although one might expect the CIA to use something of its own design."

"There's no way you're – "

"My last question," he interrupted, "is why? Or perhaps I should ask who? Did the government offer you a bounty directly, or was there some go-between?"

Kumari covered her mouth with her hand.

"Yes, you're right," Perera told me. "It hardly matters, does it?"

"Don't be a fool," I said. "I had no idea what this was. I thought it was a lighter." I turned to Kumari to explain the rest: "Leon gave it to me, the guy who owns the Rhino Eye store, the one who used to be in the JVP. He got me to hold it as part of a bet."

"He's lying," Perera said quickly.

"Didn't I almost get killed because of that thing? Twice now?"

"Not almost," he corrected, raising the pistol. He aimed for my chest.

Kumari dove at him. She drove a shoulder into his stomach hard enough to knock him back off his feet. The gun bounced once on the ground and into the field.

The driver ran towards his side of the car. I stopped him with an ankle tackle and climbed over his back to get there first.

I groped under the seat until my fingers touched the metal. The driver reached me just as I withdrew a grey pistol. He drove a fist down onto my elbow and I dropped it.

He tried a kick at my groin, but it was telegraphed. I stepped back just enough far to avoid it, then moved in with a right upper-cut. It hit the button. His head snapped back and he swayed in a circle to stay upright. I picked the gun and aimed it at his forehead.

"Go," I ordered.

Tears filled his eyes. "Please, no, sir," he moaned. "I am a family man."

I squinted as if about to shoot. "Run or die."

He ran, crouched over, zig-zagging, his arms covering the back of his head.

I turned to see Perera and Kumari struggling, both with their hands on the gun.

"Perera!" I yelled, running closer so I could put the gun to his head. "Stop now or – "

The shot cut me off. Kumari dropped to her knees. She put her hands to her stomach and brought them up red. The color drained from her face.

Perera watched her with his mouth open. His expression didn't change even as I clubbed him on the temple with the pistol grip. I hit him again, harder, on the ground, then turned to Kumari.

I knelt to hold her in my arms. "You're hurt," I said. "But you're going to be okay."

She whispered something in Sinhalese I couldn't possibly understand. Her head fell back against my shoulder and her eyes rolled up at the empty sky.

I shook her but she would not move. I felt for a pulse and found nothing. I smoothed my hands down the length of her hair, over and over.

"Don't go, Kumari," I said, knowing that she had, feeling her absence already in the hollow of my body. "Don't leave me behind."

I laid her on the ground and straightened her sarong out to cover her legs. I folded her arms across her chest.

I found myself behind the wheel of the Toyota, driving. That came to me as a surprise. I had no memory of getting in or turning the key. The sea appeared through the windshield ahead. I was nearing the coast road. I braked hard and pulled over.

My shirt was wet with blood. I groped my chest and back for a wound, but found nothing. Only then did I see the document on the passenger seat. The revolver was on top of it. Finally I understood why.

12

Taking Perera's Toyota was a risk, I knew. Not to me, to my mission. What could I lose? My life?

I mattered to no one. Least of all to myself. I was a cog, a tiny piece in the bigger wheel. No, wrong, not so much a part of things. I was alone.

I pressed my palm hard into my forehead as if I could keep the thoughts down. A mind stream? I had to plug a flood. For a good reason. I had a goal now, so I needed to focus. No distractions. No time to indulge in pity, that selfish emotion. I would not let myself slip into remorse, or grief, or anger. I would advance, relentlessly, towards my goal. If I slowed now I might get stopped by the soldiers. They might prevent me from completing my final assignment in Sri Lanka.

I parked the car under trees where it couldn't be seen from the air. I put it in neutral and revved. The engine whined under the strain but I pressed harder to hear the mechanical growl.

I tested it with a scream; I was still louder. I eased it back to idle and felt myself adrift on the purr of a hundred pieces of metal in motion. The beauty of our inventions. Our? As if we did anything together; as if I belonged.

I slid it into first gear and went slowly down a long bumpy grade, my attention not on holes in the dirt road but a gecko splayed on the windshield outside. Its tiny throat pulsated in a rapid cadence.

I eyed the wiper. Once the blade started moving, would it be quick enough to escape? Call it a sporting proposition. You move or you die. Who else gets so clear a chance to determine their fate, such a purity of options?

"Everyone," I answered out loud, disgusted with my own skittish reasoning.

I leaned half-way out the window to lift the gecko off the glass. I might even bring it along. It could be my witness. My confidant. I smiled at the thought in a way that made my cheeks ache.

I dropped the gecko onto my lap. My karma brought it to me, no? Well maybe it had some karma of its own. Maybe it had been deemed worthy of living in the United States. Or doomed to it?

Either way. I could take care of it, treat it well, bring it up, turn it into a right little reptile aristocrat, its gecko friends stuck back in some swamp astonished by the lavish cards and letters. Swimming pools and movie stars. I laughed out loud this time and called it by its new name: Dapila.

Do they let creatures like this through customs? What if it was endangered? Surely not a common lizard. Or even if. What wasn't endangered? Just let them try to take it from me.

I felt the hard outline of the gun under my thigh. When I reached down to touch the gecko's tiny head it scurried away under the seat. Whatever.

I popped one of the radio buttons and Bob Marley filled the car. Natural Mystic. That again. I turned it up until the bass filled my chest. I mouthed along with the words.

> *Things are not the way they used to be*
> *I won't tell no lies*
> *One and all got to face reality now.*

Yes. Of course. Leon.

Though I try to find the answers
To all the questions they ask
Though I know it's impossible
To go living through the past
Don't tell no lies.

Yes. That would mean me.

The radio went silent on the song's final note. That's it? One song and it's all over? I punched more buttons, fiddled with the dial, but got nothing. Maybe it had never worked in the first place.

I saw a thatch hut on my right. In front of it was a barefoot woman with a baby on her hip. She stared at me, the intruder, the big hairy creature from beyond, then shouted something back into the hut.

I stared back at her. Let her look. Get a good description, lady. You aren't about to tell anybody anyway. Her home didn't even have electricity. If you can call a smattering of sticks and leaves a home. More like a sad comment, on the planet, on modern civilization, on all of us. Yes, us. Me too. So long as I was still living, eating, using the goods. Taking up space. Here it was the late 1980s, we had computers smaller than phone books, we had stereos that fit into our shirt pockets, and these people were living without a single light bulb. No running water. A pit for a toilet.

Someone should have to answer for that too. Politicians, those power-sucking scum. Foreign elements. Everyone else in Sri Lanka blamed them, why shouldn't I? Even if that did complicate the question of just where I fit in.

I heard my own laughter bounce off the car's interior walls. Like I fit in anywhere.

The sound of a distant airplane came to me over the car engine. Maybe not so distant after all. Maybe they were on an aerial search. So what. I made a point of not looking up. Let them search. Let them find me.

It was more likely I would run into an army patrol on the ground.

The professional thugs, killers in government-issue. The man in the black cap. If anyone deserved to die. Once they'd sifted through the bodies at the warehouse, would they even care about me? Maybe. A little. Rajitpurna left before I did. If he were alive I might still be considered bait. Especially in a JVP car.

They would need to describe me. White. Tall. Bearded. If they were kind they might say something like portly, or heavy-set. More likely just fat. They get to the point here. One of their more admirable qualities. Vasudeva with his white eyes turned in, staring at what, his own brain? He would not be hard to describe. I should be even easier. Dull brown hair with touches of grey. Small brown eyes that took in a lot but lost much more. No visible scars. Armed and dangerous. For the first time in my life. I slid the gun out and laid it next to me on the seat. It bounced and spun when the car hit a bump, the barrel swinging around to point at my knee. I drove on anyway, steering into a pothole, but it didn't fire. I tucked it into my waistband. The comfort of cool steel on skin. If only I had discovered it earlier. I took it out again and slid my finger along the trigger. How hard a squeeze would it take?

I felt the bang as much as heard it. My right ear stung and then began to ring. I found myself sitting on the warm car hood with the pistol in my right hand. Was I shot? No, I must have aimed it into the air over my head, the shock waves hitting my ear the hardest. It was a test shot. That must have been it. I checked all around me. I had at least had the sense to park in the shade of some tamarind trees. I was still alone. I was still at large. They hadn't gotten to me yet. I got back in and drove on.

So that was what it took, a flex of the index finger. Nothing more than a twitch. Kumari's limp body, heavy. The soldiers would find her lying flat, arms folded, hair smoothed back, eyes closed. The same ones who came looking for rings? My left hand balled up into a fist. A hook, my second best punch.

Her parents would hear about it soon enough. But the real story? How their daughter died? Trying to save a foreigner? A fat sportswriter? They wouldn't believe it. How could anyone's karma lead them that far off course?

Where the dirt path reached the coast road I stopped and put the car in park. There were no soldiers waiting for me. Two buses and a taxi-van sped by, then a slower line of passenger cars. No one looked. I turned left and rolled on, slowly enough that cars passing me went by in a rush of air. A cow stood in an empty field staring at the ocean. A fat man with a cane sat wheezing in front of a tea hut that leaned so far over it seemed the next stiff breeze might topple it. On the left I saw the whorehouse. Already? Wasn't it miles away? But no, there was the proof, the same dirt hill, the puddle, the three shacks. My first night there. Kumari smiling as she watched me. You couldn't stop staring! I took in a long breath through my nostrils to find her fragrance in the car. No. Not a good idea. I snorted to be rid of it. There were no customers, no sign of the pimp. The drunken bastard. Maybe staring into the barrel of a gun would sober him up. A good place to work some karma out. Who knows? Maybe later, when I was done.

I parked in the empty lot of a boarded-up beach hotel. I threw the keys as far as I could into the ocean. Only after they sunk beneath the surface did I stop to think I might have kept them for later, for an escape. Either way, I decided. It was done. Vijaya's mumbo-jumbo about not clinging to things. Take the Middle Way. Fine. As long as it led to the Rhino Eye.

I leaned with one hand against a king coconut tree to catch my breath. I was a mile at least from where I'd left the car. I must have run along the water. Another mistake. The first place they would look for a foreigner. And I should have walked. I would need to start pacing myself. Conserve energy, gather strength. I left the tree to look at a rusting Nissan pick-up put up on blocks. It was pointed to the sea. I climbed into the driver's seat. The smell of mold from the upholstery mixed with the metallic tang of rust. The combination wasn't unpleasant.

The gun was in my right hand, my finger on the trigger. Even testing as far as the tension point sent a surge of pleasure through me. The beautiful technology behind it. A marvel, a masterpiece of science and art. One squeeze and out comes a piece of steel at lethal speed. The thought that these things had been around for centuries, had decided the fate of nations, made me feel like a sorry latecomer.

I spun the cylinder again and again, listening to the diminishing clicks as it slowed each time. Every chamber but one was neatly packed with its own silver missile. The gleam of the bullets. The cleanest products I'd seen in Sri Lanka. Why would it have to be for something deadly? The economics, maybe. You don't make as much on spices or batik prints. Somebody was always out for a buck first and damn the consequences. Motivation and result. Vijaya's method of testing the merit of any action. What justification could a person cite for inventing a gun? Those foreign elements again. For all their scapegoating, the locals were probably right. Although from what I'd seen, given nothing else some of them would probably club each other. Was their brutality more vicious than most or did it just seem that way in the idyllic setting?

I watched the bullets whir in their slots again and calculated the math of my task. The odds were with me. Five shots. All I needed was one. Of course I wouldn't fire until I was close. Handguns were famously inaccurate from a distance.

Leon in a state of shock as I rush into the store, his look of, what, disappointment? Yes. But mostly terror. And maybe understanding. I would plant my feet wide, knees slightly bent, both hands on the grip. A posture copied from TV, I realized, but one that made sense. One brief squeeze and I would be done with it. The flash from the barrel, the sound ringing, Leon going down.

I would talk to him first. He should know about Kumari. The way Kumari died. He should see her the way I did, the blood dripping from her fingers. How do you think that might feel Leon? Hmm? I would weave the barrel as we talked. He wouldn't know where the bullet was about to hit, where to expect the first searing flash of pain. The forehead? No. It might end too soon. The stomach? That was where Kumari got it.

I slipped the gun back into my waistband and forced myself to picture Kumari the first time I saw her. That knowing smile, at me, at everything. At the world. And didn't I smile back? Without knowing why?

It was impossible. Too many images crowded in to replace it. Random flashes from memory all competing to be seen first. Kumari on her knees, staring at her hands. She must have known what it meant. She must have seen people get killed before. Her rebel friends. The enemy. Maybe even someone she shot herself?

I pressed my temples until my skin hurt. The scene would not disappear. She knew she was about to die. She knew why. Of all her worthy causes.

"Only one way I'm ever going to get past this," I said. I looked into the rear view mirror and saw my lips moving. The voice seemed to come from someone else. "Leon has to die."

I stared into the mirror as if looking at a stranger who claimed to know me. The description struck me as apt. I was an outsider to everyone, and now even to myself. I'd never considered killing someone before. That was something other people did, people you read about in the paper, people somehow less than human. But there it was, staring back at me with blazing eyes. The face of a killer.

I scraped dried blood from my lower lip with my teeth. It must have come from my run through the trees. Or else Kumari. I might have kissed her good-bye.

"It's not murder," I announced. "Not in wartime. Kumari knew that. Leon too."

It meant also that the army could kill me. They would have to, to fill their roles too. Because I would have taken sides. Shake hands and come out fighting. But by whose rules?

The sun near the water turned my face in the mirror orange. Fuck them anyway. Newspaper people. What did they know? Convinced they're the center of every storm. As if they themselves care, as if they're even a part of things. Not for me. I'd found something worth believing in. Or at least worth dying for. Make that someone. Kumari would be my template. A meaningful life? She'd played it perfectly, until the end and her fatal mistake. She shouldn't have jumped Perera. Not for me. But that much may have been unavoidable, an act of nature, an instinct. You have to help the underdog. You have to rescue a person in peril. It didn't need to have been me. I could have been the kitten she swerved to avoid, smashing into a tree instead.

The memory of her last act passed through me with a shudder. Kumari was dead and I was the cause. Not the direct cause but close enough. If I had never met her she would still be alive. When did I slip up? Where did I lose it? I should never have gone to see Dapila, nor tried to land the Rajitpurna interview. I was playing at something I was not. Even while knowing, better than anyone ever could, how unsuited I was for it.

I felt the lines on my forehead. I was tired. I knew the logic of the depressive. Life hurts now how do you stop the pain? Passing on, we say. Death is a journey, according to Vijaya. Good thing. I'd always loved to travel. Animals slink off into the bushes to die. Maybe that's what Sri Lanka was for me. I'd been hanging on for too long and now, here, I'd reached my limit.

This was not Vijaya's way, I was sure. He would not have wanted to go out in such a muddle. He spent his energies sliding between unpalatable alternatives, but I lacked his wisdom, and wasn't bucking for nirvana. I would have to be content with simple revenge. My final move with Kumari.

The tragedy of her early passing. We regret to inform you. Ashes and dust. They never mention bones. Her father trying not to break down. The whole family distraught. Inconsolable. At such a young age. Some karma. That part didn't add up. She didn't deserve this. No one did. No one ever did. But look at how it works. The whole world. Grief at 11. You give us five minutes, we'll cram it with enough tragedy to numb you. Pick up any paper. Who got killed, who got left behind. Survived and deeply loved by. He will live on, in our hearts. Her loving memory. Juanita Velasquez, so weighted with tragedy she could hardly stand, desperate to pass some of it off to me. Would that work? Can it be portioned out and given away? The devoted husband and loving father of. How many kids? The Telegrapher had it at seven. My paper put it at four. Either way. You couldn't call it a smaller pool of grief. It can be a heart attack in 32D or the whole plane going down. Someone waiting at the airport is going to experience it complete. The full measure of sorrow. A love no longer. He's gone and nothing's going to bring him back. Vijaya's story of the mustard seed. Find a house where no one ever died. And the point? Right, the Four Noble Truths. Life is suffering, one, there's a cause, two, and the cause can be eliminated, three. What happened to the fourth? No matter. All the truth in the world wouldn't help now.

I shifted my mind to the act, settling on the details with cool, laser-like efficiency. The shooting would be easy enough. But I would need to escape afterwards. I should have been planning this part from the beginning. Killing Leon and then giving myself up would not bring Kumari back. What would she do in the same situation? She would fight. She died in battle so I would too. Maybe tonight, maybe not. I might live and fight on. But this time fighting for something. Something bigger than me. A movement.

The darkening sky sprouted stars over the sea. A breeze came in off the black water.

"I am joining the JVP," I announced as if it were a public proclamation. "Not for me, and not for anything stupid like a country. For Kumari. For what she represented. In all of us."

Leon would be my first assignment. My initiation. I would be dedicated to the task, untouched by emotion. He might yell for help as soon as I broke in. "Go ahead," I saw myself telling him in a casual tone. "It won't help you live any longer." I imagined his facade of imperturbability shattering, revealing a shivering, vile creature behind it. Or maybe he wouldn't break, wouldn't beg. Either way. I would shoot whatever face presented itself.

People would hear the firing. The whole village perhaps. But no matter. By the time they got to him I would be on the beach, the gun discarded, the document in my hands. I would head further south, to Galle, or to Unawaratuna, stay in one of the small lodges on the jungle side, something small and unpopular. Once things quieted down I could go back to Colombo. One of the wire services would help me get the corruption story out. AP or maybe Reuters. I'd promise to let them interview me later. The government couldn't censor everything. And that would take care of Perera. The other politicians on the list too. Maybe the ruling party itself. How quickly would the fires spread once I lit the match?

I left the truck and walked to the water. The slow white line of a breaking wave appeared in the distance. No moon showed yet over the jungle. A good omen. Escape would be easier in the dark.

I stared at the black horizon to empty my mind of conflict. I needed to be solid, to have my target unwavering. I dropped face down and did push-ups in the sand, 25 straight, my arms trembling on the last five. A new regimen. The mind of a fighter needed a body to go with it. I took the gun from my pants and pointed it at a spot in the water where I imagined Leon's sneering face to be. I resisted the urge to shoot and waste another bullet. No need for that now. I was in control.

Sweat from the exercise made my clothes stick. I stripped to my boxers, then took them off too. I wrapped the gun inside my pants and placed it on the sand. I dunked my shirt, then sloshed it to get out the blood. When Che Guevara was shot, women dipped their handkerchiefs into his blood. I was beyond souvenirs, even a final one from Kumari.

The water lapped warm around my knees, then my thighs. My back ached. I waded in deeper until salt water stung my face. I scrubbed with my palms to remove the blood from my cheeks, then swam out where it was too deep to touch.

I swam on further, past the waves, wondering myself when I

might stop. I went on pulling hard with each stroke. The rhythm was soothing. I could push myself like this until I was exhausted, then keep going, a marathoner in a race of one, so far out I could never make it back. The tide might bring in my body by the next morning. One more victim. Or more likely, a tourist accident. The distinction would hardly bother me as I slipped under the surface.

But Leon would survive. One thing I could not accept. I had to focus, not forget my assignment. The engaged had no room for a thought as selfish as suicide.

I lay on my back and floated with my arms spread. The stars were cold above me, something I'd never thought of before. I took solace in that. A sign that I was different, I had changed. I had crossed a line. The years of wasting my life writing about games were over.

Maybe everything would look different now. My actions would take on a significance beyond me. Motivation and result, cause and effect. Leon would be the proof. I smiled at the thought of joining Kumari's circle. I might even get closer to her, or to what she was.

I savored the new confidence building within me. I would feed on it. As I bobbed, the waves nudged me back towards the beach. I was a revolutionary now. I might die that night. A thrill swept through me, a chemical jolt of the synapses behind my eyes that struck me for the first time as enjoyable. I would feed on that too.

Back on the sand, salt water dripped from my beard. The night air tingled my skin. I stood under the sea of stars and spread my arms out wide and exalted. This is what it meant to be alive.

"I damn sure never felt this way about baseball," I said up to the sky. My own hard laughter rose above the waves.

The moon appeared as a small white disc well up in the sky, startling me. Had I been swimming that long? I pulled on my shirt. It was dry. I left it untucked to hide the gun in my belt. Juanita Velasquez. I apologize. I was wrong. I will not do it again. Nothing can bring your husband back. Yet I promise: this time I will do right.

The first mini-bus I waved at screeched to a stop. I got in with a soft step, but the gun still slipped most of the way out of my waist-band. I cringed and waited for the telling clang of metal on the floor, but it stayed tucked in. I chose an empty seat in the last row. I could watch everyone from there.

"Just up the road," I told the fare collector. He rocked his head sleepily and stared back out the windshield.

I eyed the other passengers. What impression was I making now? Would anyone of them see that I was a rebel? An armed and dangerous man? I reveled in the irony of it, this foreigner, this over-sized, soft-bellied, former hack, standing up to fight for them, and they didn't even know who I was.

A honey-skinned teenage girl behind the driver lifted her head from a nap, seemed surprised to see me there, then let her head droop again. The other passengers were either asleep or tying. The contrast was exhilarating. A boring bus ride for them, a trip to my destiny for me.

Outside a bare light bulb swung under the gate of a roadside temple, turning my side of the window into a mirror. My face came back to me as a shock. There was no sign of the boldness I felt racing through me. Instead I saw the distant and unfocused stare of the deranged. My mouth was twisted with an intensity I hardly rec-ognized as my own.

So I wasn't in complete control. No matter. I could accept that. These things are there. Everyone gets nervous. Kumari must have had her moments too. It wasn't supposed to be easy.

I got off one stop before the Rhino Eye. Fewer witnesses that way. And more time to steady myself. I had to keep calm, chan-nel my thoughts into the task. I could not lose my nerve. Not now, when there was no going back.

The coast road was empty but I left it anyway for the darker beach. All the restaurants were closed. Only a few lights were on in the private homes.

An oil lamp outside a roti stand silhouetted a lone man hunched over his plate. A dog barked in the distance, then one ahead on the beach growled. I didn't slow down or change direction. Any dog would know better now. They wouldn't try me.

From the jungle I heard the clacking of drums. It grew louder as I walked, a poly-rhythm that could have been made by one man or four. A gruff male voice lifted above the thumps, weaving in and around the rhythm with flair. It was Vasudeva, the minstrel. I felt my lips move up into a smile.

Walter's ruined boat lay ahead of me. I crouched behind the stern to look at the back entrance of the Rhino Eye. The throbbing in my neck was like a summons to move, to crash in at once before I had time to reason.

I pulled the document out of the plastic. The drumming stopped, leaving only the sound of my own rapid breathing. Secret? Not for much longer. With it and the gun, I had all I needed to start my own war.

The music came again at a more frantic pace, a rhythm barely recognizable for its urgency. The voice was forceful now, straining, almost as if the song were an admonition. Yes. A call. I had one response mapped already. I folded the document into my back pocket. Step one. Manik would be in for a surprise with the next batch of hotel mail. The scoop was his. It probably should have been from the start.

I turned to the Rhino Eye. The cold steel of the pistol felt good in my palm. I walked on tiptoes, a meaningless effort on sand but one I continued as far as the back steps.

I climbed them to reach the back door, breathing like a bellows. I forced myself to stop, to take slower breaths. A sprinter at the starting block again. Success starts when you envision success. I pictured myself bursting in with the gun already drawn. As soon as my hands stopped shaking.

Imagination would take me only as far as the initial contact. From there I was blocked. Just what would happen when I pulled the trigger? Would it feel like my own will in motion? I would need a tight grip, two hands. Aim for the heart. Hold on through the recoil.

Vijaya's family would hear the shots. But they wouldn't rush over. If I ran out the back I could be in bed before anyone reached the body. I might even join the crowd, craning my neck, faking disbelief, wondering what had happened. Or maybe not. It might be asking too much to appear so unaffected on my first night.

I eased the door open. The squeak it produced was like an alarm to my ears, but no answering sound came from inside. I slipped into the storage room. It was dark with only a shaft of light from the front marking a path through the clutter. I held the gun before me like a shield.

Leon was huddled over the counter. A single kerosene lantern over his head cast his sharp features in a yellowish tint. On the counter were stacks of money, and next to them a cloth sack. He made a tiny murmuring noise as he pulled another stack from the bag.

"Leon!" I hissed. I followed the gun in a rush to the counter, its movement like a magnet towards his chest.

He jerked back and his eyes began blinking rapidly. He stared at the gun barrel and then me. His goatee lifted up as he smirked.

"Son of a bitch," I said through an animal growl. "Go ahead and laugh."

He put the money he was holding back in the bag.

"Do not move," I ordered, my voice low. "Or I'll shoot."

"Whether I do or not," he asked, taunting. "Won't you shoot anyway?"

My insides were floating. I swallowed twice. The air was thick. I felt woozy.

His expression shifted to something suggesting only mild curiosity. Even the prospect of being killed wasn't enough to erase the implication I was boring him.

"Take your hand out of the bag," I ordered.

He did, and waited sullenly for my next move.

"Care to tell my why?" My voice quivered, but I ignored that. "Because I want to tell you what you did. You and your lighter. You killed Kumari. You understand? Do you even know who she is?"

"Of course." His narrow eyes widened, perhaps in mocking appraisal. "Comrade K."

"No. She's dead because of you!" I blurted, louder than I should have. I clamped my lips together to keep them quiet.

He nodded in agreement, then offered a tiny shrug. "It wasn't planned that way but, those are the risks, no? Kill or be killed. She knew that. As well as anyone, I should think."

"She wouldn't hurt anyone who didn't deserve it," I said. "Everybody was free to choose sides."

"Sides?" He clucked. "That may – "

"And you chose yours, you bastard. Guess what? Wrong team."

"Talison," he said slowly, shaking his head in a mild reproach. "You – "

"Maybe you want to beg for your life now," I interrupted, lowering the gun barrel so it aimed at his stomach. "Kumari never had the chance."

"You think you know a lot about this country, don't you?"

"No. I don't know anything. Except that you're evil and you're going to die. What could be more important right now?"

He tilted his head. "Nicely put."

"Why did you do it? You used to be in the JVP. I can understand you quitting. Maybe you're not interested in politics anymore. Fine. But why turn against your own people?"

He snorted. "My people."

"You mean the government is better? The army? Fascists who torch kids on the beach?"

"Don't be an ass. I'm not with them."

I shifted the gun back up to his head. "You gave me that lighter. You knew what it was."

"Of course I did." He smiled as if amused at the memory. "But I told you, I'm through with allegiances."

I started to speak but he held up his bandaged hand.

"Please. I gave you the lighter for two reasons. One, you were stupid enough to take it. And two, I got paid." He gestured to the money on his desk. He saw the look on my face. "Oh, it may be only a few rupees to you. Here it is rather a lot."

"I don't believe it," I said. "You get people killed for money?"

"No. I sell information. To the high bidder. Last month I let the JVP know about the sergeant who had those three girls raped and murdered in Galle. You may have heard of it? They got him." He shrugged. "It works out."

"You play at your evil little game and people die, people you don't even know."

He gestured with his lips towards the gun. "I don't seem to be alone in that."

"No. This is different."

"Yes?"

"This is war."

"How would you know?"

"And I'm on Kumari's side. That makes you the enemy."

He closed his eyes and sighed. As if the point wasn't worth arguing.

"No regrets?" I asked. "Kumari is dead but you've got your filthy little pile of money and that's it?"

"The lighter was there to track Rajitpurna, obviously. When I learned you were to have a personal contact, how could I resist? I'd never sold a more lucrative deal. Unfortunately I didn't realize at the time it would get Perera as well. I could have gotten more."

"Perera too?"

He frowned. "You must have heard? The news has been full of it. Both dead. Much of the Politburo captured or killed, a good portion of the Central Committee as well. What would you call it in your sports reporting, a rout?"

"All in one day? I don't buy it."

He conceded with a shrug. "Who knows? Anyway the reports on Rajitpurna and Perera must be valid. Or they would have made a broadcast by now to deny it."

I let the gun droop.

"How did they get Rajitpurna?"

"They say Perera was captured first and he led the army to him. Rajitpurna pulled out a gun and shot Perera, then the army shot Rajitpurna. So they're both dead, it's all over, happy ending."

"It's not all over. Not for the JVP. It will go on."

He sneered. "The JVP. I learned my lesson years ago. Now the rest of them will too."

"No. You didn't learn. And you're still going to pay. I owe it to Kumari. And whoever else is dead because of you and your deals."

He nodded wearily, either to agree or to be sarcastic. "As you say."

I raised the gun to sight on his forehead. The end of the barrel would not stay in place. I held the grip tighter.

"You deserve this, Leon," I said hoarsely, squinting down the barrel.

He swallowed, then licked his lips.

"Last words, Leon?" I asked in a quieter voice. My voice was no longer shaky. Because I could do it. I knew I could.

He stood up straighter and raised his chin.

"I'm not sorry about any of it," he said. "I'm not."

In the pause that followed I heard the thumping of drums again. They were joined by the thin wail of a harmonica, and then Vasudeva's rumbling voice.

"Put the money back in the bag," I ordered. He looked at me with his forehead wrinkled in puzzlement.

My finger tightened on the trigger. He stared at it, swallowed loudly, and began replacing the money. Vasudeva's voice was joined by a woman singing an octave higher.

"Talison?" Leon asked when the sack was full. "You're not a thief."

"Slide it this way."

He held it down with his bandaged hand and rolled the top with the other. He pushed it to me across the counter.

"Remember Kumari," I said, raising the gun again. I aimed for his forehead. This time it held steady. I moved the barrel slightly to the left, over his right shoulder, and squeezed. The mirror smashed behind him, the pieces cascading down in a crash that led into Leon's voice sputtering in rage.

"Damn you!" he choked out. "Shoot me."

"I remember now. The Fourth Noble Truth. It completes the circle. It's about the path to get there, beyond suffering. If I thought either of us were on it I probably couldn't do this."

I placed the gun on the table behind me. I turned and walked out the back door. I didn't bother looking back.

The shot sounded before I reached Walter's boat. I was in front of the cabana when I heard the first woman's scream.

I tucked Leon's bag tighter under my arm and joined the gathering crowd. People were streaming into the Rhino Eye, everyone talking at once. I kept walking. When their voices behind me were no louder than murmurs in the ocean breeze I turned into the jungle and went looking for Vasudeva.

epilogue

19th March 1989

My dear Gordie,

Thank you for your generosity. We donated some of the money to the monks for alms in your good name. Merits of this wholesome deed will come upon you.

I am writing this letter by electric light. Your gift has also allowed me to begin necessary repairs to my roof. For the first time in years, I now await the rainy season free of worry. My family joins me in thanking you and wishing you a happy life throughout samsara.

The best news from here of late concerns my eldest son Rohan. He has burned the bridges to his shameful past and is now in top form. His turnaround is astounding. Last month he became engaged to a girl from Matara. Together they helped build a standing stove for our kitchen to make cooking tasks easier for my wife. Rohan is currently working with a new institute for blind children opened by a local musician.

My second son Colvin has decided army life is not for him. I cannot say I am disappointed. It will mean another mouth to feed at home, but then he is a resourceful lad and I have no fears for his future.

Sadly, the economic situation in Sri Lanka is yet worse than before. As for politics, most are now too disgusted to care. Shortly after your departure some of our political leaders were discovered taking bribes from the Indian government. This caused a major scandal with one minister even losing his chair. The others somehow slipped through as the president blamed everything on subversives. Yesterday he made a speech promising to crush the remaining rebels in three months' time, but I wonder if he rather prefers to keep them around to justify an ever-larger budget for his security forces.

I continue occasional legal work, although less frequently. In my free time I try to keep current with reading, still one of my most enduring pleasures. Perhaps you'll be kind enough to send a copy of the book you're writing once it is finished, although I must admit I am inclined more to poetry than sports.

Some days I sense I am missing something as this journey winds towards its destination. But then I turn to fond memories of good friends such as yourself to brighten my disposition. One thing I have learned over the years is that life has meaning only when lived for the sake of others.

I am also meditating again. I feel I am making progress, although slowly.

Wishing you all the blessings of the Triple Gem,

Your friend Vijaya

THE END

David Tracey is a writer and environmental designer living in Vancouver, Canada. **The Mustard Seed** is based on his experiences as a journalist visiting Sri Lanka in late 1980s — but only loosely. He didn't go to cover sports, and there never was a Kumari.

For more information on the author, visit **davidtracey.ca**.

Other books by David Tracey:

Urban Agriculture: Ideas and Designs for the New Food Revolution. "David Tracey's *Urban Agriculture* is a road map to food security, to our reconnecting to the soil and the earth, even in cities, and to reclaiming our humanity as cultivators of community while we cultivate food." – Vandana Shiva.

New Society Publishers. 2011. ISBN 978-0-86571-694-0

The Miracle Tree. A laugh-out-loud tale of a young man's search for authenticity amid a media frenzy about a tree that might make wishes come true.

Pure Wave Media. 2010. ISBN 978-0-9865055-0-8.

Ebook: http://www.smashwords.com/books/view/7035

Guerrilla Gardening: A Manualfesto. A fast-paced and funny guide to planting public spaces for the public good. Resistance is fertile.

New Society Publishers. 2007. ISBN 978-0-86571-583-7